PAUL JENNINGS'
TRiCKIEst stoRIEs

ALSO BY PAUL JENNINGS

Unreal!
Unbelievable!
Quirky Tails
Uncanny!
Unbearable!
Unmentionable!
Undone!
Uncovered!
Unseen!

Tongue-Tied!

Paul Jennings' Funniest Stories
Paul Jennings' Weirdest Stories
Paul Jennings' Spookiest Stories

The Cabbage Patch Fibs

The Cabbage Patch series
(illustrated by Craig Smith)

The Gizmo series
(illustrated by Keith McEwan)

The Singenpoo series
(illustrated by Keith McEwan)

Wicked! (series) and Deadly! (series)
(with Morris Gleitzman)

Duck for Cover
Freeze a Crowd
Spooner or Later
Spit it Out
(with Terry Denton and Ted Greenwood)

Round the Twist
Sucked In . . .
(illustrated by Terry Denton)

For adults

The Reading Bug
. . . and how you can help your child to catch it.

For beginners

The Rascal series

Novel

How Hedley Hopkins Did a Dare . . .

More information about Paul and his books can be found at
www.pauljennings.com.au and www.puffin.com.au

PAUL JENNINGS'
TRiCKIEst stoRIEs

VIKING
an imprint of
PENGUIN BOOKS

VIKING

Published by the Penguin Group
Penguin Group (Australia)
250 Camberwell Road, Camberwell, Victoria 3124, Australia
(a division of Pearson Australia Group Pty Ltd)
Penguin Group (USA) Inc.
375 Hudson Street, New York, New York 10014, USA
Penguin Group (Canada)
90 Eglinton Avenue East, Suite 700, Toronto, Canada ON M4P 2Y3
(a division of Pearson Penguin Canada Inc.)
Penguin Books Ltd
80 Strand, London WC2R 0RL England
Penguin Ireland
25 St Stephen's Green, Dublin 2, Ireland
(a division of Penguin Books Ltd)
Penguin Books India Pvt Ltd
11 Community Centre, Panchsheel Park, New Delhi – 110 017, India
Penguin Group (NZ)
67 Apollo Drive, Rosedale, North Shore 0632, New Zealand
(a division of Pearson New Zealand Ltd)
Penguin Books (South Africa) (Pty) Ltd
24 Sturdee Avenue, Rosebank, Johannesburg 2196, South Africa

Penguin Books Ltd, Registered Offices: 80 Strand, London, WC2R 0RL, England

Individual stories copyright © Lockley Lodge Pty Ltd
First published by Penguin Books Australia Ltd
You Be the Judge, Clear as Mud from Undone, 1993
For Ever, Just Like Me, Backward Step from Uncovered, 1995
One Finger Salute, Ticker, Guts from Unseen, 1998
There's No Such Thing from Unbelievable!, 1987
Nails from Unbearable, 1990
Cry Baby, Ex-Poser, Sloppy Jalopy, Eyes Knows, from Unmentionable, 1999
The Hat, Shake from Tongue-Tied! 2002
Sucked In first published as Together Again in The Paul Jennings 1996 Superdiary, 1995
A Watery Grave from The Paul Jennings 1997 Superdiary, 1996
The Spitting Rat from Spit It Out, 2003

Burp first published by Addison Wesley Longman Australia Pty Limited, 1991

This collection published by Penguin Group (Australia), 2008

10 9 8 7 6 5 4 3 2 1

This collection copyright © Lockley Lodge Pty Ltd, 2008
Illustrations copyright © Bob Lea, 2008

The moral right of the author and illustrator has been asserted.

Text and cover design by Adam Laszczuk © Penguin Group (Australia)
Cover illustration by Bob Lea
Typeset in 13.5/17 pt Joanna by Post Pre-press Group, Brisbane, Queensland
Printed in Australia by McPherson's Printing Group, Maryborough, Victoria

National Library of Australia
Cataloguing-in-Publication data:

Jennings, Paul, 1943-
Paul Jennings' trickiest stories / Paul Jennings.
ISBN: 978 0 670 07184 5

A823.3

puffin.com.au

Contents

A person who eats someone else is called a cannibal. But what are you called if you drink someone? Like I did.

No, no, no. Don't put down the book. This isn't a horror story. It isn't even a horrible story. And it's not about vampires and ghouls. But it sure is a weird tale. Really weird.

Now you can say that you don't believe me if you like. But I tell you this – I don't tell lies. Well, that's not quite true. I did tell one once. A real big one. Did I do the right thing? I don't know. You be the judge.

1

It began the day Dad and I moved to the end of the world.

There we were. In the middle of the desert. The proud new owners of the Blue Singlet Motel. There was no school. There was no post office. There was no pub. There were no other kids. There was nothing except us and our little cafe with its petrol pumps. And two rooms out the back for rent.

The red desert stretched off in every direction.

And it was hot. Boy was it hot. The heat shimmered up off the sand. When you walked outside you could feel the soles of your shoes cooking.

'Paradise,' said Dad. 'Don't you reckon?'

'Ten million flies can't be wrong,' I said, waving a couple of hundred of them away from my face.

'Don't be so gloomy,' said Dad. 'You'll love it. The trucks all stop here on their way to Perth. It's a little goldmine.'

Just then I noticed the dust stirring in the distance. 'Our first customer,' said Dad. A huge truck was buzzing towards us at great speed. Dad picked up the nozzle of the petrol pump. 'He'll probably want about a hundred litres,' he said with a grin.

The truck roared down the road. And kept roaring. Straight past. It vanished into the lonely desert.

Poor old Dad's face fell. He put the nozzle back on the pump. 'Don't worry,' he said. 'There'll be plenty of others.'

But he was wrong. For some reason hardly any of the trucks pulled up. They just tore on by. There were a few tourists. They stopped and bought maps and filled up their water-bottles and topped up with petrol. Some even stayed the night. It was a living. But it wasn't a goldmine.

But to be honest it wasn't too bad. And Dad had a plan. A plan to attract customers.

2

'It's called a Wobby Gurgle', Dad said, waving an old faded book at me. 'There's a legend that the Wobby Gurgle lives around here in the desert.'

'What's it look like?' I said.

Dad looked a bit embarrassed. 'No one's ever seen one,' he said.

'Well, how do you know there's any such thing?'

'Stories,' said Dad. 'There are stories.'

'Well, what does a Wobby Gurgle do?' I asked.

'Drink.'

'Drink?'

'Yes,' he went on. 'It, ah, likes to drink water.'

I scoffed. 'There isn't any water around here. Only what we bring in by truck. There isn't a waterhole for hundreds of miles.'

Dad wasn't going to give up. 'Well, maybe it sort of saves water up. Like a camel.'

'It would have to be big. It hasn't rained here for twelve years,' I told him.

Dad tried to shush me up. He was getting all excited. 'Imagine if it was true,' he said. 'People would come from everywhere to see it. We could sell films and souvenirs. Lots of petrol. We could open a museum. Or a pub.'

Dad was getting excited. His face was one big happy grin.

'Like the Loch Ness Monster,' he yelped. 'No one's ever really seen it. But people go to Loch Ness from all over the world – just hoping to catch a glimpse.'

'So?' I said.

'So we let people know about the Wobby Gurgle. They'll come for miles to see it.'

'But what if there isn't one?' I said. 'Then you would be telling a lie.'

Dad's face fell. 'I know,' he said. 'But we'll keep our eyes open. If we see one it will be like hitting the jackpot.'

3

Well, we didn't see anything. Not for a long time anyway. Time passed and I started to enjoy living at the Blue Singlet Motel. We didn't make a lot of money. But we got by.

I liked the evenings the best. After the sun went down and the desert started to cool. Sometimes a gentle breeze would blow in the window. I would sit there staring into the silent desert, wondering if anything was out there.

'Never go anywhere without a water-bottle,' Dad used to say. 'You never know what can happen out here in the desert.'

Anyway, this is about the time that things started to get weird. One night I filled my water-bottle to the brim and put it on the windowsill as usual. I fell off to sleep quickly. But something was wrong. I had bad dreams. About waterfalls. And tidal waves. And flooding rivers.

I was drowning in a huge river. I gave a scream and woke up with a start. I was thirsty. My throat was parched and dry. I went over to my water-bottle and opened it.

Half the water was gone.

I examined it for holes. None.

Who would do such a thing? Dad was the only other person around and I could hear him snoring away in his bedroom. He would never pinch my water. He was the one always giving me a lecture about never leaving the property without it.

I looked at the ground outside. My heart stopped. There, on the still-warm sand, was a wet footprint.

I opened my mouth to call out for Dad. But something made me stop. I just had the feeling that I should handle this myself. It was a strange sensation. I was scared but I didn't tell Dad.

I jumped out of the window and bent over the footprint. I touched it gently with one finger.

Pow. A little zap ran up my arm. It didn't hurt but it gave me a fright. It was like the feeling you get when lemonade bubbles fizz up your nose. Like that but all over.

I jumped back and looked around nervously. The night was dark. The moon had not yet risen. All around me the endless desert spread itself to the edges of the world.

The warm sand seemed to call me. I took a few steps

and discovered another footprint. And another. A line of wet footprints led off into the blackness.

I wanted to go home. Turn and run back to safety. But I followed the trail, still clutching the half-empty water-bottle in my hand.

4

How could someone have wet feet in the desert? There was no pond. No spring. No creek. Just the endless red sand.

The footprints followed the easiest way to walk. They avoided rocks and sharp grasses. On they went. And on.

I was frightened. My legs were shaking. But I had to know who or what had made these prints. I was sure that a Wobby Gurgle had gone this way.

I could run and get Dad, but the trail would have vanished by then. The tracks behind me were evaporating. In a few minutes there would be no trail to follow.

If I could find a Wobby Gurgle we would be set. Visitors would come by the thousands.

A cricket chirped as I hurried on. A night mouse scampered out of my way. Soon the cafe was only a dark shadow in the distance. Should I go on? Or should I go back?

I knew the answer.

I had to go back. It was the sensible thing to do. Otherwise I might be gobbled up by the desert. I was in my pyjamas and slippers. And only had half a bottle of water. That wouldn't last long. Not once the sun came up.

The footprints were fading fast. I looked back at the cafe. Then I headed off in the opposite direction, following the tracks into the wilderness.

I had never been one to do the sensible thing. And anyway, if I could spot a Wobby Gurgle we would make a fortune. Tourists would come from everywhere to look for it. That's what kept me going.

On I went and on. The moon rose high in the sky and turned the sand to silver. The Blue Singlet Motel vanished behind me. I was alone with the wet footprints. And an unknown creature of the night.

The moon started to lower itself into the inky distance. Soon the sun would bleach the black sky. And dry the footprints as quickly as they were made. I had to hurry.

My eyes scoured the distance. Was that a silvery figure ahead? Or just the moon playing tricks?

It was a tree. A gnarled old tree, barely clinging to life on the arid plains. I was disappointed but also a little relieved. I wasn't really sure that I wanted to find anything.

I decided to climb the tree. I would be able to see far ahead. If there was nothing there I would turn around and go home. I grabbed the lowest branch of the tree.

5

I can't quite remember who saw what first.

The creature or me.

I couldn't make sense of it. My mind wouldn't take it in. At first I thought it was a man made of jelly. It seemed to walk with wobbly steps. It was silvery and had no clothes on.

It let out a scream. No, not a scream. A gurgle. Well, not a gurgle either. I guess you could call it a scurgle. A terrifying glugging noise. Like someone had pulled out a bath plug in its throat.

It was me that let out a scream. Boy, did I yell. Then I turned and raced off into the night. I didn't know where I was running. What I was doing. I stumbled and jumped and ran. I felt as if any moment a silvery hand was going to reach out and drag me back. Eat me up.

But it didn't. Finally I fell to the ground, panting. I couldn't have moved another step, even if I'd wanted to. I looked fearfully behind me. But there was nothing. Only the first rays of the new day in the morning sky.

Soon it would be hot. Unbearably hot. I stood up and staggered on towards where I thought the Blue Singlet Motel should be.

I wandered on and on. The sun rose in the sky and glared down on me. As I went a change came over me. My fear of the Wobby Gurgle started to fade. And be replaced by another terror. Death in the desert. I was hopelessly lost.

The water-bottle was warm in my hand. I raised it to my lips and took a sip. I had to make it last.

By now my face was burning. Flies buzzed in my eyes. My mouth felt as if I had eaten sand for breakfast. My slippered feet were like coals of fire. My breath was as dry as a dragon's dinner.

Stupid, stupid, stupid. To leave home in the middle of the night. With only a little water. And no hat. Dressed in pyjamas. The heat was sending me crazy.

How long I walked for I couldn't say. Maybe hours. Maybe days. My throat screamed for water. In the end I guzzled the lot in one go. I was going mad with thirst.

I laughed crazily. 'Wobby Gurgle,' I shouted. 'Come and get me. See if I care.'

Finally I stumbled upon a small burrow under a rock. There was just enough room for me to curl up in its shade. I knew that without help I would never leave that spot.

6

Night fell. I dozed. And dreamed. And swallowed with a tongue that was cracked and dry. I dreamed of water. Sweet water. I was in a cool, cool place. A wet hand was stroking my face. A lovely damp hand, fresh from a mountain stream.

I opened my eyes.

It wasn't a dream.

Or a nightmare.

It was the Wobby Gurgle.

Normally I would have screamed and run. But in my near-dead state I only smiled. Smiled as if it was perfectly normal to see a man made of water.

He had no bones. No blood. No muscles. His skin was like clear plastic. The nearest image I can think of is a balloon filled with water. But a balloon shaped like a man. With arms and legs and fingers. All made of water.

For a silly second I wondered what would happen if I stuck a pin in him. Would he collapse in a shower and seep away into the sand?

His water lips smiled sadly. His hand on my cheek tingled like fizzing snow. Cool, cool, so cool.

Inside his chest a tiny, dark red fish circled lazily. I knew that I must be losing my mind. There is no such thing as a man made of water. With a fish swimming inside him.

It was then that he did the weirdest thing of all. He placed the end of one finger in my mouth. It was cold and fresh and filled me with sparkling freshness. A little electric shock ran all over me.

I felt a trickle of pure water on my tongue. The clearest, coolest, freshest water in the world. I sucked like a calf at a teat. The Wobby Gurgle was feeding me. With himself.

The freshness was so good. I was greedy. I swallowed until I could take no more.

'Thanks,' I managed to croak.

He didn't answer. Well, not in speaking. He just gave a gentle gurgle. Like a mountain stream trickling over a rock.

He stood up and started to move off. 'Don't leave me,' I said. 'Don't go.'

The Wobby Gurgle looked up at the sky. The sun was already rising. I had to get home that night. Another day in the desert would finish me.

And him? Would it finish him too? Where did he live? In a cool burrow somewhere? I didn't know. But I remembered Dad's words. Maybe he stored up water like a camel. Maybe he was carrying twelve years supply.

I staggered after him, somehow realising that he was leading me in the right direction. Every now and then he would give a low gurgle, as if to encourage me.

The sun beat down mercilessly. I wondered how he could stand it. My throat was dry. I wanted water. But I didn't like to ask. I knew I would never make it without regular drinks.

7

So did Wobby Gurgle. He seemed to know when I couldn't go on. Every fifteen minutes or so he would come and put his cool finger into my mouth. And I would feel the trickle of fizzing liquid flowing across my tongue.

He was so gentle. So generous. Waiting. Leading me on. Giving me a drink. Pure, pure water.

After several hours I felt much stronger. But the Wobby Gurgle seemed to be moving more slowly. His steps were shorter. And was it my imagination or had he shrunk?

On we went. On and on. With the cruel sun beating down. We stopped more often for a drink and after each one the Wobby Gurgle walked more slowly.

I looked at him carefully. The tiny fish seemed bigger as it floated effortlessly inside his arm. It wasn't bigger. He was smaller.

I was drinking him.

'No,' I screamed. 'No. I can't do it. You're killing yourself for me. You'll soon be empty.'

He seemed to smile. If a water face can smile.

Once again he placed his finger in my mouth. And like a greedy baby at its mother's breast I sucked and swallowed.

The day wore on and the Wobby Gurgle grew smaller and smaller with every drink. I clamped my jaw shut. I refused to open my mouth. I wasn't going to let him kill himself for me. No way.

But it was no use. He simply pointed at my mouth and let fly with a jet of water. It ran down my chin and dripped onto the dry sand, wasted. He wasn't going to stop until I swallowed. I opened my mouth and accepted the gift of life.

As the afternoon wore away, so did the Wobby Gurgle. By now he was only half my size. A little bag of liquid. His steps were small and slow. Like an exhausted child.

I tried to stop him feeding me. But it was no good. He simply poured himself onto my face if I refused.

In the end he was no bigger than my fist. A small figure, wearily leading me on at a snail's pace. I picked him up in one hand and looked at him. The fish almost totally filled his body. He held no more than a few cupfuls of water.

'That's it,' I said. 'I'm not taking any more. I'd sooner die myself. If you give me any more I'll run off. You'll never catch me.'

He looked up sadly. He knew that he was beaten.

And so was I.

The sun set once again. And the far-off moon, unknowing, uncaring, rose in the night sky.

I thought that I could last until morning. But the tiny Wobby Gurgle, how long could he last?

We both fell asleep. Me and my little friend – the bag of water.

Later I woke and with a fright saw that the Wobby Gurgle was lying on his back, not moving. The dark red fish inside him floated upside down.

'Hey,' I yelled, 'wake up.'

There was no movement. He looked like a tiny, clear football that had been emptied of air. I knew he was dying.

8

Tears trickled down my cheek. How I had enough moisture to make tears I will never know. I was so filled with sorrow that I didn't see the watcher. The sad, silent watcher.

A woman. A water woman. With a gasp I saw her out of the corner of my eye. She seemed to flow across the desert sand rather than walk.

'Quick,' I yelled. 'Here.'

I pointed to the tiny, deflated figure on the sand.

She didn't look at me but just bent over the still figure and gently kissed him on his water lips.

It was the most beautiful sight I had ever seen. Water flowed from her lips into his. She was filling him up. From herself. It was like watching a tyre being inflated. He grew larger and she grew smaller. The fish once more began to swim. The kiss of life went on and on until both Wobby Gurgles were the same size. About my size. Three kids in the desert.

Well, no. One kid. And two wonderful half-empty Wobby Gurgles.

They both smiled. So gently. Then the woman held out her water-filled arm and pointed. In the distance I could see a red glow. It was the neon light of the Blue Singlet Motel.

'Thanks,' I yelled. It seemed such a small thing to say. I could never repay them for what they had done. I turned around to try and tell them how I felt.

But they had both gone. I was alone in the night.

I walked towards home. As I got closer I could see the police cars. And the search helicopter. Dad would have lots of customers.

But not as many as he would have when the word about the Wobby Gurgles got out.

People made of water.

Visitors would come from everywhere. Australians. Americans. Japanese. Germans. Clicking their cameras. Buying their films. There would be museums. Hotels. Pizza parlours. Probably even poker machines. We would be famous. And rich.

Dad came rushing out with tears streaming down his face. He hugged me until I couldn't breathe.

'How did you stay alive?' he said. 'With no water? Did someone help you?'

I looked at him for a long time. The police were listening – everyone wanted to know what had happened. I thought about the Wobby Gurgles. Those shy, generous people. Who had given the water of life to a greedy boy. Then I thought about the crowds with the cameras. And the noise and pizza shops that would follow.

I thought about all the plants and flowers that had vanished from this country for ever.

'Well?' said Dad.

He was a good dad. But I knew that he would want to find the Wobby Gurgle.

That's when I looked at him and told a lie. 'No,' I said. 'I never saw anyone.'

Did I do the right thing? You be the judge.

There's No Such Thing

Poor Grandad. They had taken him away and locked him up in a home. I knew he would hate it. He loved to be out in his garden digging the vegies or arguing with old Mrs Jingle next door. He wouldn't like being locked away from the world.

'I know it's sad,' said Mum. 'But it's the only thing to do. I am afraid that Grandad has a sort of sickness that's in the head. He doesn't think right. He keeps seeing things that aren't there. It sometimes happens to people when they get very old like Grandad.'

I could feel tears springing into my eyes. 'What sort of things?' I shouted. 'I don't believe it. Grandad's all right. I want to see him.'

Mum had tears in her eyes too. She was just as upset as I was. After all, Grandad was her father. 'You can see him on Monday, Chris,' she said. 'The nurse said you can visit Grandad after school.'

On Monday I went to the sanatorium where they kept Grandad. I had to wait for ages in this little room which had hard chairs and smelt of stuff you clean toilets with. The nurse in charge wore a badge which said, 'Sister

Gribble'. She had mean eyes. They looked like the slits on money boxes which take things in but never give anything back. She had her hair done up in a tight bun and her shoes were so clean you could see the reflection of her knobbly knees in them.

'Follow me, lad,' said the nurse after ages and ages. She led me down a corridor and into a small room. 'Before you go in,' she said, 'I want you to know one thing. Whenever the old man talks about things that are not really there, you must say, "There's no such thing." You are not to pretend you believe him.'

I didn't know what she was talking about, but I did know one thing – she shouldn't have called Grandad 'the old man'. He had a name just like everyone else.

We went into the room and there was Grandad, slumped in a bed between stiff, white sheets. He was staring listlessly at a fly on the ceiling. He looked unhappy.

As she went out of the room Nurse Gribble looked at Grandad and said, 'None of your nonsense now. Remember, there's no such thing.' She sat on a chair just outside the door.

2

Grandad brightened up when he saw me. A bit of the old twinkle came back into his eyes. 'Ah, Chris,' he said. 'I've been waiting for you. You've got to help me get out of this terrible place. My tomatoes will be dying. I've got to get out.' He looked at the door and whispered. 'She watches me like a hawk. You are my only chance.'

He pulled something out from under the sheets and pushed it into my hands. It was a small camera with a built-in flash. 'Get a photo,' he said, 'And then they will know it's true. They will have to let me out if you get a photo.'

His eyes were wild and flashing. I didn't know what he was talking about. 'Get a photo of what?' I asked.

'The dragon, Chris. The dragon in the drain. I never told you about it before because I didn't want to scare you. But now you are my only hope. Even your mother thinks I have gone potty. She won't believe me that there is a dragon. No one will.'

A voice like broken glass came from the corridor outside. It said, 'There's no such thing as a dragon.' It was Nurse Gribble. She was listening to our conversation.

I didn't know what to think. It was true then. Poor old Grandad was out of his mind. He thought there was such a thing as a dragon. I decided to go along with it. 'Where is the dragon, Grandad?' I whispered.

'In Donovan's Drain,' he said softly, looking at the door as he spoke. 'Behind my back fence. It's a great horrible brute with green teeth and red eyes. It has scales and wings and a cruel, slashing tail. Its breath is foul and stinks of the grave.'

'And you've seen it?' I croaked.

'Seen it, seen it. I've not only seen it, I've fought it.

Man and beast, battling it out in the mouth of Donovan's Drain. It tried to get Doo Dah. It eats dogs. And cats. It loves them. Crunches their bones. But I stopped it, I taught it a thing or two.' Grandad jumped out of bed and grabbed a broom out of a cupboard. He started to battle an imaginary dragon, stabbing at it with the broom and then jumping backwards.

He leapt up onto the bed. He was as fit as a lion. 'Try to get Doo Dah, will you? Try to eat my dog? Take that, and that, you smelly fiend.' He lunged at the dragon that wasn't there, brandishing the broom like a spear. He looked like a small, wild pirate trying to stop the enemy from boarding his ship.

Suddenly a cold, crisp voice cut across the room. 'Get back in bed,' it ordered. It was Nurse Gribble. Her mean eyes flashed. 'Stop this nonsense at once,' she snapped at Grandad. 'There is no such thing as a dragon. It's all in your head. You are a silly old man.'

'He's not,' I shouted. 'He's not silly. He's my Grandad and he shouldn't be in here. He wants to get out.'

The nurse narrowed her eyes until they were as thin as needles. 'You are upsetting him,' she said to me. 'I want you out of here in five minutes.' Then she spun around and left the room.

'I've got to escape,' said Grandad as he climbed slowly back into his bed. 'I've got to see the sun and the stars and feel the breeze on my face. I've got to touch trees and smell the salt air at the beach. And my tomato plants – they will die without me. This place is a jail. I would sooner be dead than live here.' His bottom lip started to tremble. 'Get a photo, Chris. Get a photo of the dragon. Then they will know it's true. Then they will have to let me out. I'm not crazy – there really is a dragon.'

He grabbed my arm and stared urgently into my eyes. 'Please, Chris, please get a photo.'

'Okay, Grandad,' I told him. 'I'll get a photo of a dragon, even if I have to go to the end of the earth for it.'

His eyes grew wilder. 'Don't go into the drain. Don't go into the dragon's lair. It's too dangerous. He will munch your bones. Hide. Hide at the opening and when he comes out take his photo. Then run. Run like crazy.'

'When does he come out?'

'At midnight. Always at midnight. That's why you need the flash on the camera.'

'How long since you last saw the dragon, Grandad?' I asked.

'Two years,' he said.

'Two years,' I echoed. 'It might be dead by now.'

'If it is dead,' said Grandad, 'Then I am as good as dead too.' He looked gloomily around the sterile room.

I heard an impatient sigh from outside. 'Visiting time is over,' said Nurse Gribble, in icy tones.

I gave Grandad a kiss on his prickly cheek. 'Don't worry,' I whispered in his ear. 'If there is a dragon I will get his photo.' The nurse was just about busting her ear-drums trying to hear what I said but it was too soft for her to make out the words.

As she showed me out, Nurse Gribble spoke to me in her sucked-lemon voice. 'Remember, boy, there's no such thing as a dragon. If you humour the old man you will not be allowed back.'

I shook my head as I walked home. Poor Grandad. He thought there was a dragon in Donovan's Drain. I didn't know what to do now. I didn't believe in dragons but a promise is a promise. I would have to go to Donovan's Drain at midnight at least once. I tried to think of some other way to get Grandad out of that terrible place but nothing came to mind.

3

And that is how I came to find myself sitting outside the drain in the middle of the night. It was more like a tunnel than a drain. It disappeared into the black earth from which came all manner of smells and noises. I shivered and waited but nothing happened. No dragon. After a while I walked down to the opening and peered in. I could hear the echo of pinging drips of water and strange gurglings. It was as black as the insides of a rat's gizzards.

In the end I went there five nights in a row. I didn't see Grandad in that time because the nurse would only let me visit once a week. Each night I sat and sat outside the drain but not the slightest trace of a dragon appeared. It gave me time to think and I started to wonder if perhaps

Grandad's story could be true. What if he had seen a dragon? It could be asleep for the winter – hibernating. Perhaps dragons slept for years. It might not come out again for ten years. In the end I decided there was only one way to find out.

I had to go in.

The next night I crept out of the back door when Mum was asleep. I carried a torch and Grandad's camera and I wore a parka and two jumpers. It was freezing.

I walked carefully along the drain with one foot on either side of the small, smelly stream that ran down the middle. It was big enough for me to stand upright. I was scared, I will tell you that now. It was absolutely black to the front. Behind me the dull night glow of the entrance grew smaller and smaller. I didn't want to go but I forced myself to keep walking into the blackness. Finally I looked back and could no longer see the entrance.

I was alone in the bowels of the earth in the middle of the night. I remembered Grandad's words. 'Don't go into the dragon's lair. It's too dangerous. He will munch your bones.'

I also remembered Nurse Gribble's words. 'There's no such thing as a dragon.' I almost wished she was right.

The strong beam of the torch was my only consolation. I shone it in every crack and nook. Suddenly the idea of a dragon did not seem silly. In my mind I could see the horrible beast with red eyes and dribbling saliva, waiting there to clasp me in its cruel claws.

I don't know how I did it but I managed to walk on for a couple of hours. I had to try. I had to check out Grandad's tale. I owed him that much.

Finally the tunnel opened into a huge cavern. It was big enough to fit ten houses inside. Five tunnels opened into the cavern. Four of them were made out of concrete but the fifth was more like a cave that had been dug out by a giant rabbit. The earth sides were covered in a putrid green slime and deep scratch marks.

I carefully made my way into the mouth of this cave. I wanted to turn and run. I wanted to scream. I half wished that a dragon would grab me and finish me off just to get it over and done with. Anything would be better than the terror that shook my jellied flesh.

I stumbled and fell many times, as the floor was covered in the same slime as the walls. The tunnel twisted around and upwards like a corkscrew. As I progressed a terrible smell became stronger and stronger. It was so bad that I had to tie my handkerchief over my mouth.

Just as I was about to give up I stood on something that scrunched under my feet. It was a bone. I shone the torch on the floor and saw that small bones were scattered everywhere. There were bones of every shape and size – many of them were small skulls. On one I noticed a circle of leather with a brass tag attached. It said 'Timmy'. I knew it was a dog's collar.

As I pushed on, the bones became deeper and deeper until at last they were like a current sweeping around my knees. My whole body was shaking with fear but still I pressed on. I had to get that photo. The only way to get Grandad out of that sanatorium was to prove he wasn't mad.

Finally the tunnel opened up into another cavern that was so large my torch beam could not reach the roof. And in the middle, spread out across a mountain of treasure, was the dragon.

4

His cruel white jaws gaped at me and his empty eyes were pools of blackness. He made no movement and neither did I. I stood there with my knees banging together like jackhammers.

The horrible creature did not jump up and crunch my bones. He couldn't. He was dead.

He was just a pile of bones with his wings stretched out in one last effort to protect his treasure. He had been huge and ugly. The dried out bones of his wings were petrified in earthbound flight. His skull dripped with slime and leered at me as if he still sought to snap my tiny body in two.

And the treasure that he sought to hoard? It was poor indeed. Piles of junk. Broken television sets, discarded transistor radios, dustbin lids, old car wheels, bottles, a broken pram, cracked mirrors and twisted picture frames. There was not a diamond or a gold sword to be seen. The dragon had been king of a junk heap. He had saved every piece of rubbish that had floated down the drain.

Now I could get what I came for. I could take a photo. I stood on a smooth rock and snapped away with my camera. This was the evidence that would save Grandad. I took about ten photos before my foot slipped and the torch and camera spun into the air. I heard them clatter onto the dragon's pile of junk. The torch blinked as it landed and then flicked out. I was in pitch blackness. Alone with a dead dragon.

I felt my way carefully forward trying to find the camera. The rock on which I had stood was not a rock at all. It was a smooth type of box with rounded corners. I felt it carefully with my fingers, then I started to grope my way forward. I had to find the camera and the torch but in my heart I knew that it was impossible. They were somewhere among the dragon's junk. Somewhere under his rotting bones. I knew I would never find either of them in the dark.

As I started to grope around in the rubbish I bumped into an old oil drum. It clattered down the heap making a terrible clacking as it went.

Suddenly I felt the damp ground tremble. The noise had loosened the roof of the cave. Pieces of rock and stone started to fall from above. The cave was collapsing. The earth shook as huge boulders fell from the roof above. I had to get out before I was buried alive. I stumbled back through the rubbish to the tunnel and fought my way through the piles of bones. I often hit my head on a rock or slipped on the slimy floor. I could hear an enormous crashing and squelching coming from behind. Suddenly a roaring filled the air and a blast of air sent me skidding down the corkscrew passage. The whole roof of the cavern must have fallen in.

I skidded down the slippery tube on my backside. The floor was rough and the seat was ripped out of my pants as I tumbled down and down.

At last I landed upside down at the bottom. I was aching all over and although I couldn't see anything I knew I must be bleeding.

A bouncing noise was coming from above. Something was tumbling down after me. Before I could move, a hard, rubbery object crashed into me and knocked me down. It was the smooth box-thing that I had stood on.

I just sat there in the gurgling water and cried. It had all been in vain. I had seen the remains of the dragon and taken the photo. But the camera and the dragon and his rubbishy treasure were all buried under tonnes of rock. The dragon was gone for ever and so was Grandad's hope of getting out of the sanatorium. There was no proof that the dragon had ever lived.

5

I could feel the box-thing move off down the drain. It was floating. I decided to follow it downstream and I think that it probably saved my life. By following the floating cube I was able to find my way back without a torch.

At last – wet, cold and miserable – I emerged into the early morning daylight. The whole adventure had been for nothing. Everyone would still think that Grandad was crazy and I was the only one who knew he wasn't. All I had to show for my efforts was the rubbery cube. I had no proof that a dragon had once lived in the drain.

I looked at the cube carefully. It looked like a huge dice out of a game of Trivial Pursuit except it had no spots on it. It was heavy and coloured red. I could see it had no lid. It was solid, not hollow. I decided to show it to Grandad.

I carried the cube back home and had a shower. Mum had gone to work. I got into some clean clothes and went round to the sanatorium. The mean-eyed nurse sat in her glass prison warder's box at the end of the corridor.

'Well,' she said sarcastically, 'Where is your dragon photo?'

'I haven't got one,' I said sadly, 'But I have got this.' I held up the cube.

'What is it?' she snapped.

'It's from the dragon's cave,' I said weakly.

'You nasty little boy,' she replied. 'Don't think your lies are going to get the old man out. You make sure that when you leave that smelly box leaves too.'

I went down to Grandad's room. His face lit up when he saw me but it soon grew sad as he listened to my story.

'I'm finished, Chris,' he said. 'Now I will never be able to prove my story. I'm stuck here for life.'

We both sat and stared miserably at the cube. Suddenly Grandad sat up in bed. 'Wait a minute,' he said. 'I've read about something like that in a book.' He pointed at the cube. 'I think I know what it is.' He was smiling.

As he spoke, I noticed a crack appearing up one side. With a sudden snap the whole thing broke in half and a little dragon jumped out.

'It's a dragon's egg,' shouted Grandad. 'Dragon's eggs are cube shaped.'

The little monster ran straight at my leg, snapping its teeth. It was hungry. I jumped up on the bed with Grandad and we both laughed. Its teeth were sharp.

The dragon was purple with green teeth. Smoke was coming out of its ears.

'I'm getting out of here,' said Grandad. 'They can't keep me now. We can prove I saw a dragon in the drain. This little fella didn't come from nowhere. I'm free at last.'

'Hooray,' I shouted at the top of my voice. 'It really is a dragon.'

Just then I heard the clip, clop sound of Nurse Gribble's shoes. The little dragon stood still and sniffed. He was looking at the door. He could smell food.

Nurse Gribble stepped into the room and started to speak. 'There's no such thing . . .' Her voice turned into a shriek as the tiny new-born dragon galloped across the room and clamped its teeth onto her leg. 'Help,' she screamed. 'Help, help. Get it off. Get it off. A horrible little dragon. It's biting me.' She hopped from one side of the room to the other with the dragon clinging on to her leg tightly with its teeth. She yelled and screamed and jumped but the dragon would not let go.

Grandad headed for the door carrying his suitcase.

Nurse Gribble started to shriek. 'Don't go, don't go. Don't leave me alone with this dragon.'

Grandad looked at her. 'Don't be silly,' he said. 'There's no such thing as a dragon.'

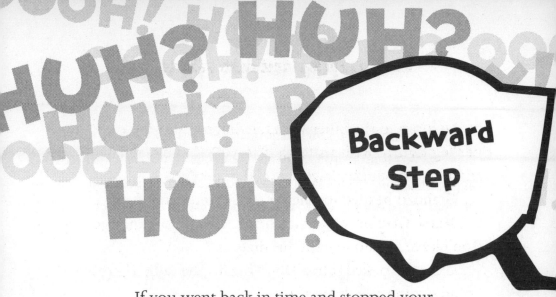

HUH? HUH? HUH? HUH? HUH? HUH? HUH?

Backward Step

If you went back in time and stopped your grandparents from meeting each other you would never have been born. But then if you had never been born you wouldn't be able to go back and stop them. Would you?

'John,' said Mrs Booth to her five-year-old son. 'You just sit there and watch "Inspector Gadget" on the TV while I go down the street and get some milk. I'll be back by the time it's over.'

'I love "Inspector Gadget",' said John.

Mrs Booth reached the front gate and then stopped. She felt a little guilty, leaving her son alone in the house. But she knew he wouldn't budge. Not for another twenty minutes. Not until the show was over.

'Excuse me, Mrs Booth,' said a voice.

She jumped in fright and then stared into the eyes of a teenage boy. He thrust an old exercise book into her hand. 'Read this. Please, please, please read it.'

'I'm not interested in buying . . .' she began to say.

'I'm not selling anything,' he said. 'And it's not a religion. This is important. This can save your life. You're in great danger. Please read it.'

'Now?' she said.

'Right away. Please, it's really important.'

There was something about the boy. He seemed very nervous. And she felt as if she knew him. The boy's hands were shaking. 'Well,' she said. 'Just for a second.' She gave a little sigh and opened the old exercise book.

1

I am fourteen. Nine years ago I was also fourteen. And nine years before that I was fourteen too.

It is creepy. It is weird. But I think I have figured it all out. It makes sense to me now. It is the only explanation. No one will believe me, of course. They will just say I am crazy.

Look – I'll try and explain it to you as simply as I can. I've put one and one together and come up with two. Or should I say I've put nine and five together and come up with five.

No, no, no, that's just talking in riddles. I'll start at the beginning. Or is it the end?

Sorry, there I go again. Look, have you ever wanted strange powers? You know, to be able to fly or read thoughts or be very strong? I'll bet you think it would be great. But think again. It could be dangerous. You could end up hurting yourself. Like I did.

I am famous. Yes, there wouldn't be too many people around here who haven't heard of me. I'll bet you think it would be great to be famous. Pictures in the paper. On television. People wanting your autograph. That sort of thing.

It's not really that good. You never know whether people want to be your friend because they like you or because you are well known. And then there are kids who get jealous and give you a hard time and push you around. I would rather be ordinary and have ordinary problems.

I became famous at five. They called me the boy from nowhere. There was a great fuss. It was in the papers. A five-year-old boy just suddenly appeared sitting in the back seat of the class. Right next to a girl called Sharon Coppersmith.

That boy was me.

Sharon Coppersmith screamed and screamed when I arrived. Or appeared. According to her I just popped out of nowhere. One minute the seat was empty. The next minute there was little old me. Five years old, sitting next to her in a history class.

All the big kids crowded around. They were glad to have something break up the lesson. They laughed and offered me lollies and made a great fuss. The teacher thought that I had wandered in from the street.

I just looked up and started crying. I was only five but I remember it just like it was yesterday. Who were all these big kids? Where was my mummy? Where was the nice big boy who wanted to help me?

'What's your name, little fella?' said the teacher.

For a while I couldn't get a word out. I just sat there sobbing. In the end I managed to say, 'John Boof, Firteen

Tower Street, Upwey, seven five four, oh, oh, six two free free.'

'John Booth,' said the teacher. '13 Tower Street Upwey. Phone 754 006233. Well done. Don't cry, little fella. We'll have you home in no time.'

2

The principal's office seemed huge. He wore a pair of those little half-moon glasses and kept peeping over them at me while he spoke into the phone. 'Are you sure?' he said. '754 006233. No John Booth? Never heard of him. How long have you lived there? Three years. Well, sorry to have troubled you.'

I just kept licking the salty tears that were rolling down my cheek and wondering how I got there.

I had been watching 'Inspector Gadget' on television. I remember the man saying something like, 'a brand new episode'. Then a big boy was talking to me. He just popped out of nowhere. He was nice. I was holding his hand and then 'poof', he was gone and there I was sitting in this school-room full of big kids. With everyone looking at me and wondering where I had come from.

'Look,' said the principal to his secretary. 'Pop him in your car and see if he can show you where he lives. If he can't find the place you'll have to take him to the police station. His parents will come for him sooner or later.'

I knew that I didn't have a father. But I didn't know that my mother had died nine years earlier.

The secretary was nice. She strapped me into the seat next to her and gave me a little white bag with jelly-beans in it. 'Don't worry, love,' she said, 'We'll soon find Mum. You just show me the way to go. All you have to do is point.'

She drove around for a bit and I thought I recognised some of the houses and places. But they were different. Looking back I can describe it as like being in a dream. The streets were the same but different.

'There,' I suddenly yelled. It was the water tower. I could see it in the distance. It was right next to our house.

'What?' said the nice lady. 'The water tower? You couldn't live there, love.'

'Neks door,' I said.

She smiled. 'Now we're getting somewhere.'

There was only one house next to the water tower and it was my house. At least it was like my house. It had the same rock chimney and the same fountain in the front yard. But it was painted green instead of blue. And the trees were huge. And the chicken shed had gone. But it was still my house.

'Mummy,' I shouted. I had never been so happy in my life. I didn't stop to think that you can't paint a house in one day. And the trees can't grow overnight. When you are five you think adults can do anything. I pelted up to the front door and ran inside. Then I just stopped and stared. Our furniture had gone. There was no television. My photo wasn't on the wall.

'Mummy,' I screamed. 'Mummy, Mummy, Mummy.' I scampered into the kitchen. A very old lady looked down at me. Then she looked at the secretary who had followed me in and started to scream.

The old lady thought we had come to rob her.

After all, we had just walked into her house without even knocking.

3

Well, after a lot of talking, the secretary managed to calm the old lady down. They had a cup of tea and the old lady gave me some green cordial. 'Mummy,' I said. 'I want my mummy.' I didn't know what this old lady was doing in our house. I didn't know where my toys had gone. I didn't like the new carpet and the photos of strange people. I wanted everything to be like it was before. I also wanted to go to the toilet.

I ran upstairs, through the big bedroom and into the little toilet at the back. When I came back I heard the secretary saying, 'How did he know where to go?'

The old lady just shook her head. None of us knew what was going on.

The secretary took me out to the car but I didn't want to get in. I didn't want to leave the house that was supposed to be my home. But the secretary was firm and she put me in the front seat. As we drove off she checked the house number. '13 Tower Street,' she said to herself with a puzzled look.

The police were puzzled too. 'We'll look him up on our computer,' said the sergeant. 'His parents have probably reported him missing by now.'

He tapped away for several minutes. Then he scratched his head and just sat there staring at the screen. 'There is a John Booth missing,' he said. 'He disappeared nine years ago, aged five. That would make him fourteen by now.'

'Well, this little boy is not fourteen,' said the secretary. She squatted down and looked into my eyes. 'Are you John?'

'I'm five,' I said.

The sergeant tapped for a while. 'The missing boy lived around here,' he said. '13 Tower Street.' He crouched down and patted me on the head. 'Where were you when you lost your mum?' he asked kindly.

'Watching "Inspector Gadget",' I said.

'Is that still on?' said the secretary.

The sergeant rummaged through a newspaper. 'No channel has "Inspector Gadget" on,' he said. 'Not any time this week.'

'Maybe he's from another state,' said the secretary.

The sergeant went off for a while and the secretary tried to read me a story. But I didn't want it. I only wanted my mother. Finally the sergeant returned. 'I rang Channel Two,' he said. '"Inspector Gadget" is showing in fifteen countries but nowhere in Australia. The nearest place is New Zealand.'

'Maybe he's a Kiwi,' said the secretary.

The sergeant squatted down again. 'Say fish and chips,' he said.

'Fish and chips,' I said.

'Nah,' said the sergeant. 'He's a dinkie di Aussie, aren't you, mate?'

I didn't know what it meant but I nodded anyway.

After that the secretary left and a policewoman looked after me. Everyone was getting more and more excited. 'Wait until the papers get hold of this,' said the sergeant.

They were looking at an old newspaper. There was a picture of a mangled car. And a picture of a five-year-old me standing in front of the water tower.

The sergeant shook his head. 'A kid goes missing nine years ago,' he said. 'Then an identical kid turns up today. He says he lives at the same address. He says he has the same name. He knows all about "Inspector Gadget" which hasn't been shown here for nine years. He is even wearing the same clothes. This boy is the world's first time traveller. He has jumped forward nine years.'

There was only one thing they didn't tell me for a long time. I wanted my mum but they couldn't go and fetch her. She was killed the day I disappeared. A car knocked her down while she was crossing the road to the milk bar.

Talk about a fuss. Everyone wanted to see me. Take my photo. People from university wanted to study me. Fortune tellers and mystics claimed they had moved me in time. I was on television all over the world.

In the end my grandma came and got me. At first I didn't recognise her because she was much greyer and had more wrinkles. But as soon as she spoke I knew it was her. 'You're coming with me, John Boy,' she said. There was no arguing with that voice. I ran over and hugged and hugged her until my arms ached.

She tried to stop them taking photos. She tried to keep off the professors and psychics. She tried to give me a normal life. But of course she couldn't. She was old and she didn't really want to bring up a child again. 'Your mother was enough,' she said. 'Having a child and looking after it with no father. And now it's me looking after you.'

So here I am nine years later. An oddity. Grandma is doing her best. But she is old and tired and we are both unhappy. I have no friends. No mother. No father. I'm famous. Everybody knows me. But nobody likes me. Being famous has mucked up my life.

Nine years ago I travelled in time. Today I found out that I can do it again.

4

I was walking along the street in a sort of a daze. There was a lot of traffic. Trucks, cars, motorbikes. The air was full of fumes and noise. I checked the time on my watch. Four o'clock.

A huge petrol tanker was bearing down. I didn't see it. I just stepped out in front of it without looking. There was a squeal of brakes. Blue smoke and a blaring horn. There was no time to get out of the way.

I knew that I was gone. There was no escape.

Suddenly, 'poof'.

I was lying on a seat on the other side of the road. An old man sitting next to me looked as if a ghost had just appeared in front of him. He screamed and ran off as fast as he could go.

What had happened? How did I get there?

I looked at my watch. Half past four. Where had that half hour gone?

Suddenly it all fell into place. I was the boy who could travel in time. I must have been run over by the truck and badly injured. Maybe people had carried me over to the bench. I would have wished that I could go back in time to just before the moment I stepped in front of the truck. And that's what happened. For just a second there would have been two of me on the footpath. The injured me would have grabbed the hand of the other me before he was hit. And wished ourselves half an hour in the future.

But then the injured me would never have been injured. In fact he would have missed those thirty minutes too. So he never did any of it. He never happened. He must have disappeared as soon as I landed on the seat where he had started from.

And the old man saw a boy appearing out of nowhere. I had come from half an hour in the past.

I had gone back in time. And saved myself by bringing

me into the future. I could travel in time just by wishing it to happen. There was no doubt about it. Thirty minutes. If I could do thirty minutes I could do eighteen years. I could go back to the time when I was watching 'Inspector Gadget'. I could stop my mother going to the shop. Then she wouldn't be killed and I wouldn't have to live with Grandma. I would be happy growing up with my mother.

But what if it went wrong? What if I made a mistake and arrived too late? Something deep inside was warning me. I felt as if I had been in this situation before. I was cautious. Then it struck me.

I *had* been there before.

I remember me at age five watching 'Inspector Gadget'. It was just as the closing credits were rolling. The end of the show. A big boy had just appeared out of nowhere. He was upset. He was searching around the house calling out 'Mum'. He looked out of the window. There was a policeman coming up the drive.

Suddenly I realised what had happened all those years ago. The fourteen-year-old me had gone back nine years in time. But I had arrived too late. 'Inspector Gadget' was over. My mother was dead. A policeman was coming up the drive to tell the five-year-old me that his mother was dead. I wouldn't have let that happen. I wouldn't have left him to live all those years with an old grandma who didn't want him. That's when I would have panicked. When I didn't think clearly.

I must have grabbed my hand. The big me must have

grabbed the hand of the little me. And wished us nine years into the future. I wanted to take the five-year-old into the future and look after him.

'Poof.' The five-year-old me landed nine years into the future. The fourteen-year-old me just vanished. By taking his five-year-old self nine years into the future he ceased to exist. He had missed all those nine years and hadn't grown up. He was the boy who never was.

Suddenly a five-year-old child landed in the future. On his own. He didn't know how he got there. And neither did anyone else.

That's what I think happened anyway. That's my explanation of how I jumped nine years.

5

I went home and sat in my room. Grandma was taking a rest. She was tired. Much too tired to be worried about me.

What if I went back again? What if I was really careful? What if I went back to the front gate just as my mother reached it? At the beginning of 'Inspector Gadget'. I could tell her not to go to the milk bar. Then she would not be run over.

I closed my eyes and wished myself back.

Mrs Booth closed the exercise book and stood up. She could hear the strident voices of 'Inspector Gadget' floating through the window. She looked at the fourteen-year-old boy carefully. She was sure that she had seen him before. But she was a little cross. 'Why have you picked on our family?' she said. 'You have described me and my mother and my child. You've been snooping around. Why didn't you do your assignment on your own family?'

The fourteen-year-old boy was crying. 'You are my own family, Mum,' he said.

She still gripped the exercise book tightly in her hand. Her mind was in a spin. The boy was crying real tears.

'Your story doesn't make sense,' she said. 'If I go back inside, obviously I won't get run over. And none of what you have written will happen.'

'That's right,' he said.

'And you will never have been here.'

The boys lips trembled just a little. 'That's what I want,' he said.

Mrs Booth turned and walked back to the house. When she reached the door she turned and looked back. She felt as if she had been talking to someone.

But there was no one there.

One-Finger Salute

Every day after school Gumble sticks his finger up at me. Every day. He sits on the fence at the end of our street and gives me the one-finger salute. He has a bunch of toughs for friends and they all laugh like crazy every time he does it.

It might not sound like much. A one-finger salute. I mean it doesn't actually cause pain. Not like getting your ear twisted or your arm shoved up behind your back. But it hurts all the same. It hurts my feelings.

I can't stop thinking about it. It's like a stone in my shoe. Or a dog barking in the night. All day at school I'm thinking about the one-finger salute Gumble will give me on the way home tonight.

My dad says it's extremely rude to stick your middle finger up in the air at someone.

And I personally have never done it.

Don't get me wrong. I'm no angel. But there are a number of reasons why I don't stick my middle finger up at Gumble.

1. He's bigger than me.
2. He has really mean mates who would make my

life even more miserable than usual.

3. I don't have any middle fingers to stick up at him. The last reason it the main one I don't do it.

So here I am. Walking home from school. And there are Gumble and Smithy and Packman sitting on the fence, waiting.

'Hey, Digit,' yells Gumble. 'Cop this.' He sticks his middle finger up in the air and starts moving it up and down in a very insulting way. Smithy and Packman start doing it too. They laugh like crazy.

I walk by, hating them as usual. What can I do? I could stick my little finger up at them. I could stick my thumb up at them. But it's just not the same. You have to stick the middle finger up. The big finger is the one that gives the big insult.

I hurry off down the street. I'm mad and embarrassed. Their insults follow me down the street like a cloud of flies. Even after I reach home I can hear their laughter ringing in my head.

2

I look at my hands. Eight fingers. Or six fingers and two thumbs if you want to look at it that way.

I started off with ten fingers but lost two of them when I was a little kid.

I was only three at the time. Mr Watson, the guy next-door, was cutting his lawn. He left the motor of his lawn-mower running and went round to the backyard to empty the grass clippings. I wandered over to the lawn-mower and stuck my hands underneath to see what was whizzing around under there.

That's what I was told I did anyway. I actually don't remember anything about it. But my mum and dad do. They rushed me to hospital. Nothing could be done. My two middle fingers were cut right off. They were so mangled that they couldn't be sewn back on.

Mr Watson moved away to another house. It wasn't his fault, but he felt bad every time he saw me. He couldn't bear to think about it.

I don't really blame him. You shouldn't go putting your hands under lawn-mowers.

3

So here I am back in school. Another day with the long walk home at the end of it. Another day to get the one-finger salute from Gumble.

I *should* feel happy. I got eighteen out of thirty for maths today. That's good for me. And Mrs Henderson put my science project up on the wall. So I *should* be smiling. But I'm not.

Instead I spend every second thinking about paying back Gumble for picking on me. I'll get even with him if it kills me.

I can't stick my middle finger up at him so I'll have to think of something else.

It's free-reading time and I start to leaf through my

scrapbook. I've read it a thousand times.

But I read it again.

I start with the bit about worms. It's really interesting. You know what happens when a worm sticks its head out of the ground and a bird grabs it? The worm hangs on. It doesn't want to be breakfast for a bird. So the bird pulls and the worm squirms. The bird pulls more and the worm starts to stretch like an elastic band. Something has to give. And it does.

Twang, the worm breaks in half. The bird eats its end and flies off.

And then. Wait for it. This is the good bit. The worm grows a new tail.

I turn the pages. Now this is really weird. There is a type of frog that can grow new toes. I look down at the pictures and shake my head. I wish I was a frog like that.

See, I have all these clippings in my scrapbook.

And I have something else as well. In my bedroom at home. In an empty ice-cream container. Yes, I have a drop-tail lizard. A live one.

If a kookaburra grabs a drop-tail the lizard drops its tail. The kookaburras just can't catch the whole drop-tail lizard. All they get is its tail.

Drop your tail and run away – live to fight another day. That's the drop-tail lizard.

But, even better than that. The fantastic thing is –

The lizard grows another tail.

Now, why can't people be like that?

Just imagine it. I mean it would change history. Henry the Eighth chops off his wife's head. And she grows a new one. Ace.

4

It's time to walk home, but today Elaine walks with me. She's the girl next-door. She moved in when Mr Watson moved out.

Elaine's not bad for a girl. When she smiles her freckles all bunch up and I feel like reaching out and touching them. With my eight fingers.

Thinking about Elaine makes time fly for once. Before I know it we've come to our street. There's no sign of Gumble. I start to feel good, like I'm walking on air. For once I'll get home without any hassle.

But wait. What's that sticking up over the fence? It's an arm. And a hand. And a finger.

He's doing it again. He's giving me the one-finger salute.

There's another arm. And another. There's laughing. And sniggering. My face goes red. How I'd love to do it back. How I'd love to grab Gumble's arm and shove it behind his back until he squeals. But there are too many of them. I don't have the guts.

Elaine does though. She jumps up and grabs one of the fingers. Then she twists it. She twists it real hard.

There is an enormous scream. 'Ow. Ouch. Let go. Let go.'

She's got Gumble. I'd know that voice anywhere.

She twists his finger until she can't twist it any longer. Gumble's head pops up over the fence. I start to run.

'You're history, Digit,' yells Gumble. 'You're dead meat.'

Elaine runs after me, laughing. It's all right for her. They think I did it. I'm the one who'll be dead meat.

'That showed 'em,' she says. She laughs and all her freckles bunch up. My stomach turns over.

I wish I could impress Elaine. I wish I could pay Gumble back. But I don't have the fingers for it.

'See you tomorrow,' I say. I walk inside with love and hate buzzing around inside me. And the love isn't for Gumble, I can tell you that.

5

No one's home. Mum and Dad aren't back from work yet. My cat, Slurp, is there, looking for something to eat as usual. I love Slurp partly because she has a similar problem to me. Missing parts. She has no ears. They were ripped off by the dog next-door in a fight. A big mongrel with no tail.

I go to my bedroom and lock Slurp out. Then I take my lizard out of the ice-cream container. His name is Droplet. I make sure that I don't pick him up by the tail. I don't want him dropping it on me.

No, really I don't.

I put him on the floor and watch him run around. He really is the cutest lizard. Outside, Slurp starts to meow. She would love to get in and eat Droplet. She'll eat anything. I open the door and peer out.

'No way,' I yell. 'Go and find yourself a mouse.'

Flash.Whizz. Pow. Oh, no. Slurp shoots across the room after Droplet. Quick as a flash she pins him down by the tail.

And quick as a flash Droplet drops his tail and runs under the bed. The tail squirms and squiggles under Slurp's paw.

I grab Slurp and lock the silly cat in the laundry. 'Bad girl,' I say.

Then I crawl under the bed. Poor Droplet is hiding under a pair of underpants. I gently grab him and hold him in the palm of my hand. Now he has a stumpy little tail instead of a long pointed one.

It doesn't hurt them when they drop their tails, though. Drop-tail lizards are meant to do that. It's just nature.

All the same, I decide to give the little lizard his freedom. I walk out into the garden and put Droplet in the flower-bed. 'Bye, Droplet,' I say. 'Don't worry about it. You're going to grow a new tail.' He wriggles off into the bushes. 'Drop in any time,' I say.

I go back to my bedroom and shut the door. I look at the lizard's tail lying there on the floor. It's still wriggling and jiggling like a crazy worm. After a bit it stops. I get an idea.

No. Look, I'll be honest. The idea came to me a long time ago but I couldn't pick Droplet up by the tail on purpose. Not pull off his tail. I just couldn't. But now it's happened anyway. By accident. So I might as well give my idea a try.

I carefully pick up the lizard's tail and take it into the kitchen.

I put it on a plate and stare at it. Can I do it, though?

I get out some pepper and salt. And a bit of bread. I shake the tomato sauce all over the tail. This isn't going to be easy. Or pleasant.

But I have to do it. It's the only way.

I take out a very sharp knife.

No. No, no, no. I can't do that. I can't cut it up. Not when it's still wriggling around. It's too awful.

Suddenly I grab the tail. I close my eyes. I shove the tail onto my mouth and swallow. Straight down without chewing. The tail has gone to a better place.

Oh, wow. My stomach turns over. And it's not because of Elaine because Elaine isn't even here. The tail gives a couple of squiggles inside me. Then it lies still.

What have I done? Why have I done it? Will it work?

I don't know the answer to all these questions. But I do know one thing. I will never ever tell anyone that I ate Droplet's tail.

6

I go to bed early and I toss and turn and have a terrible dream about an octopus.

When I wake up my whole world has changed.

At first I think it's still the dream. Then I wonder if I've gone crazy.

I look at my hands. I just can't believe what I see. I have ten fingers. Yes. Ten fingers. I've grown a new one on each hand. Both of them are perfect.

Gently I touch them. They feel normal. They look normal. I bend one, very carefully. Yes, it works. I touch my nose. I scratch my ear.

'Yes, yes, yes.' It worked. The lizard's tail has done the trick.

I want to rush out to tell Mum and Dad. I want all my friends to know. I want to scream it to the world. 'I've got new fingers.'

But then I stop and think.

No. There's one person I want to see my fingers first. And he's not a friend. No way.

I get dressed, bolt my breakfast and race out of the door. If I'm quick I'll be able to catch Gumble.

There he is, sauntering along with his mates. Elaine's on the other side of the street.

Gumble hears me coming up behind him. He turns and grins.

Then he does it. Yes, just like I knew he would.

'Cop this,' says Gumble.

He gives me the one-finger salute.

And . . .

And . . .

Oh, yes.

I give it back.

I stick the new finger on my right hand up and give the first one-finger salute of my life. Brilliant. Elaine's eyes nearly pop out of her head.

Gumble doesn't think it's brilliant.

He scowls. He growls. He can't believe what he's seeing. He thinks it's a trick. He thinks I've made fake fingers out of clay or plastic or something.

I hold up both of my new middle fingers and wiggle them around. I put them right up under his nose.

Oh, this is good. All my life I've wanted to get even and do this back to Gumble.

Quick as a flash Gumble moves. He grabs my new fingers to see if they're fakes.

I grin. 'They're real,' I say. 'Real, real, real.'

Gumble yanks my fingers.

Splot.

My new fingers break away.

Gumble looks at his hands and grins. He thinks that he has pulled off fake fingers. But he hasn't. They're real. Flesh and blood. Two knuckles on each. And little bones sticking out of the end. Gumble stares at them carefully. Then he starts to scream. The fingers are squirming and worming around in his hands. Just like the lizard's tail.

Gumble's mates start to scream too. They shriek like they've just seen a headless ghost. Gumble throws the fingers into the air and watches in horror as they land on the ground and twist around with a life of their own.

Gumble and Smith and Packman turn and run. They just run screaming down the road to school. I pick up my new fingers. They won't go back on no matter what I do.

I look at my hands. The stumps have already healed over. I'm back where I was before. Eight fingers. Useless.

By the time I get to school I feel a bit better. After all, I don't think Gumble will give me the one-finger salute again.

And I'm right. He's terrified of me. He knows that he's ripped my fingers off. He thinks he's going crazy. He's too scared to come near me.

There's nothing to worry about any more. Especially when I see what's happening to me. Yes, it's happening. Right in front of my eyes. I'm growing another pair of middle fingers. Awesome. I'm stoked.

7

All day long at school I keep my new fingers to myself. I'm not going to rush into things. Life could be complicated with drop-tail fingers. So I don't want anyone to know about them. Not just yet.

I think about what's happened. This morning I ate a drop-tail lizard's tail. And now I've grown removable middle fingers. One pull and off they come.

Okay, so new ones grow straight away. Just like the tail on lizards.

In one way it's great. But in another way it's not. I'm the only person in the world who can grow new fingers.

Maybe I'm a freak.

I could be on television. In the papers. Everyone will want to see the teenager who can grow new fingers. People will gawk at me. They might even laugh.

I don't want everyone looking at me like I'm the Elephant Man in a sideshow. So I keep my secret to myself. And my hands in my pockets.

Gumble and his mates can't figure it out. Now they're not so sure that they did pull my fingers off this morning. And I'm not telling them anything.

At lunch time I go into the loo and sit down in one of the cubicles. I take my two spare fingers out of my pocket and look at them.

Gumble pulled them off and ran away screaming. No wonder. The fingers still give a little wriggle every now and then. They've been doing this all morning. I've seen people looking at me and wondering what's going on in my pants. It's very difficult to explain.

What am I going to do with these fingers? They're part of me. I can't just flush them down the loo.

I'd like to give them a proper burial. I'd like to say a few words before they're interred. But I can't bury them while they're still wriggling. I'll have to wait until they are well and truly dead.

8

After school I walk home alone with my secret.

Mum asked me to stop off at Knox City Shopping

Centre and buy food for Slurp. I make my way to the pet shop and get some chicken loaf. Then I take the escalator up to the first floor.

Is it my imagination or are people staring at me? The people on the down escalator seem to be grinning as they go by. I turn around and see them peering back.

What are they looking at? What's wrong with me? Do I have a big pimple on my nose or something?

I touch my face. With my four fingers.

One of my fingers has gone. It's fallen off. But where is it? I look down at the escalator. It's nowhere to be seen.

It must be back down below, wriggling around on the floor somewhere. I have to find it quickly. If someone picks up a human finger they'll take it to the police and everyone will know I'm a freak.

I turn around and start running down the up-escalator. As I go people jump out of the way.

'Disgusting,' says an old man.

'Aaagh,' screams a little girl.

I reach the bottom of the escalator and look around to find that everybody in the whole world is staring at me. Some are laughing but most are just gawping.

Both hands are in my pockets. I move my fingers around and discover something else. The other finger's gone too. They've both gone and new ones are growing. But that's not what everyone's looking at. They can't see my hands inside my pockets.

So what *are* they staring at?

I race over to a shop window and peer at my reflection.

Oh, no, no, no. Horrible, horrible, horrible.

One finger has come off in my earhole. It's sticking out from my head and twitching around like a bit of live sausage.

Everyone's laughing and screaming. One kid's putting his finger into his mouth, making out he's going to puke.

This can't be for real. I feel like puking too.

I pull the finger out of my ear and turn and run.

My nose starts to itch. Right up inside. I'm not thinking clearly. If I was I wouldn't do the next stupid thing.

Pick my nose.

Now the crowds are shrieking with laughter and yelling about how revolting I am.

I look in the shop window and see the other finger hanging out of my nose.

I pull it out and bolt out of the entrance.

9

It's a long way home from Knox City and I'm out of breath. My feet hurt and my T-shirt feels like armour around my chest. My underpants are riding up and cutting into me. But I keep running. I just want to get home.

I bunch up my fists and swing my arms as I run. I can see that my two new fingers have already grown.

And in my pockets are four spare fingers. They're twitching and twisting like worms on a hook.

This thing's going mad. I have to tell Mum what's happened. She won't tell anyone or let it get into the newspapers.

I hope.

Finally I reach our street. Home.

But not quite. Sitting on our front fence is Elaine. She gives me a big smile. Which turns into a grin. Which turns into a laugh. My stomach feels queasy, but it's not because of her freckles.

'What's so funny?' I say.

'There's something sticking out of your bottom,' Elaine says politely.

'What?' I say. I feel the blood draining out of me as I realise what's happened. Oh, please don't let it be true.

While I was running I must have scratched . . .

I feel behind me. I did. It's true. The worst thing in the world. Oh, horror. A finger is sticking out of the crack of my backside. It must have come off when I scratched at my tight jeans. I've run all the way home with a finger sticking out of my bum.

I pull my finger out and run inside without a word.

All I can think about are these stupid fingers. I don't want fingers that come off. I just want to go back to like I was before with one finger missing from each hand.

Eight fingers isn't so bad.

Outside, Slurp is clawing at the door and meowing. She wants to come in. I throw up the window and yell. 'Shut up. Buzz off.'

I've never ever spoken to Slurp like that before. I love Slurp. Now I feel guilty because she's slinking off with her tail between her legs.

I sit on the bed and stare at my hands. One has five fingers and the other four.

I wiggle the horrible drop-tail finger. I don't want it. I hate it.

I grab the finger. And pull. *Splot*. It comes off and starts to wiggle around. I throw it angrily onto the bed and pull the other spare fingers out of my pocket.

I put those five spare fingers on my bed too. Sometimes one or two of them give a bit of a twitch.

I hold my hands in front of my face. Now they're both the same. Four fingers on each hand. But for how long?

I wait for the new fingers to grow.

Minutes pass. Hours pass. Nothing happens.

Brilliant. Wow. Oh, yes. No new fingers are growing. I must have used them all up. Even a drop-tail lizard must run out of tails some time.

Clunk. I hear the front door. Mum's home.

I run downstairs, yelling as I go, 'Mum, Mum, guess what happened.'

10

Mum listens very carefully to the whole tale. 'Very clever, dear,' she says. 'You should write it up at school.'

'It's not a story,' I yell. 'It's true.'

'Come on,' says Mum. 'Get real. We all know you have a good imagination. But really.'

'I can prove it,' I yell.

I run into the bedroom to get the six spare fingers.

But they're gone. A breeze blows gently through the open window. I poke my head out of the window. There's no one there. Not even Slurp.

So that's that. Mum doesn't believe me. No new fingers grow on my hands. Thank goodness.

Everything goes back to normal.

Except for one or two things. Gumble stays well away from me. He never puts a finger up at me again.

Slurp is different too. She bites at people's fingers when they pat her. She seems to like the taste. And she grows new ears. But they don't last for long because she keeps scratching them off. And they get eaten by the dog next-door – the big mongrel with the long tail.

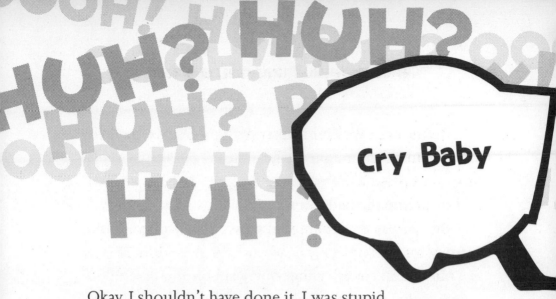

Cry Baby

Okay. I shouldn't have done it. I was stupid.

'Who is responsible for that?' said Mr Kempsy. He was pointing at the pin board.

'Cry Baby,' said one of the kids.

'Stand up, Gavin,' said Mr Kempsy.

He needn't have asked me to stand up. I'd been standing up all week. I faced the class. Outside the window I could see the desert stretching off into the distance. I wished I was there. 'Did you do that drawing?' said Mr Kempsy. He knew it was mine. That's why he was asking. I nodded my head. 'Now,' he said, 'tell us how you did it.'

Everyone looked at the wall where my picture was pinned. I had called it 'Elephant Ears' because that's what it looked like.

'Well,' said Mr Kempsy. 'We're waiting.' He knew how I did it. Otherwise he wouldn't have been asking.

I breathed deeply. 'Last week I went into the staff room after school,' I said.

'Yes,' he growled.

'Then I pulled down my pants, sat on the photocopier and pressed the button.'

Well, you have never heard anything like it. The class cracked up. They laughed till the tears ran down their faces. I just stood there feeling stupid. My face was red and so was my burnt bottom.

Mr Kempsy didn't laugh though. He suspended me from school for a week.

Mum didn't laugh either. She went on and on and on about it. The way parents always do.

That's the worst of being a kid. You never know when you are going to cop it. You can get into trouble at any time. One minute everything is fine and then 'boom' – you are dead meat. Things can turn nasty just when you least expect it.

Like what happened the next day after the elephant ears and Mr Kempsy. Let me put you in the picture. I had to stay home from school. Mum wouldn't talk to me so I moped around feeling awful. After she went out I did a whole heap of jobs without even being asked. I tried to make up for what I had done. When I had finished the washing-up I stood in the lounge and watched TV.

2

Mum had left her new writing pad on the coffee table. Now that might not seem like much to you but you have to remember that she had once told me this: 'Gavin, you are never to touch this writing pad. It was Aunt Nellie's and there are only a few pages left. They are precious pages.'

Aunt Nellie had drowned when she paddled her canoe in front of a ship carrying rainforest timber. The boat broke her canoe in half and she was never seen again. Mum kept Aunt Nellie's picture on the kitchen wall and she often stood staring at it.

Anyway, like I said, I was standing there watching TV – a movie called *The Old Man and the Sea*.

The writing pad was on the coffee table. It was made of delicate, thin paper with a design on the top. Trees – a lovely forest spreading across the top of the page. I wanted a closer look. I didn't want to write in it. I didn't want to tear out a page. I just wanted a look. There was nothing wrong with that really. Was there?

So I picked it up and sat down.

Now you are going to find out why they call me Cry Baby. See, all week I had been forgetting about my burnt behind. Every time I sat down it hurt so much that tears sprang into my eyes.

As you have probably guessed, the tears started to flow. Right down onto Mum's special writing pad. Even though I jumped up straight away the whole thing was drenched. I mopped up the tears but it was no good. The trees were all bent and twisted and the leaves were running off the branches. The paper was wet and stained.

My heart started to thump. That was it. This was death. I was gone. First the elephant ears and now the paper. Mum was going to kill me. I thought about rushing down the street to buy another pad. But I knew that I would never find one. Aunt Nellie's pad was as old as the hills.

My stomach felt weak. Any time now Mum would come back. I went outside to see if there was any sign of her. Grandpop was in the front yard packing up his truck for another venture into the desert. 'What are you looking for this time?' I asked.

He held up a photo. 'The best one,' he said. 'The water-holding frog.' He was so excited that his hands were shaking. All his life he had wanted to find a specimen of the water-holding frog. His old face was wrinkled with a huge smile. His eyes twinkled. This was going to be the tenth trip looking for this frog. I was scared that he was going to die before he found one. I could feel tears welling up in my eyes because the thought of it was so sad.

I tried to get my mind off it by thinking of something else. That wasn't so hard. I just thought about what Mum was going to do to me when she came home.

'Did I ever tell you about the water-holding frog?' Grandpop asked. I nodded but he started telling me again anyway.

'This frog,' he said, 'lives in the desert. Before the summer comes it fills itself up with water and burrows into the ground. It can stay down there for years and years, waiting for the rain. Then, one day the rains come. Water seeps through the sand and wakes up the sleeping frog. It burrows out and sings in the rain. Wonderful. Marvellous.' He was all excited. His whiskers were fairly bristling with joy.

Grandpop slammed the door of the truck and took out his keys. 'Tell your mother that I'll be back the day after tomorrow,' he said in his croaky old voice. He jumped into the truck and started up the engine.

A cloud of dust was approaching in the distance. It was Mum's Land Rover. I felt sick inside. I couldn't face her.

3

Okay, I shouldn't have done it. I was stupid.

But I did. I pulled open the back door of Grandpop's truck and climbed in. I knelt down and hid under a blanket. I was careful not to sit on my burnt bottom, I can tell you that. The truck was full of exploring equipment. A curtain was drawn across behind Grandpop's seat. I felt quite safe snuggled down among the tents and pans. The roar of Mum's Land Rover went by outside.

I had to stay hidden until we reached our destination. If Grandpop found me before we got there he'd just turn back. The truck bumped and jolted. It was hot and I started to get thirsty.

Grandpop started to sing. He was making up the words as he went. It was a sad little song about the water-holding frog. It told how the raindrops fell and woke up the sleeping frogs. 'Oh, what a sight that would be,' he said to himself.

Suddenly, more than anything else in the world, I wanted to help Grandpop find a water-holding frog before he died. Being in Mum's bad books didn't seem important at all any more. I was so excited that I even forgot how thirsty I was.

The truck bumped on and on. I lay on my stomach in the back, dreaming that I would be the one to find the water-holding frog. Grandpop would be happy. Mum would be happy too because she loved Grandpop so much. She probably wouldn't even go crook at me about running away or ruining the writing pad. I had to find a water-holding frog. For everyone's sake.

Just then I heard a blast from a horn. I peeped out of the back and saw two blokes in a hotted-up car. It was a red Ford with big, fat tyres. The driver was trying to make Grandpop go faster. The dirt road was narrow and they couldn't get past. They were really mean-looking guys. The driver was covered in tattoos. The bloke next to him was picking his nose and glaring at us at the same time.

Poor old Grandpop. 'All right, all right,' he said in a trembling voice. 'I'm going as fast as I can.' I could hear him through the curtain that he had stretched behind the front seat. He couldn't see me staring out of the back.

But the two men in the Ford could.

Okay, I shouldn't have done it. I was stupid.

But I just couldn't help myself. I bent one finger and held the knuckle up under my nose. It looked like my finger was going right up inside my nostril. Then I twisted my wrist and with my other hand, pointed at the guy who was picking his nose.

Well, he went right off. His face turned red. The big Ford suddenly lurched off the road and tore past in a swirl of dust. The driver blasted his horn and cut us off. The truck bumped and skidded on the edge of the road. For a second I thought we were going to turn over.

But we didn't. Somehow or other Grandpop managed to keep the truck on the road. 'Idiots,' he yelled as the Ford disappeared into the distance.

I sure hoped we weren't going to meet those blokes again.

4

My throat was parched. There was a water barrel in the back but I couldn't get to it without shifting some boxes. Grandpop might hear me.

After another four hours the truck stopped. I heard Grandpop get out. I peeped through a window and saw that we were at one of those lonely little petrol stations in the middle of the desert. A big sign said LAST STOP BEFORE ALICE SPRINGS. Behind the sign I saw a red Ford parked in the shade.

Grandpop started filling the truck with petrol.

This was my chance to get a drink. The water was in

a large drum with a tap at the bottom. I grabbed a mug and filled it up. Boy, was I thirsty. I drank mug after mug full. I was just filling my fourth mug when I heard shouting.

I peeped outside. The big tattooed guy and his mate were pushing Grandpop around. They had his hat and were throwing it to each other. Poor old Grandpop had no one to help him. Except me. I forgot all about the water that was pouring into the mug. I just dropped everything and leaped out of the car.

Grandpop jumped and hopped like a little kid, trying to get his hat back. He was really old and I could see it was hard for him to move. His breath came out in noisy wheezes. Sweat was pouring down his cheeks. Or was it tears?

Now I'm quite good at basketball, if I do say so myself. I took a flying leap up onto the back of the tattooed one and snatched the hat. He fell down in the dust onto his knees.

Grandpop was amazed to see me. 'Gavin,' he yelled. Half happy, half mad.

The two big guys came towards us. They were not half happy and they were not half mad. They were completely furious. They started to walk towards us. We backed away.

But at that exact moment the owner of the garage came out. He was the biggest man I had ever seen. His legs were like tree trunks. His fists were like boulders.

'What's going on?' he said.

'Nothing,' said the nose picker. Both men headed towards their car muttering beneath their breath. As they drove off I held my knuckle up to my nose for one more time. They saw me but they kept going. I felt quite safe standing there with a giant next to me. Lucky for us we never saw them again.

Grandpop gave me a big lecture but I could see that he was glad to have me there. He went inside the garage and rang Mum. I waited outside feeling nervous. After a bit Grandpop came out. 'She said you can come with me,' he said.

'Did she say anything else?' I asked.

He gave me a wink. 'She said she's busy writing letters on her new pad.'

Whew. What a relief. She wasn't angry with me any more. Now we could get on with it. And find a water-holding frog.

It was good not to be in any trouble. It was good not to feel guilty for messing things up. I climbed into the back of the truck and knelt behind Grandpop's seat. We headed off into the burning desert which was nearly as hot as my burning bottom. Neither of us knew that I had left the water tap turned on in the back.

5

Grandpop was so pleased to have me. 'That water-holding frog will amaze you,' he said. 'The rain falls after the drought. It soaks into the ground. And the little frog digs its way up.' He was so happy. It was enough to bring tears to your eyes.

I wasn't so sure though. I looked out at the bleached desert. It was in the middle of summer. 'How will you find a frog?' I said. 'They'll all be underground.'

'Dig,' he said. 'The ground will be rock-hard and digging is the only way.'

We turned off the main road and headed across the hot red earth. Spinifex and mulga bushes were the only plants in the barren soil. Grandpop often stopped to check his compass. Each time he did we had a swig from his water bottle. You sure got thirsty out there in the middle of nowhere. I loved the feel of that cool water trickling down my throat.

After four hours we reached the waterhole. I say waterhole but, of course, at that time of the year it was only a claypan. Just a shallow, dry hole.

The truck bumped to a stop. 'Just in time,' said Grandpop. 'The radiator is boiling.' Sure enough, clouds of steam came whooshing out of the bonnet. 'It doesn't matter,' he said. 'I've brought plenty of water.'

We went around to the back of the truck to unpack.

You know what I said about never knowing when you were going to be in trouble? Well, when Grandpop found out that we had no water, it was worse than ever. Once again I had mucked things up.

He didn't go crook because I left the tap on. He didn't tell me off. He just stood there looking very worried. Very worried indeed. In a way, it was worse than being yelled at. I felt terrible. It was all my fault.

'What will we do?' I said.

'We stay here,' replied Grandpop. 'The first rule in the desert is to stay with your vehicle. Someone will come and look for us.'

'No one knows where we are,' I said.

'They know roughly where we are,' he said. 'Anyway, we don't have any choice. The car is no good without water. And we don't have a drop to spare.'

I tried to cheer him up a bit. 'We can look for the water-holding frog while we wait,' I said.

He shook his head. 'We have to conserve our energy. All we can do is wait for help without moving too much.'

I felt so guilty. Now he was never going to find his water-holding frog. And it was all my fault.

We put up a canvas shelter on the side of the truck to stop the heat of the sun. Grandpop handed me the water bottle. 'Take two swigs,' he said. I held back my head and took two swigs. I couldn't have taken three swigs even if I'd wanted to. There was none left. Grandpop had given me the last of the water. That's the sort of bloke he was.

6

I wondered how long we could last with nothing to drink. Grandpop would go first. I was young and strong. He was old and weak. What if I lived and he died? I couldn't bear the thought of it.

Hours passed. Night crept up. Mosquitoes whined. Things moved in the night. The moon rose. It became cold and we wrapped ourselves in blankets.

The next morning it grew hot quickly. My mouth was dry and dusty. I could hardly swallow. Grandpop dozed and mumbled. He seemed to be off in a dream.

The sun rose higher and higher. 'Frog. Little water-holding frog,' mumbled Grandpop. His eyes were wild. He didn't seem to know what was going on. The heat was getting to him. He crawled on his hands and knees into the middle of the claypan. He started scratching at the sand with his bent fingers. 'Frog, little frog,' he croaked.

I gently led him back to the shade. 'I'll get you a frog,' I said.

Only one thought filled my mind. Find Grandpop a water-holding frog. I didn't care about being rescued. I didn't care whether I lived or died. Grandpop was off his head but it didn't make any difference. All I wanted was to put one of those frogs into his hand.

Everything was my fault. He would die soon, without water, I knew that. I had to grant his life-long wish. I had to find one of those frogs.

I grabbed a shovel and trudged into the middle of the claypan. I whacked the point down into the ground. Wham. It was as hard as rock. The shock hurt my fingers.

The hot sand shimmered. Flies buzzed around my eyes. Dust covered my skin. But on I dug. On and on. Each time I hit the ground with the shovel I collected a small pile of sand. 'Frog,' I said. 'Little frog, where are you?'

But there was no answer. The water-holding frogs were all buried deep, waiting for the first drops of water to fall and wake them from their long sleep.

My fingers started to bleed. Large blisters grew and burst on my palms. I had managed to dig out a hole about the size of a shallow bath. But still no frog. It was no good. I would never find one. My tongue felt like a piece of shrivelled leather.

Grandpop lay there in the shade. I could tell he was still alive because his chest was going up and down. But he didn't have much longer to go. Not without water. I had to find a water-holding frog before it was too late. I couldn't give up.

Grandpop mumbled to himself, 'Little frog, little water-holding frog.'

I wrapped a rag around my blistered hand and started to dig again. Painfully. Slowly. Bending, scraping, digging only a few grains at a time. My head started to spin. It was no good. I just couldn't lift the shovel any more.

7

I tried to dig with my grazed fingers but they made no impression on the baked ground.

It was useless. I couldn't go on. I stood and looked at the empty horizon. Grandpop would never get his water-holding frog. He would die without his dream coming true. And it was all my fault. It was so sad.

Okay, I shouldn't have done it. I was stupid.

I sat down in despair. Wow. Did my bottom sting. It was still red and sore. The pain was terrible. Tears streamed down my nose and plopped onto the hard ground. A regular waterfall of tears. A little wet patch formed on the sand just beneath my cheek.

Suddenly, in the middle of the damp sand, a small green leg appeared. And then another.

My tears had woken a water-holding frog from its sleep. Two eyes blinked at me. Two wonderful, wonderful eyes.

'I've got one, Grandpop,' I screamed. 'I've got one.' Gently I picked up the glistening frog. I walked over to Grandpop and placed the tiny creature in his hand.

I wouldn't have believed that one little frog could have had such an effect. Grandpop leaned up and gave the biggest grin I had ever seen. He looked at me with love in his smile. Love for me. And the frog. We both had tears in our eyes.

It was such a magic moment that neither of us noticed the storm clouds gathering. We just sat looking at that frog until the first raindrops fell. And the pool began to fill. The songs of a thousand frogs filled the air.

It was a real downpour. The heavens seemed to be weeping as I stood there and rubbed my behind. 'Cry, baby,' I said to the sky. 'Cry, baby, cry.'

Ex Poser

There are two rich kids in our form. Sandra Morris and Ben Fox. They are both snobs. They think they are too good for the rest of us. Their parents have big cars and big houses. Both of them are quiet. They keep to themselves. I guess they don't want to mix with the ruffians like me.

Ben Fox always wears expensive gym shoes and the latest fashions. He thinks he is good-looking with his blue eyes and blonde hair. He is a real poser.

Sandra Morris is the same. And she knows it. Blue eyes and blonde hair too. Skin like silk. Why do some kids get the best of everything?

Me, I landed pimples. I've used everything I can on them. But they still grow and burst. Just when you don't want them to. It's not fair.

Anyway, today I have the chance to even things up. Boffin is bringing along his latest invention — a lie detector. Sandra Morris is the victim. She agreed to try it out because everyone knows that she would never tell a lie. What she doesn't know is that Boffin and I are going to ask her some very embarrassing questions.

Boffin is a brain. His inventions always work. He is smarter than the teachers. Everyone knows that. And now he has brought along his latest effort. A lie detector.

He tapes two wires to Sandra's arm. 'It doesn't hurt,' he says. 'But it is deadly accurate.' He switches on the machine and a little needle swings into the middle of the dial. 'Here's a trial question,' he says. 'Are you a girl?'

Sandra nods.

'You have to say yes or no,' he says.

'Yes,' replies Sandra. The needle swings over to TRUTH. Maybe this thing really works. Boffin gives a big grin.

'This time tell a lie,' says Boffin. 'Are you a girl?' he asks again.

Sandra smiles with that lovely smile of hers. 'No,' she says. A little laugh goes up but then all the kids in the room gasp. The needle points to LIE. This lie detector is a terrific invention.

'Okay,' says Boffin. 'You only have seven questions, David. The batteries will go flat after another seven questions.' He sits down behind his machine and twiddles the knobs.

This is going to be fun. I am going to find out a little bit about Sandra Morris and Ben Fox. It's going to be very interesting. Very interesting indeed.

I ask my first question. 'Have you ever kissed Ben Fox?'

Sandra goes red. Ben Fox goes red. I have got them this time. I am sure they have something going between them. I will expose them.

'No,' says Sandra. Everyone cranes their neck to see what the lie detector says. The needle points to TRUTH.

This is not what I expected. And I only have six questions left. I can't let her off the hook. I am going to expose them both.

'Have you ever held his hand?'

Again she says, 'No.' And the needle says TRUTH. I am starting to feel guilty. Why am I doing this?

I try another tack. 'Are you in love?' I ask.

A red flush starts to crawl up her neck. I am feeling really mean now. Fox is blushing like a sunset.

'Yes,' she says. The needle points to TRUTH.

I shouldn't have let the kids talk me into doing this. I decided to put Sandra and Ben out of their agony. I won't actually name him. I'll spare her that. 'Is he in this room?' I say.

She looks at the red Ben Fox. 'Yes,' she says. The needle points to TRUTH.

'Does he have blue eyes?' I ask.

'No,' she says.

'Brown?' I say.

'No,' she says again.

I don't know what to say next. I look at each kid in the class very carefully. Ben Fox has blue eyes. I was sure that she loved him.

'This thing doesn't work,' I say to Boffin. 'I can't see one kid who doesn't have either blue eyes or brown eyes.'

'We can,' says Boffin. They are all looking at me.

I can feel my face turning red now. I wish I could sink through the floor but I get on with my last question. 'Is he an idiot?' I ask.

Sandra is very embarrassed. 'Yes,' she says in a voice that is softer than a whisper. 'And he has green eyes.'

Sloppy Jalopy

My sister Helen looked around the schoolyard and then pointed to my ear. 'You're mad wearing an earring to school,' she said.

'Smacka Johns,' said a voice behind me. 'Come here at once.'

It was Ms Cranch, the vice principal. She held out her hand. 'Give me that earring.'

'But it's only a sleeper,' I said as I handed it over.

'No jewellery is allowed at school,' she snapped.

Before I could get another word out she turned round and headed off towards her office with my earring.

'I told you,' said Helen.

'She's the crabbiest teacher I ever met,' I grumbled. 'I wonder what she does with the earrings. She must have millions of 'em.'

'She wears them,' said Helen. 'I saw her wearing mine down the street once.'

'She wouldn't,' I said scornfully. 'Even crotchety old Cranch wouldn't nick stuff from kids.'

All day I thought about my earring. I got madder. And madder. And madder. By the time school was over

I had made a decision. There was only one thing to do. Buy another earring and wear it to school as a protest. Teachers aren't allowed to steal from kids.

I went straight home and strode into the lounge. 'Dad,' I said. 'Can you take me into town? I want to buy a new earring.'

Dad smiled. 'Sure,' he said. 'I'm just on my way out.'

Earrings didn't worry Dad. He used to wear one himself once. He's not your regular sort of dad. He is always doing crazy, wild things. To be perfectly honest, sometimes he is a bit of an embarrassment.

We walked out to the car. Dad had always wanted a sports car but he couldn't afford it. So he cut the top off our Holden and now we could only use it when it wasn't raining.

On the way to town I complained about the car. 'I don't know what you're going on about,' said Dad. 'This is a fabulous car. No one else in town has got one like it. Who wants to be like everyone else?'

I smiled. He was right. I didn't want to be like everyone else. Little did I know that in a very short time my wish was going to come true in a big way.

2

We finally reached town and Dad pulled up behind a filthy-looking tanker truck. He pointed to a shop. 'There,' he said. 'They sell earrings.'

The shop was dingy and cobwebbed. It looked spooky

inside. I felt a bit nervous. 'I've changed my mind,' I said to Dad. 'I don't like the look of this place.'

'Rubbish,' said Dad. 'Hurry up, I've got my own shopping to do.' He pushed me through the door into the shop.

I banged straight into an enormous man dressed in shorts and a blue singlet. He clutched an earring between his fingers. He smelt terrible. Awful. 'Watch it,' he growled. He brushed past me and swept through the door.

'Sorry,' I mumbled.

An old man with an incredibly wrinkled face was serving at the counter.

'I'm looking for an earring,' I said.

The shopkeeper smiled at me. 'I usually only sell them in pairs,' he said. 'But that gentleman talked me into letting him have just one. You can have the matching one if you want. They were second-hand. I bought them from a palm reader.'

It was just what I wanted so I handed over five dollars. Then I put the earring in my pocket. We walked out into the street and jumped into the Holden.

A horrible stench filled the air. It was coming from the tanker truck in front.

Straight away I knew what it was. Newman's Pond. The Council has been emptying it and taking the contents to their depot. It was the most putrid pond in the whole world. Drains from the fertiliser works, the fish factory and the oil refinery poured into it. Everything was dead for metres around. Green slime covered the surface. Stifling fumes bubbled into the fetid air. Horrible lumps floated in the slime.

The Council workers had to wear gas masks while they were sucking the squelching goo into the trucks. The sludge in that tanker was the stuff of nightmares. My nightmares as it turned out.

The guy in the blue singlet drove the truck out onto the road. We followed in our convertible. I was longing for fresh air. But I didn't get it.

Little brown flecks flicked off the truck and onto our windscreen. Dad turned on the wipers but they only made things worse. A foul smear made it almost impossible to see. The spattering turned into a shower. Filthy specks of putrid liquid covered us like freckles.

'What a nerve,' yelled Dad. 'Look what he's doing to my car.'

I wasn't worried about the car. I was worried about me. I was splotted with dreadful droplets. I shuddered to think where they came from.

The back of the truck had a large valve for connection to a pipe. I could just imagine what had been sucked in through it.

Dad beeped the horn. 'Pull over,' he screamed. 'You idiot. You're polluting the whole town.'

I myself would not have called the driver an idiot. Not a big guy like that. But Dad never thinks of the consequences. He pulled out next to the truck and shook his fist at the guy in the blue singlet. 'Pull over, you fool,' Dad yelled through his brown smeared lips.

The truck lurched over to the side of the road and stopped.

3

The driver stepped out. Dad stepped out. I did not step out.

'You're flicking foul muck all over the street,' said Dad. 'Tighten that valve up.' Dad pointed to a wheel on top of the valve.

'Did you call me an idiot?' said the driver. He was an awfully big bloke.

'Well,' said Dad, trying to laugh. 'Look what you've done.' They stared at our splattered car. I pretended I wasn't there.

'An idiot, eh,' said the driver. 'An idiot, am I? I guess I'm so dumb that I couldn't even tighten the valve up properly.' He jumped up on the back of the truck and began turning the wheel. 'Oh dear,' he said. 'I seem to be turning it the wrong way.'

'Aghhhh . . .' I screamed. 'No. Mercy. No, no, no.'

But I was too late. An enormous jet of bilious brown sludge hit me in the head. It flooded. It surged. It filled the car to the top of the doors and poured down onto the street.

I gagged and gasped in the middle of my own private

cesspool. Horrible lumps floated by. A rotting fish head swirled by in its own polluted sea.

Our car had been transformed into an ecological disaster.

I fumbled for the door handle and was swept out onto the footpath by the unspeakable flow.

My ears and eyes and nose were choked with the filth. I coughed and spluttered and dragged myself across the footpath. People on the street jumped back in horror. They held handkerchiefs to their noses.

They glared at me as if I was a monster spewed up from dark and hideous places. I stood up and shook myself like a dog coming out of the water. A moaning sigh of horror swept across the passers-by. They fell back in fear as my spray scattered in the breeze.

The smell was terrible. I stank like a sewer. I dripped with dung. Foulness fell like melting manure from my putrid skin. I choked with each tortured breath.

The guy in the blue singlet thought it was funny. He started laughing. He turned off the terrible flow, jumped in his truck and drove off.

Dad just stood there staring at his contaminated car and shaking his head.

'Help,' I gurgled. Brown bubbles formed on the end of my nose as I spoke. I felt weak. The fumes were making my head spin. Suddenly my brown world turned to black. I collapsed on the footpath.

4

When I awoke most of the muck had gone. Dad stood squirting me with a hose that the butcher had lent him. 'You'll be okay,' said Dad with a grin. 'It's all part of the rich pageant of life.' He took a deep breath, blew up his cheeks and started to hose out the car. Every now and then he dashed away and gulped fresh air.

But there was no fresh air for me. I stank. I staggered over to a flower-box outside a shop. I swear that the flowers wilted in front of my eyes. People crossed the street to avoid the mad father flushing out his car. And his horrible, stinking son.

It was a hot day and a lot of the gunk had become baked on the car. Dad couldn't get it off. The butcher approached with a handkerchief over his nose. 'Look,' he said. 'You'll have to get that thing out of here. I'm losing business.'

Dad opened the car door.

'Get in,' he said to me.

'You're joking,' I gasped. 'It'll never start.'

'Get in,' he said again.

I did as I was told. I squeezed into the sodden, foul seat. Dad turned over the engine. It started first go. I couldn't believe it.

'They don't build 'em like this any more,' Dad said with a smile.

We set off down the road throwing a brown shower out behind us. Talk about embarrassing. Now it was us who were polluting the neighbourhood. The following cars tooted and bipped. Drivers shook their fists at us as freckles of foulness spattered their windscreens.

'Step on it,' I said to Dad. 'I can't take much more of this.' Chitty Chitty Bang Bang had nothing on this car.

After what seemed about ten years Dad finally reached our house. 'You go in and have a shower,' he said. 'I'm taking the car into town to get it steam-cleaned.'

I was already halfway to the door before he'd finished talking. A shower. Oh, how I longed for a shower. I stayed under the water for at least an hour. I scrubbed. And rubbed. I soaped and soaked. I had to get every bit of gunk off my skin.

This was pollution of the worst type. Who knew what chemicals had been dumped in that pond?

At last I jumped out of the water. I dried myself and put on my new earring. Then I examined my reflection in the mirror. Something was wrong. Maybe the sludge had seeped into my skin. I sniffed myself all over like a dog. I didn't seem to smell. But something was different. My skin tingled. It felt strange. Still, after what had happened it was no wonder.

I walked down to the kitchen. That's when everything started to go wrong.

5

A movement in the corner caught my eye. Someone had thrown a used tissue there. It was flapping in the breeze. Except there was no breeze. Without warning, the tissue sort of flapped and twirled and then flew across the room. It plastered itself onto my face.

I gave a little scream and tore it off. It twisted and squirmed in my hand. I screwed it into a ball and threw it down on the floor. The tissue bounced and then shot back and stuck itself onto my nose.

I heard a noise. 'Dad,' I yelled. But it wasn't Dad. An empty sardine tin slid towards me. It sped across the floor and attached itself to my right foot. I pulled it off and threw it into the corner where it stayed for about half a second. Then it sped straight back to its place on my foot.

I rubbed my eyes. This was crazy. First the tissue and now the sardine tin. Sticking to me like glue. What was going on? I pulled on my clothes like a crazy man.

Something had happened to me. Something awful. I tried to peer at myself in the mirror. But before I could even catch a glimpse of my face my vision was blotted out. About twenty tissues flew out of the waste-paper basket and covered my face.

Hairs trapped in the plug-hole of the sink started to move. They twirled and then, like flicked rubber bands, shot through the air and stuck to my jumper.

My mind swirled. Was I going crazy? Was this really happening?

It was.

Rubbish. I was attracting rubbish. Like a magnet.

'Newman's Pond,' I said to myself. 'The stinking

waste has made me magnetic. Filth is attracting filth.'

A gnarled old toothbrush swooped towards me. Two empty drink bottles followed.

I looked around for somewhere to hide. By the door was our phone box. One of those old-fashioned red ones that used to be on street corners. I had laughed when Dad bought it. But now I wasn't laughing.

I bolted into the phone box and slammed the door behind me. I made it just in time. The bottles glued themselves to the glass. The toothbrush tried to jiggle its way under the door.

I tried to think. I was shivering with fear. Rubbish of every sort was seeking me out. My life was in danger. I could be buried. Suffocated. Bits of fluff and dust were wriggling under the door. Spent matches and bottle tops followed and splotted onto my knees.

My brain wouldn't work. 'Think,' I said to myself. 'Think.'

I was sure that the water from Newman's Pond had done something to my skin. That man in the blue singlet. He was responsible. He lived with that stuff every day. He must have some sort of soap to cure it.

I grabbed the phone book and flipped through the pages. 'South Barwon Council Depot,' I said to myself. 'Got it.'

My fingers fumbled with the dial. I heard the phone ringing at the other end. 'Come on,' I said. 'Come on, come on.'

But there was no answer. The man with the blue singlet was probably out in the yard emptying the revolting contents of his truck.

The phone box was almost completely covered in garbage. Junk was hurtling across the room and flapping on the glass as if it was alive. At any moment the glass might break.

It was time to make a run for it. I was just about to force the door open when my heart froze in terror.

Our garbage can was rattling. It jiggled and wiggled as if demons inside were trying to burst out.

I turned back to the phone book and looked up the taxi company. I dialled with a shaking hand. 'Address?' said a voice.

'Fifteen Henry Street,' I gasped.

'Going to?' asked the voice.

'South Barwon,' I said. 'The Council Depot.'

'Please wait,' said a voice on the other end of the phone.

'Hurry,' I yelled. 'It's an emergency.'

'Ten minutes,' said the voice.

I stared out of the phone box at the bulging bin over by the sink. At any moment it might burst. I could be trapped in the phone box if I stayed much longer.

6

More and more rubbish flattened itself against the glass door. A newspaper flew across the room and flapped over to join the attack. The phone box door was creaking and cracking under the strain. There wasn't much time left.

'Hurry,' I shouted. 'Hurry.'

A horn sounded from outside. I groaned with relief. A pane cracked next to my ear. Glass and junk exploded into the phone box. I charged out of the house. Our garbage bin rattled and jumped as I ran past it. Debris followed me as I fled.

I yanked open the taxi door and jumped into the back seat. I slammed the door just in time to keep out most of the garbage. 'Where to?' said the taxi driver. He was a little, nervous-looking guy. His eyes nearly bugged out of his head when he saw my coating of junk.

'South Barw . . .' I started to say. I never finished the sentence. The contents of the taxi's ashtray flew through the air straight into my mouth. Filthy cigarette butts, ash and dead matches crammed themselves between my lips. I choked and spluttered and spat them out. They stuck to my face like glue.

'What the . . .' shouted the taxi driver. 'Get out of my . . .'

We both looked out of the window as a loud bang filled the air. The lid had shot off our garbage bin as if it had been dynamited. The contents were bouncing and flying down the path towards us. They smattered onto the back of the taxi and rattled on the rear window.

Plastic bags full of refuse were bouncing our way

along the track. 'Quick,' I screamed. 'Quick. Move it or we're history.'

An empty can of cat food hit the taxi window like a mortar shell. With a loud scream the driver put the car into gear and shot forward. Rubbish bounced and banged along after us.

We screeched along the track and out onto the road. The back of the car was piled with cans, paper bags, take-away food boxes and other unmentionables. Suddenly the driver hit the brakes. A dog. A dog was on the road.

'Don't stop,' I yelled. 'Whatever you do, don't stop. We'll be buried alive.'

The dog was trotting by with a bone in its mouth. The bone started to jiggle. The dog growled and pulled back as if someone was trying to pull the bone out of its mouth. Suddenly the bone shot out of the dog's jaws and flew through the air towards us. The dog charged after it, barking and yelping like crazy. The bone banged onto the back of the car and joined the putrid pile on the boot. The back window blacked out as more and more junk gathered.

The driver raced around the dog and down past the fish factory. 'No, no. Not that,' I screamed. Too late. Hundreds of dead, stinking fish slid out of the factory garbage bins. Flying fish. Dead flying fish. They splattered against the car and flapped on the side windows in their thousands.

'My car. My lovely new car,' groaned the driver.

'Go,' I yelled. 'Faster, faster, faster.'

7

The driver gunned the engine and we raced along the road and out onto the highway. I thought that the rubbish might fall off as we bounced and lurched around the traffic. But no luck. Every piece of rubbish clung on, trying desperately to get inside. Other junk stirred and flew up as we passed but we were too fast for it. Bits of roadside rubbish fell back like cowboys giving up the chase.

'We're safe as long as you keep going,' I shouted over the din of the banging rubbish.

'What happens when we run out of petrol?' he yelled back.

'A man in a blue singlet,' I said. 'At the Council Depot. He knows about it. He must. It's all his fault. Find him.'

'Find the man in the blue singlet,' mumbled the driver. He slowed to take a corner and two mouldy cabbages bounced out of a roadside vegetable stall and lobbed onto the bonnet.

Well, I won't say much about the rest of the journey. Except to say that it was a nightmare. As we moved further into the countryside I thought it would be better. But it wasn't. Every time we slowed down, cow pats in the paddock stirred and flew towards us. They splotted on top of our coating of junk and formed a thick, brown crust.

Only a small clearing on the windscreen remained. The windscreen wipers groaned under the strain. It was me the junk was chasing so I stayed well to the back of the car to attract it away from the windscreen.

Finally we reached a fence with a dirty sign hanging on the gate. South Barwon Council Depot. We only just made it. The car was covered. It was ten times its size. A slowly moving mountain of litter. We stopped. 'I can't see a thing,' said the driver. 'This is the end.'

I looked at the poor guy. He was terrified. 'It's okay,' I told him. 'It's me. I attract rubbish. When I get out it'll all follow me. You'll be okay.'

'What about my taxi?' he asked through the gloom. 'It's covered in filth.'

'It will all drop off and follow me. Don't worry about it,' I said.

He looked at the meter and held out his hand. 'Twenty-five dollars sixty,' he said. 'And it should be two hundred.'

Suddenly I felt weak. I went cold all over. I patted my jeans desperately. I searched every pocket. 'Oh no,' I groaned. 'I've left my wallet at home.'

I closed my eyes in despair. When I opened them I saw that the taxi driver had changed. He wasn't his normal self at all. His face was red. He looked as if he was going to explode.

'What?' he screamed. 'After all this you haven't even got the fare?' He leaned over and grabbed my T-shirt. He was so mad that he was spitting as he yelled. 'Right. What have you got then?'

I fumbled with the strap of my watch. 'You can have this,' I said. 'It's real valuable.'

He looked at my watch scornfully as he strapped it on his wrist. 'Pull the other one,' he growled. Then he pointed to my ear. 'I'll have that as well.'

I was in no position to argue. I took out my new earring and handed it over. He looked in the mirror and threaded it into a hole in his ear. Then he grinned at me – daring me to object.

I had nothing else to give. And I had to get out of there. I heaved open the door of the car and plunged out through the rubbish. I rolled over on the ground like a soldier avoiding bullets. Then I folded my head into my arms and waited for the rubbish to hit.

8

Nothing. Nothing happened. Not for a second or two anyway. I looked down at my clothes. I was as clean as a whistle.

Suddenly a terrible scream came from the taxi. The rubbish was piling into the open door. 'Help,' yelled the driver. 'Help, help, help.' He was completely covered in the seething junk. The pieces of rubbish were like rats pouring into a food bin.

I looked around the depot for something to pull the rubbish away from the poor man. But it was a very clean yard. Strangely clean for that sort of place. There was nothing I could grab.

I ran over to a little shed in the corner of the yard. I tried to get in the door but I couldn't. The shed was filled to the roof with the seething junk. 'Help,' came a deep voice from inside. 'Help.'

I'd heard that voice before. It was the guy in the blue singlet.

My head began to spin. The taxi driver was covered in junk. And so was the tanker driver. But the junk wasn't after me any more. Why?

Suddenly it came to me. The earrings. Both earrings came from the same shop. And the same pair. The earrings were attracting the junk, not the sludge from Newman's Pond.

I ran over to the taxi. 'The earring,' I yelled. 'Take off the earring.'

There was muttering and spluttering from inside. Suddenly the junk collapsed. Like cans in a supermarket falling, the rubbish tumbled out onto the ground. The taxi driver began to clamber out. He was shaking like a leaf.

I turned my attention to the man in the blue singlet. 'Take off your earring,' I shouted into the junk pile. 'The earrings attract rubbish when you put them on.'

There was more muttering and spluttering as the

tanker driver reached up and pulled the earring out. Then without warning, his pile of junk collapsed too. His head poked out of the top like a fairy on a horrible Christmas tree. He climbed out towards us. 'This thing is dangerous,' he said. 'I'm getting rid of it.'

'Me too,' said the taxi driver. They threw back their arms. They were going to hurl the earrings into the paddock.

'No,' I said. 'Don't throw them away.' I picked up an empty jar and held it out towards them.

9

The next day I walked slowly into the grounds.

'I'm showing these to one of the science teachers,' I said to Helen. 'We could be rich and famous.'

She looked around the schoolyard and then stared at my jar. 'You're mad bringing more earrings to school,' she said.

'Smacka Johns,' snapped a voice behind me. 'Come here at once.'

It was Ms Cranch, the vice principal. She held out her hand. 'Give me those earrings.'

'But I'm not even wearing them,' I said as I handed over the jar.

'No jewellery is allowed at school,' she said.

Before I could get another word out she turned round and headed off towards her office with my earrings.

'I told you,' said Helen.

I mooched around sulking for about five minutes. Then I suddenly cheered up. All around the yard the garbage cans had started to rattle. They jiggled and wiggled as if demons were trying to burst out.

Loud bangs filled the air as the bins burst their lids. I started to laugh as the contents bounced across the yard towards Ms Cranch's office.

Eyes Knows

The people are so far below they look like little pins. I am scared and lonely. If I let go of the ladder I will fall. Down, down, down. Tumbling and turning. I can't bear to think about it. The wind whistles in my hair. The ladder on the crane reaches up towards the sky. I don't know whether to go up. Or down. My fingers are cold and numb. Who can help me? Only my little robot man.

My arm is curled tightly around the ladder but I can just reach him with my hand. I'm scared that I'll fall. I edge the little robot man out of my pocket with trembling fingers. If I drop him I'll never know what to do. 'Little robot man,' I say. 'You are my last chance.' I pull his nose and his eyes begin to spin.

2

It is only four hours since my little robot man started telling me what to do. And it is twenty-four hours since Mum and Dad broke my heart. 'Harry,' said Dad. 'We've got bad news. Your Mum and I are going to split up. We don't love each other any more.' He said a lot of other things but that's the only bit I remember. I ran to Mum and hugged her. My face made hers all wet. Or was it the other way round?

Then I ran to Dad and hugged him. He was crying too. 'What about me?' I said. 'What about me?'

Dad looked at me sadly. 'You have to choose,' he said. 'Mum's going interstate. You can go with her or stay here with me. We're not going to force you. It's up to you. Take a bit of time to think about it. You have to choose.'

How could I make a choice like that? I felt like a nail between two magnets. One magnet pulling me one way. And one the other. I was stuck in the middle.

I looked at my parents. I loved them both. I didn't know what to do. That night there was a terrible storm. I snuggled down inside my blankets. And cried a lot.

In the morning I started to dress myself. There were two pairs of socks. A green pair and a red pair. I couldn't make up my mind which to put on. I put out my hand for the green pair but then stopped. It felt wrong. I reached out for the red ones but that wasn't right either. I couldn't choose.

That's when my little robot man came to the rescue. See, he has two pairs of eyes. They spin like poker machines when you pull his nose. Sometimes the green eyes show and sometimes the red ones. You never know which it's going to be.

I took him down from the shelf and pulled his nose. His eyes spun in a blur. Then they stopped. On green. 'Green eyes – green socks,' I said. I put on my green socks and finished dressing. Then I ran into the kitchen for breakfast.

Dad had already gone to work but Mum was still there. 'Cornflakes or muesli?' she asked. I looked at both packets. I couldn't decide. I reached for the cornflakes but changed my mind. I decided on muesli. But that wasn't right either. What should I do?

There was a quick way out. I pulled the nose of my little robot man. 'Green for cornflakes,' I said. The eyes spun and stopped on red. 'Muesli it is,' I shrugged.

3

I kissed Mum goodbye, grabbed my little robot man and headed for school. I walked slowly. My feet dragged. I really felt down. Before long I was going to have to choose between Mum and Dad. I just couldn't do it. Life is full of terrible choices.

I trudged along, staring at my feet. Suddenly I stopped. There on the footpath was a little furry caterpillar. It was alive, but not moving. It had fallen off the branch of a tree and couldn't get back. Someone would probably stand on it and squash it. All I had to do was bend down, pick it up and put it back on the tree.

I didn't know whether to save the caterpillar or not. I decided to ask my little robot man. I gave his nose a tug and set his eyes spinning. 'Green for yes, red for no,' I said. The eyes spun swiftly and then slowed down. They stopped on green. 'This is your lucky day, caterpillar,'

I said. I gently placed it on a leaf on the tree and it started munching straight away.

I felt a bit better. I had saved the caterpillar. My little robot man was good at making choices. I turned the corner and saw an amazing sight. My heart failed for a second. About a thousand caterpillars were wriggling helplessly on the footpath. I guessed that the storm must have knocked them all off the trees.

'Do I save them? Yes or no?' I asked the robot with a trembling voice. The eyes spun. And stopped on green. 'Yes,' I said. 'The answer is yes. Oh no.' I crouched down and started to pick up the caterpillars. Down up, down up. Each one clung gratefully to its leaf and started to munch.

The minutes ticked by. Half an hour passed and I hardly seemed to have saved any of them. I knew I was going to be late for school. My little robot man was getting me into trouble. In the end it took me an hour to put all the caterpillars back on the tree. Every one was munching happily.

I looked at my watch. I was an hour late for school. Mr Hanson would be peering out of his office. He would pounce like a snake as soon as he saw me crossing the yard. I was in big trouble. I looked at my little robot man. 'You've really done it now,' I said. 'That's the last time I ask you to decide anything.' The little robot man was bad luck. I could see that now.

The hairs on the back of my head started to stand up. Someone was watching me. I could just feel it. I looked around and saw her. Mrs Week, a friend of Mum's. She was on her knees, weeding her garden. She was smiling at me. She called me over with a crooked finger. 'Wait here,' she said in a bright voice. She shuffled inside her house and left me standing alone. She took ages and ages. Finally she came back carrying a little envelope.

'I saw you saving those caterpillars,' she said. 'What a kind boy. No one else would do such a thing. Here's a little reward for you.' She pushed the envelope into my hand.

Should I take it? Yes or no? I wasn't sure. So I pulled the nose on my little robot man. Green. The green eyes blinked at me. It was green for yes. Mrs Week was already walking back inside with a big smile on her face. 'Thanks,' I yelled. 'Thanks a million.'

4

I hurried towards school. I was going to be later than ever. I tore the top off the envelope and looked inside. I stopped walking. Fifty dollars. There was a fifty-dollar note inside. I couldn't believe it.

My little robot man was bringing me incredible luck. Every time I asked it anything it came up with the right answer. Things worked out.

But what about school? Nothing could save me from the beady eyes of Mr Hanson. Or could it?

I thought of another question. Something to ask my little robot man. 'Shall I wag school? Not go at all?'

I pulled his nose. And his eyes stopped on green. Two green eyes telling me to wag it.

This was the way to decide things. This was definitely the best method to find out what to do. Everything my little robot man told me to do worked out all right. I slowed down. Some old people were blocking the way. They were waiting outside a take-away hamburger place. A very crabby nurse was bossing them around:

'Don't block the path,' she snapped at a poor old lady. 'Wait here,' she ordered. 'I'll get your salads.'

'Please, nurse,' said an old man. 'Can we have a hamburger?' Their faces lit up. 'Hamburgers,' said another old man. 'Yes, hamburgers.' They started to chant. 'Hamburgers, hamburgers, hamburgers.' Their eyes shone. Their wrinkles cracked into smiles. 'Hamburgers, hamburgers, hamburgers.'

'Stop this noise at once,' snapped the nurse. 'You'll get what you're given.' She was talking to them as if they were little kids. Their smiles fell from their faces like caterpillars dropping off a tree. The nurse walked inside the shop.

'What have you got there?' said a voice. It was one of the old people. He nodded at my little robot man. He was a nice man. He told me that his name was Fred. He listened carefully while I explained. So did all the others. They gathered around and nodded and chuckled while I told them how the little robot man worked.

Fred shook his head. 'I don't like the sound if it,'

he said. 'It's like trusting to luck.'

But the others were all excited. 'Try it out,' said an old man. 'Yes,' yelled someone else. 'Give us a demo.'

5

I looked up at the smiling faces. Why not? I took out my fifty dollars. 'Should I spend this?' I said aloud. I pulled the nose on the little robot man. His eyes spun. 'Green,' I yelled. 'That means yes.'

'Hamburgers,' said one crafty old guy with no teeth. 'Ask it if it wants to buy fifteen hamburgers.'

'Okay,' I said. 'Will I buy fifteen hamburgers? Yes or no?' I pulled the little robot man's nose. The eyes turned up red. Toothless was disappointed.

'Twenty,' he screeched. 'Ask if it wants twenty hamburgers.'

'Yes, yes,' said all the others. 'Twenty hamburgers. Twenty.'

I asked the little robot man and this time his eyes turned up green. Everyone cheered. I went into the shop and bought twenty hamburgers. The nurse wasn't anywhere to be seen. I guess she must have been in the washroom.

The old folks munched into the hamburgers. They were really hungry. Some of them patted me on the back. I felt good helping all these people and giving them such a good time. Fred wouldn't take a hamburger. He just shook his head in a kindly sort of way. 'I'll wait for the salad,' he said.

'Try something else,' said Toothless. 'Ask it something else.' He started to get excited. He stared at their bus that was parked by the side of the road. 'The bus,' he said. 'Ask if we should nick the bus.' They all started to grin wickedly with mouths full of hamburger. 'The bus,' they chanted. 'The bus, the bus, the bus.'

I wasn't so sure about this. The nurse was in charge of the bus. But what the heck. 'Do we take the bus?' I said to the little robot man. I pulled his nose. His eyes spun. Green. It was green for yes.

The old people pushed and shoved and scrambled on the bus. 'Nick the bus,' they chuckled. 'Nick the bus.' I was swept on with the rest.

Toothless jumped into the driver's seat and started up the engine. 'I used to race cars at Phillip Island,' he chuckled. 'Five firsts and six seconds. Eleven trophies.' He let out the clutch and the bus roared off. I looked back and saw the crabby nurse run out from the hamburger joint. She was yelling and waving her fists.

Everyone cheered and waved back. Some of them made rude signs at her with their fingers. Fred sat at the back looking worried.

The bus rocketed through the traffic at enormous speed. We were approaching a T-intersection. 'Which way?' yelled Toothless. 'Left or right?'

'I don't know,' I yelled.

'Ask him,' screeched Toothless.

I pulled on the nose. 'Left,' I screamed. 'Yes or no?'

The eyes rolled. The bus plummeted on. Into the intersection. Cars screeched and swerved. A brick wall seemed to rush towards us. The eyes stopped. Red. 'Right,' I yelled. 'Turn right.'

Toothless pulled on the wheel. The bus lurched around. The tyres screamed. Blue smoke swirled through the air. We missed the brick wall by about one centimetre. Other drivers sounded their horns. Boy, were they mad. But our passengers cheered and screamed. They were loving every minute of it.

'Put my foot down? Yes or no?' yelled Toothless. The answer was green. Toothless did as he was told. He stepped on the accelerator. The bus screamed along the road. Suddenly I heard something. A police siren. The police were giving chase.

'Pull over or run for it?' yelled Toothless.

'Pull over,' said a voice. It was Fred. He leaned across and pulled out the ignition key. 'This has gone far enough,' he said. The bus bumped to a standstill and the old folk got off the bus. They were all still grinning with excitement as the police walked up.

I edged towards the back of the crowd. 'Run for it, yes or no?' I whispered. I pulled the nose and my little robot man's eyes rolled. Green. I looked for somewhere to run.

That's when I saw the crane. With the ladder straight up the side. 'The crane,' I whispered again. 'Yes or no?' I was hoping it was going to be red. But it wasn't. The eyes spun to green.

'Give me that,' said Fred. He took the little robot man from my hands and turned it over. There was a little door on its back. Fred opened the door and started to fiddle around inside. He was doing something to it.

'No,' I yelled. 'Give it back.' I snatched the little robot man from his hands.

A large policeman yelled at the crowd. 'Who's responsible for all this?' he said in a stern voice.

There was dead silence. Then Toothless turned around and pointed at me. 'Him,' he yelled. 'Him.'

I started to run. I belted along the street towards the crane. The police set out after me. And the old folk. And the nurse. 'Stop,' they screamed. 'Stop.' They yelled and called and stumbled. I fled for my life. Towards the crane.

I looked up. My legs trembled. My head felt as if it was a ball on the end of a piece of string. I didn't want to go. But the little robot man had given his orders. I put my foot on the bottom rung. And started climbing. Up, up, up. Hand over foot. Higher and higher. I looked up at the clouds. I dared not stare below.

6

So here I am. Stuck halfway up the ladder. I am too scared to go up. And too scared to climb down. The people are like little pins far beneath. I have been here for ages. My hands are getting tired. My feet are numb. If I don't do something soon I will fall. Over and over and over.

Like a caterpillar falling off a leaf. Only no one will pick me up and put me back.

Someone is starting to climb up. It's hard to see so far below but I think it is Dad. What if he falls? It will be my fault. I don't know what to do. I reach for my little robot man and pull his nose. I stare at the eyes as they spin. They stop. 'Oh no,' I say. 'Oh no.'

I start to climb down to my doom. Slowly. Painfully. One foot after another without looking. I am scared I am going to fall. But I don't. Finally I get to the bottom and Dad and Mum hug me. The old people all cheer. Fred smiles at me.

The police are angry. 'He could have killed himself. Or someone else,' says the policeman.

'He's not himself today,' says Dad. 'We told him we are getting divorced. He's upset.' Mum is crying. We are still crying when we get home.

I hope that Mum and Dad will change their minds now. And not split up. But they don't. I still have to choose between them. Will I go interstate with Mum? Or stay with Dad? I sit on my bed and decide to give my little robot man one more go. I pull his nose. 'Green for Dad,' I say. The eyes spin. And stop. Just like they did on the crane.

I toss the little robot man out of the window and walk into the lounge-room. Mum and Dad are sitting there. 'I've made up my mind,' I yell. 'You're getting divorced. Not me. You choose. It's your problem, not mine.' They both look at each other. They know I am right.

7

So. It all turns out to be not so bad. Mum and Dad split up. But Mum doesn't go interstate. She rents a house in the next street. Sometimes I stay with her and sometimes I stay with Dad. I can choose whichever I like. If Dad's in a bad mood I stay with Mum for a couple of days. Then I go back. It could be a lot worse.

And the little robot man? Some passing kids find him on the footpath. It makes me smile and remember what Fred did. 'Look at this little robot,' says one of them. 'He has got one green eye and one red one.'

For Ever

Every kid in the class was laughing at Richard.

Well, everyone except Tim. He felt more like crying. After all, Richard was his brother.

Even Ms Fish, the teacher, had to bite her tongue to stop herself chuckling. She stared out of the window, watching Richard leap around in the playground. 'Tim,' she said.

Tim sighed. Then he picked up his crutches and swung his way to the door. Another gale of laughter rocked the room as he left. Richard was at it again. Toilet paper. Why was Richard so mad about toilet paper? Why couldn't it be newspaper? Or paper bags? Why did it always have to be toilet paper?

Today it was worse than usual.

In the past Richard had wrapped up letter-boxes and sticks and garden spades. But today took the cake. Richard had wrapped himself. He looked like a mummy risen from the dead. Bound head to foot in toilet paper. Loose bits flapped in the breeze as he danced around the playground.

Tim hobbled across the yard. 'Come on,' he said

gently to his brother. 'Come back inside.'

'Aargh, aargh, aargh,' barked Richard.

'Aargh' was his only word. If you could call it a word. Richard had never spoken a sensible sentence in his life.

As Tim approached, Richard pranced around like a dog when someone tries to take a ball from its mouth. He darted in and out – wanting and not wanting to be caught at the same time.

'Oh no,' Tim said as he saw Richard glance at a nearby gum tree.

Tim tried to shepherd his brother away. But the crutches and his tired arms slowed him down. In a flash Richard was scrambling up the tree trunk.

Tim suddenly felt very tired. The crutches chafed his armpits. And his head throbbed. The pain that always gnawed at his chest was worse than ever. He lowered himself to the grass. 'Please come down, Richard,' he said. 'I can't climb trees.'

'Aargh, aargh, aargh,' barked Richard.

Tim looked towards the school. The teachers had agreed to give Richard a trial. Two months to see if they could handle him. If not, he would have to find another school. Tim shook his head. Nobody could handle Richard. Except Tim. He had to think of something. Otherwise there would be a fuss. And Richard wouldn't be allowed to stay. 'Come on, Richard,' he yelled. 'Please come down.'

The bell rang and kids started streaming out into the

yard. Soon there was a big circle standing around the tree. Laughing, pointing, joking. Richard waved a white toilet roll in one bandaged hand.

'Please don't,' Tim said to himself.

Richard started to unroll his treasure. Soon a long ribbon was fluttering out from his arm. Longer and longer like a never-ending flag. Flapping and waving in the sunshine. Finally it broke. The wind caught the fragile paper and lifted it above the head of the crowd. Kids jumped and reached, yelling and laughing. The toilet paper twisted and snaked towards the school. Finally it drifted down and the mob grabbed it wildly, pulling the sheets apart and throwing them into the wind.

Richard swung around in the tree like a ghostly monkey. He began pulling his paper bandage away and throwing it down on the laughing mob of kids.

Tim's heart dropped as he saw teachers coming with a ladder. He had to get Richard down before they frightened him. Otherwise he might fall on someone. Or hurt himself. If that happened Richard might be sent home. For good.

Tim closed his eyes and tried to shut out the angry blood-red clouds that swirled inside his head.

'Think of snow,' he said to himself.

A wonderful picture filled his mind. Soft, silent flakes of snow fell gently to the ground. Imaginary houses carried banks of whiteness. Every branch bowed beneath a cold burden. A snowman stood watching without a word.

Peace. Nothing disturbed this wintry peace.

Now Tim knew what to do. The snow had never let him down.

2

Tim opened his eyes. Teachers were hustling across the yard with a ladder. Kids were jumping and shouting, enjoying the show. He had to hurry. He limped towards the tree on his crutches and then started fishing around in his pocket. 'Hurry, hurry, hurry,' he said to himself. And then, 'Got 'em.'

He pulled out two squashed sachets of honey that his Dad had brought back from a motel. The type that have just enough for one slice of toast. Tim quickly pushed them both into a hole in the side of the tree. 'Hey, what's this in here?' he called in a loud voice. He pretended to be very interested in the hole. Out of the side of one eye he could see Richard peering down. 'Oh, look,' he shouted to himself. 'Honey.' He pulled out one sachet and made a great show of peeling back the lid and slurping the contents. He sucked and chewed noisily.

Richard watched from above.

'I wonder if there's any more,' Tim yelled into the hole.

In a flash Richard dropped lightly to the ground and thrust his hand into the tree. He pulled out the sachet and shoved it into this mouth without opening it. He munched happily, not knowing or caring that the whole school was watching. Finally he spat out the plastic container.

'Well done, Tim,' said Ms Fish.

The two boys headed for the classroom. Tim paused as a pain growled inside his chest. He winced and then kept going. He wondered how long the teachers would go on letting Richard disturb the class. He didn't seem to be learning anything at all. And he was annoying everyone else.

That night Richard sat in the corner of the lounge and fiddled with a toilet roll. He turned it over and over. He seemed hardly aware that Tim and his mother and father were in the room.

Dad tossed Richard two sachets of honey. 'Here,' he said. 'Give one to Tim.'

Richard turned them over in his hand. He looked at Tim for just a second and then shoved both into his mouth.

'Aren't you going to share?' said Mum.

'A bit late for that,' Tim grinned. He gave Richard a friendly punch. 'One day,' Tim told him. 'One day me and you are going to the snow.' He closed his eyes and described what he saw. Richard fiddled with the toilet paper, not taking his gaze from it for a second.

'That snow,' said Tim, 'is as fresh as an apple still on the tree. It is as cool as the breeze across a deep, deep lake. Oh, I see that snow like it is here now. Me and you there, Richard. We are sliding down the slope on skis.

And there is a snowman. And you know what? You know what the snowman is doing, Richard? You know what the snowman is doing? Is he just standing there? Is he just silent under the blue sky?

'No. That snowman is dancing, Richard.

'Oh, you should see him. He is leaping around and skipping and throwing up his arms. He is picking up snow and throwing it into the air. Oh, that snowman. He is full of joy. He doesn't care that the sun will melt him away. He doesn't worry about what is coming. He is king of the snow. There is no tomorrow for him. Oh, look at him dance, look at him dance.'

Tim smiled beneath his closed eyes.

'We will see him, Richard. We will. You and me. One day we will see snow. One day we will go to the mountains. One day we will see the snowman dance.'

Tim opened his eyes and the snow-covered scene vanished. 'I'm going to lie down,' he said. 'I don't feel too good.' He picked up his crutches and swung out of the room.

Richard turned over the toilet roll. Over and over. 'Aargh, aargh, aargh,' he said.

The boys' mum and dad looked at each other with tear-filled eyes.

'Tim will never see snow,' said Mum. 'Not in Australia in December.'

'He might make it,' said the father. 'It sometimes snows in the mountains in June.'

'June will be too late,' said Mum.

'I should have taken him last year,' said Dad.

'Don't blame yourself,' said Mum. 'The doctor wouldn't allow it, remember.'

'Aargh, aargh, aargh,' barked Richard. The noise was louder and more violent than usual. He hugged the toilet roll to his chest and rocked like a baby.

Mum glanced over at Richard. 'Do you think he knows?' she said.

Dad scowled as a truck changed gear on the road outside. It sounded its horn loudly. 'He doesn't know about anything. Except toilet rolls. Here we go again.'

Richard's face lit up. He raced out the door. 'Aargh, aargh, aargh.' At the front gate he jumped up and down waving his arms crazily. The truck has a large toilet roll painted on the side. Underneath was written 'SOFT AS DAWN'. The driver leaned over and wound down the passenger side window. Then he threw something into the air.

It turned over and over and then bounced crazily into the front yard.

Richard scampered after his prize. One tightly wrapped roll of toilet paper. He grabbed it eagerly and clutched it to his chest. 'Aargh, aargh, aargh,' he yelled happily.

Another truck rounded the corner and the driver also threw out a toilet roll. He tooted and laughed as Richard gathered up the bouncing paper. A third and a fourth truck did the same. Each driver enjoyed this daily ritual.

Passers-by stopped and stared at the strange sight.

Richard ran back inside with the loot. He headed towards his favourite place. The loft. A large, warm space in the roof of the house. He climbed up the ladder and disappeared through a manhole.

3

'Geeze, I don't know,' said Dad. 'All these blasted toilet rolls. We have to put a stop to it. It's just making him worse. We're the laughing stock of the neighbourhood. Harry James asked me if we're going to build a public toilet in the front yard. I'll bet the factory doesn't know their drivers are throwing away rolls and rolls every day. It's been going on for years.'

'Have you looked at his face?' said Mum. 'It's the only time Richard ever smiles. When those toilet rolls come bouncing over the fence he's happy. You can't stop that.'

'It's a fire risk,' said Dad. 'All that paper up inside the roof. The whole place could go up in smoke.'

'Think of it as free insulation,' said Mum.

'Have you been up there lately? Go and have a look. And don't let him see you or you'll cop the usual.'

Mum silently climbed the ladder and peered in the loft. Her eyes widened. A huge castle made of toilet rolls filled the entire space. It was so much bigger than before. Turrets and walls and a tall, arched entrance. Paper stairs made their way to the top of the ramparts. Dolls and teddy bears were propped up like archers peering down at the enemy. The whole loft was crammed with thousands and thousands of toilet rolls.

'Aargh, aargh, aargh.' Richard's face appeared over the battlements. He began to fire on the intruder. A shower of bouncing toilet rolls peppered Mum. She quickly ducked down and closed the loft hatch above her.

'Right,' yelled Dad. 'That's it. I'm not putting up with this nonsense for one more second.' He climbed quickly up the ladder and opened the hatch. 'Richard, get down from there. I'm putting a stop to this. Tomorrow I'm going to the factory to stop those drivers throwing out toilet rolls. And all of this is going. Every last one. It's ridiculous. Now come down here at once.'

'Aargh, aargh, aargh.' Toilet rolls fell around Dad like mortar shells. He shook his fist at Richard as the angry boy lobbed the rolls over the castle walls. Dad ducked and hit his head on the side of the hatch. Then he fell, screaming and grabbing at the rungs of the ladder. He crashed heavily to the floor.

'Damn and blast,' he yelled.

Mum tried to smother a smile. 'Are you okay, dear?' she asked.

'No I'm not. It's not funny. I mean it. Every last bit of paper is going out of that loft.'

Another hailstorm of toilet rolls bounced down on top of him and the hatch banged shut.

4

In his room nearby, Tim lay on his bed and listened to the commotion. He shook his head. He knew what the toilet roll castle meant to Richard. Terrible things would happen if he lost the toilet rolls. He had been collecting them for years. Building with them. Wrapping things up. His loft was a refuge. A place to go to. A warm world of his own. Angry red clouds rolled in Tim's head. Why couldn't Richard talk? Why did he always have to live in a lonely world of his own?

Tim looked at his crutches propped against the bed. Life wasn't fair. He closed his eyes. And thought of snow.

Gentle, falling snow. Drifting down. Cleaning the world with its whiteness. Covering the streets and the cars. Happy children threw snowballs and laughed.

And there he was. The best bit of all. The snowman. Dancing, dancing. Lifting his black hat with a snowy arm. Winking with his coal-black eyes. Beckoning Tim. Calling him. 'Oh, look at that snowman dance,' said Tim. A wonderful peace filled his mind. He lay back on his pillow and for a while the pain in his chest melted away.

'I'd love to see snow,' he said to himself. 'If I could see snow. Just once. I'd be happy for ever.'

Tim opened his eyes and the vision vanished. Outside the window the summer sun cooked the brown grass.

'Oh no,' said Tim.

A figure was loping across the lawn, dragging a

large garbage bag behind him. 'Aargh, aargh, aargh,' said Richard.

Tim could see that Richard was angry. He knew that his brother was running away from home. Taking his most precious possessions with him.

'Come back, Richard,' yelled Tim. But he was too late. Richard had already disappeared along the footpath. Tim struggled out of bed and searched frantically for his shoes. Where were they? Under the bed. He grabbed a crutch and hooked them out. He quickly put on the shoes and limped outside. 'Richard, Richard,' he yelled. His voice echoed along the empty street. Richard was nowhere to be seen.

Tim set off along the road. His crutches rubbed under his arm and with every step the pain in his chest grew worse. He knew that he was supposed to take it easy. Not strain himself. 'Richard,' he called. 'Richard.'

Tim was worried. He should have told Mum and Dad so they could use their car to search. But Dad was angry with Richard. That might be the last straw.

Richard could be in danger. He would often run across roads without looking. At this very moment he might be on top of someone's roof. Or hanging off a bridge over a river. Or crawling down a drain.

Blood-red clouds began to swirl in Tim's mind. But there was no time to call the snowman to drive them away. Sweat began to form on his brow and he felt faint.

5

Tim wandered the streets for hours. Up and down. Along and around. He couldn't find Richard anywhere. He had tried all of the usual places. The bridge. The station. The river. Nothing.

Finally Tim leaned his crutches on a wall and sat down. He felt very, very tired. He had just decided to give up and go home when something caught his eye. A letter-box. A letter-box wrapped in toilet paper.

Richard had been this way.

Tim struggled on. A dog ran past. A dog wrapped up in a paper bandage. This dog had met Richard for sure.

The houses gave way to fields. A herd of black cows grazed lazily in the sunshine. Twenty black cows. And one white one. A farmer was cursing and pulling away the shroud of paper which entwined his mooing animal.

Tim hobbled on, following the paper trail. He found it hard to breathe. He was hot and the pain in his chest grew worse and worse. But he kept going. He had to.

Finally he stopped. A long stream of paper fluttered in the gutter. It wound like a country road through the long, brown grass to a barbed-wire fence. A few strands of paper were impaled on the wire. The trail led through the fence and onto . . .

'The train line,' gasped Tim. He rolled under the fence and climbed up onto the tracks. Cold sweat formed on his brow as he followed the steel and paper trail. His breath came in gasps. His chest seemed to be enclosed in a ring of iron which grew tighter and tighter. The tips of his crutches slipped and jarred on the heavy stones between the tracks.

Tim knew what lay around the corner. He tried not to think about it. 'Think of snow,' he said to himself. 'Think of snow.' But the snow would not come. The dancing snowman had deserted him. There was nothing but angry, red clouds. And a railway line running across a tall, tall bridge.

In the centre of the bridge a tiny figure danced crazily, waving a long, white stream of paper. A fragile rope which suddenly broke and fell uncaringly into the river far, far below.

6

Tim stopped when he reached the bridge. It stood on huge wooden legs which spanned the river beneath. At the top it was narrow with one set of tracks which ran along close to the edge.

Gentle vibrations, growing strongly, came up through Tim's crutches. The train was somewhere on the other side of the bridge. Tim wanted to run onto the bridge and grab his brother. But he knew in his heart that if he did, neither of them would come back.

'Richard,' he screamed. 'Richard. The train is coming. This way, quick. Get off the bridge.' He took one wobbling step towards his brother but could go no further. One crutch lodged in a gap in the planks. Tim fell sprawling between the tracks. His chest hurt terribly. And one leg was bleeding freely. For a second he just wanted to stay there. Just stop and let things happen. Blood-red clouds swirled. He lay back and shook his head. Then he closed his eyes. 'Where are you?' he said. 'Where are you? Don't let me down now.'

And through the mists of his mind came the wonderful, dancing snowman. Calling, calling, calling. Beckoning with a snowy finger.

Tim smiled. He opened his eyes and crawled towards his crutches which were balanced on one of the rails. He moved his fingers like the legs of a spider. He could just reach the crutches and scratch them towards himself. In a second he had them and was up on his feet. The vibrations from the tracks grew stronger and stronger. He looked towards the other side. In the distance a train whistle sounded.

'Richard,' he shouted. 'This is for you.' He rummaged in his pocket and pulled out a sachet of honey. He lifted his arm and threw it with all his might. The tiny container arced into the air and then fell down, down, down until it disappeared in the pebbles by the river.

The train was on the bridge. Thundering towards Richard. Brakes screaming. Sparks flying high into the air.

Richard looked down after the honey. He looked at Tim. He looked at the train behind him. 'Aargh, aargh, aargh,' he screamed. Then he ran, stumbling towards his brother. Fleeing before the steel monster which screeched and roared towards him. He fell at Tim's feet.

The train was upon them. Richard peered down the grassy slope towards the river, searching with his eyes for the honey. Then he jumped off the tracks and bounded over the fence and down the hill.

Tim had no strength. He simply fell, like a tree teetering after the axeman's last blow. He toppled sideways, away from the train. The thundering wheels crunched his crutches to splinters. Tim rolled like a log. Down the gentle bank and under the fence. At last he stopped by a small stand of bushes.

'Aargh, aargh, aargh,' came Richard's voice from the river far below. He scrabbled among the rocks, looking for the honey.

'Stupid little idiots,' came a fading voice from the last carriage of the train as it rushed into the distance.

Richard struggled back up to his brother with the sachet of honey. He held it out in one hand. But Tim was too tired to even notice.

7

Later, at home, the doctor pulled the sheet back up to Tim's chin and looked at the sleeping figure. 'He's a very sick little boy,' he said to the two parents. 'He must have walked ten kilometres. On crutches. And that fall down the bank. It was too much for him. It was getting near the time anyway. You should think about putting him into hospital soon.'

Tim's dad shook his head. 'We've talked about this over and over,' he said. 'We knew this day was going to come. And we're ready for it. We want him to spend his last days in his own bed. At home with us.'

Above their heads, in the bedroom ceiling, an eye swivelled and stared down through a small hole. The eye moistened and formed a tiny droplet. The tear wobbled for a second and then fell. It spun glistening through the warm air and plopped onto Tim's cheek. His mother wiped it away, thinking it was her son's. She was right. And she was wrong. 'He's crying in his sleep,' she said. The eye in the ceiling blinked.

'He wanted to see the snow,' said Dad. 'He's never been to the snow. He's never seen a snowman. Or a snowstorm. It's the only thing he's ever wanted.'

They all looked out of the window. Insects buzzed in the warm summer air.

'And now he never will,' said Mum. 'I wish he could see snow before he . . .' She found it almost impossible to say the word. 'Dies.'

The eye in the ceiling vanished. A terrible banging and crashing came from above. A long barking howl filled the air. 'Aaaargh, aaaargh, aaaargh.'

'What on earth . . .?' said the doctor.

They all looked up at the ceiling. 'It's Richard,' said Dad. 'He's had a bad day. Don't worry. I'll get him down. He'll be okay.'

After the doctor had gone Dad climbed the ladder to the loft. The noise grew worse and worse. Dad pushed up the hatch and peered inside. A hail of toilet rolls drove him back.

'What's happening?' said Mum.

'He's gone crazy. He's completely wrecked the castle. Demolished the whole thing. Toilet rolls everywhere.'

Suddenly the noise stopped. Mum climbed the ladder and peeped in.

'Well?' said Dad.

'He's angry about something,' said Mum. 'He's sitting there with a toilet roll. He's pulling it to shreds. Just biting it and ripping it to bits like a wild animal.'

She quietly lowered the hatch and climbed down.

'Do you think he knows?' said Dad. 'About Tim?'

'Who knows what he knows,' said Mum. 'But just for once we are going to have to forget about Richard. And worry about Tim.'

8

Two days passed and Tim grew weaker and weaker.

In the ceiling above all was quiet. Richard refused to come down. Every time the hatch was lifted a furious hail of toilet rolls met the intruder.

'Just leave him,' said Dad. 'He'll get sick of it up there and he'll come down like he always does.'

'He's hardly touched the food I put up there,' said Mum. 'But I've got something special. I've been keeping it for an emergency.' She fetched a two-litre jar of honey from the kitchen. 'This ought to bring him down.' She climbed the ladder and carefully lifted the hatch. Then she waved the honey jar through the opening. 'Richard,' she said softly. 'Look what I've got.'

There was no reply. Then, before she could blink the honey disappeared. Snatched from her hand. 'Rats,' she yelled. 'He's grabbed it. Now he'll never come down. We'll just have to leave him.'

Both parents went down to Tim's room. They were shocked by what they saw. 'Get the doctor,' said Dad. Tim was pale and sweaty. His eyes rolled wildly in his head and his breath came in heavy gasps.

Above them in the ceiling an eye stared down and then disappeared.

Outside the warm summer breeze was swinging around and becoming cooler.

The doctor arrived within twenty minutes and gave Tim an injection. 'Stay with him,' he said. 'I'll wait in the lounge. It's not going to be long now.'

Tim opened his eyes and tried to sit up. His father lifted him so that he sat upright on the pillows. 'I want to look out,' said Tim. 'At the garden.'

His father pushed the bed until it was hard up against the window. Without warning something crashed onto the path outside.

Dad stared out. 'A tile,' he gasped. 'A tile's come off the roof.' Another tile hurtled down and smashed into a thousand pieces. And then another and another.

'It's Richard,' said Mum. 'He's on the roof. And he's wrecking the place.'

Like a furious fiend Richard grabbed tile after tile and threw them to the ground. Then he crawled up and over to the other side of the roof. He grabbed tiles wildly and tossed them into the air. Soon there was a yawning hole on both sides of the roof.

The wind dropped completely. It was the stillness that always comes before a cool change in Melbourne.

9

And still the tiles fell.

'Get the fire brigade,' said Mum. 'We have to get him down.'

'No,' said Dad. 'This is one time when Richard is not getting all the attention.' He took his wife's hand and led her back to their fevered son.

'What's going on?' said Tim weakly.

'Nothing for you to worry about,' said Dad. 'You just like back there and think about . . .'

'Snow,' said Mum softly. She nodded through the door at the doctor. He quietly left the room and went outside.

He placed a ladder against the wall and climbed to the top. 'Good grief,' he said as he stared into the roofless house. He turned and scrambled back down. He beckoned Mum through the window.

'What's up?' she whispered.

'He's taken off all his clothes,' said the doctor. 'And he's smeared honey all over himself. And those toilet rolls. He's . . .'

A cold breeze stirred and turned into a gust.

'He's torn up all those toilet rolls into little scraps. There's not one left.'

The gust became a gale. And lifted a billion tiny pieces of toilet paper into the air.

From his bed by the window Tim's eyes grew wide. He stared in amazement at the eddying cloud of white flakes.

'Snow,' Tim choked. 'Oh, it's snowing. Oh, just look at that snow. That snow,' said Tim, 'is as fresh as an apple still on the tree. It's as cool as the breeze across a deep, deep lake. Oh, I thought I'd never see it.'

Another gust lifted the paper and drove it crazy like a billion white bees swarming in furious silence over a winter garden.

Then the wind dropped. And the paper began to settle. It filled the air and flurried down covering the brown grass with a snow-white coat. Branches bowed in reverence. The car disappeared like a cake under Christmas icing.

Drifts formed on the window. Distant houses vanished under the swirling clouds. The world was white, white, white.

'Look,' called Tim. 'Look. Yes, it is. I'm sure it is.

A snowman. Oh, can you see that snowman?'

And there, faintly emerging from his private storm, was Richard. Paper stuck to the honey. A wild, snowy figure. Prancing and dancing amongst the flurries. The finest snowman ever. Dressed in a warm, white coat.

Tim gazed in wonder as his dream came true before his staring eyes. 'Just look at that,' he said in wonder. 'A snowman. Look at him go.' He gave a happy laugh.

His last laugh.

He lay back on the pillows with an enormous smile on his face.

His last smile.

Then he closed his eyes for the last time.

And went off to dance with the snowman.

For ever.

Just Like Me

I love you.

Now that's a thing no self-respecting twelve-year-old would say to a girl.

Well, you couldn't really, could you? Not when she was the most beautiful girl in the class. In the school. In the country. In the whole world. In those days I would have said the whole universe.

A skinny, dorky kid like me couldn't have said it to her.

Here I am, a grown man. Twenty-one years old and my stomach still gets the wobbles when I think about Fay.

Maybe it's because I might see her again. In five minutes or so.

See, we buried a time capsule in the wall of the old school. And Mr Wheeler made us promise to come back exactly nine years later. When all the kids would be twenty-one years old. I feel a bit foolish actually. Probably no one else will turn up. They will have forgotten. I'll be the only idiot there. And I've flown all the way out from England.

I turn my car into Brewer Road. Soon I'll be at the

school. Everything looks different. Where did all those office blocks come from?

The old park has gone. And the fish and chip shop. And the pond where we used to catch frogs.

Oh, oh, oh. No. It isn't. It can't be. It must be a mistake. Look what they have done. No, no, no.

The school is not there.

There's a dirty big shopping centre. With a car park and thousands of cars. Signposts. Balloons. Loud speakers. Escalators. Security guards.

They have pulled down the school and the trees and the bike shed. They have pulled down my dreams and built a nightmare.

I park my car and wander in through the huge doors. Jaws, more like it. I ride the escalators to the top of the mall and look down at the fountain far below. There are hundreds of shoppers. People sipping coffee, staring into windows, pushing trolleys, dragging children, carrying parcels.

There is no one digging out a time capsule from a school wall. There is no one from Grade Six at Bentleigh West State School. And even if there was I wouldn't recognise them.

All I have left is memories.

I think back and remember what I wrote when I was twelve. The letter I put in the time capsule. The letter that has gone for ever. That no one will read. The letter I wrote to a girl I will never see again.

Dear Fay,

My Mum and Dad are moving to England. So it looks like I will never see you again. Not till I'm twenty-one, anyway. And that's ancient. Anyway, that's how old you will be when you get this letter. If you are there. When they dig out the time capsule, I mean.

I will be there for sure.

I feel stupid writing this. But no one will know. If Luke Jeffries knew he would give me heaps. So would his nerdy mates. They pick on me. Just because I've got freckles. I hate them, I hate them, I hate them.

My first day at this school was awful. I knew I would cop it. I'm not like you. See, you are the netball captain. You are good at everything. You get As for every subject. The teachers always pick you to do jobs. They hold up your work out the front.

You are good-looking. No – scrub that. You are better than that. I'll tell you what I think about you. It will be all right because no one will read this until the time capsule is opened.

You are gorgeous. If I was a cat you would be the cream. If I was a dog you would be the bone. If I was a rock you would be the waterfall running over me.

You are the top and I'm the bottom. I'm not any good at anything. Except drawing. Mum says I'm a good drawer.

Anyway, I'm getting off track. I want to tell you about my first day at school. There I was standing out the front with nowhere to sit. In the end I had to use Mr Wheeler's chair. He said, 'You can sit there for the present.'

Everyone gawked at me. You were the only one who smiled.

When the bell went I stayed on my seat. Mr Wheeler said, 'What are you waiting for, Ben?'

I said, 'I'm waiting for the present.'

Everyone packed up. They all laughed like mad. Except you. My face was burning, I can tell you that. Talk about embarrassing.

After that my problems just got bigger and bigger. I couldn't get out what I was thinking. When they picked on me I couldn't say a thing.

I would like you to be my friend. But you are popular and I'm not.

You sit at the desk in front of me. Your ponytail hangs down and swishes across my books. It is gold like the tail of an angel's horse. I would like to touch it but of course I never would.

My stomach goes all wobbly when I look at you.

I wanted to give you something. But I didn't have any money. Mum is always broke. 'Make something,' she said. 'It's the thought that counts. If you want to give a present make it yourself.'

Well, it was coming up to Easter so I decided to draw on an Easter egg. Seeing as how I am good at drawing.

I got an egg and put a little hole in each end. Then I blew out all the insides and started painting.

Three weeks. That's how long it took. I sat up every night until Mum went crook and made me put out the light. It was going to be the best egg ever in the history of the world. I painted rabbits. And a gnome with a fishing rod. And a heart with your initials on it. All covered in flowers.

Mum reckoned it was a little ripper. 'Ben,' she said. 'That is beautiful. It is the most lovely Easter egg I have ever seen.'

So I wrapped it up in cotton wool and put it in a box.

Then I started to get scared. What if you didn't like it? What if you showed everyone and they laughed? What if you laughed?

Oh geeze. I'm scared, Fay. I'm glad you won't get this until I'm twenty-one.

It turned out worse than I thought.

As soon as I walked in the school gate I was in trouble. Luke Jeffries grabbed the box. 'Look at this,' he yelled. 'Ben has a cute little egg for Fay. I wonder why?'

All the kids gave me heaps. They really rubbished me. 'Give it back,' I whispered. My face was burning like an oven.

Luke Jeffries threw the box on the ground. 'This is an egg,' he said. 'So we will hatch it.' He sat down on the box and clucked like a hen. The egg was smashed to bits.

I turned and went for it. I just ran and ran and ran. I didn't care about wagging school. I didn't care about anything. Except a present for you.

I ran into the kitchen and grabbed another egg. There was no time to blow it out. There was no time to paint rabbits and gnomes and things. I put on some boiling water to hard-boil an egg. Then I tipped in some dye.

And that's when it happened. I was angry and rushing around. I slipped over with the saucepan in my hands. The water sloshed onto my cheeks. Oh, the pain. Oh, my face was burning. Oh, it hurt. I'm not a sook. But I screamed and screamed and screamed.

I didn't remember anything else till I woke up in hospital.

My face still burned. But I couldn't touch it. I was wearing a mask. Bandages. I looked like a robber. There were little holes for my mouth and eyes and nostrils.

'Your face will be okay,' said Mum. 'But you will have to wear the mask for a long time while it heals.'

'I'm not going to school like this. No way.'

'You have to,' said Mum. 'You have to wear the mask for six months or your face won't heal properly.'

So I walked in the classroom late. Looking like a burglar. With my mask on.

No one laughed.

Because someone else was just like me.

You.

Not burned. But just sitting there with a mask around your face.

Where did you get it? I don't know. And you kept on wearing it for weeks.

And I have never said thank you. And tomorrow my parents are moving to England. I want you to know that I . . . No, scrub that.

You will get this when they dig up the time capsule. I want you to know that I . . . No, I just can't get it out.

Yours sincerely . . . No, scrub that.

Yours with thanks . . . No, scrub that.

Aw, what the heck . . .

Love,

Ben.

Well, that's what I wrote all those years ago. Something like that anyway. And here I am exactly nine years later. In the shopping centre. The school has gone. There is no Mr Wheeler and his grown-up class there to open the time capsule.

There is just me and a million shoppers. I can't even tell where the school was. It would take half an hour to walk from one end of the centre to the other.

My face healed up long ago. I don't even have any scars. I should feel happy but the school has been knocked down. And there is no time capsule with my letter in it. I guess the bulldozers must have uncovered it. Or it could still be buried, deep under the shops and fountains and car parks. Maybe some of the letters inside were sent to the kids. Who knows? No one would have been able to contact me – on the other side of the world.

One of the other kids might be here in the shopping centre. Maybe, like me, they have come because they didn't know the school was knocked down. But I would never recognise them. Not after all these years. Not now we are grown.

I make my way sadly through the happy shoppers. I don't notice the shouting and jostling and laughing. I reach the door.

And for a moment my heart misses a beat.

For standing there I see something that takes me back in time. Silently standing by the door is a person wearing a burns bandage on her face. Children are staring at her. They shouldn't do that. Neither should I. But my heart is beating fast and I don't know what I am doing.

The woman's eyes meet mine and slowly she starts to take off the bandage. The children gasp. And so do I as her hair falls down behind her like the golden tail of an angel's horse.

Just for a moment I am twelve again. I catch my breath. My stomach wobbles.

I stare at the woman in front of me.

I know that my life is going to be happy. Because she is smiling the biggest smile.

Just like me.

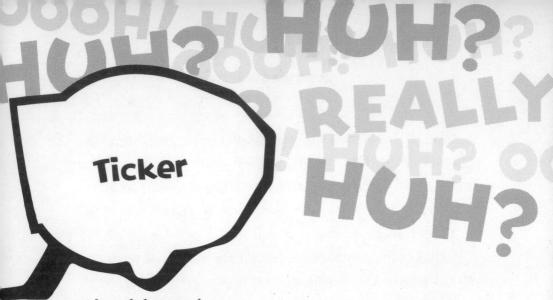

Ticker

I hated the wind.

Especially that night.

Oh, yes, the wind. It ripped and tore at Grandad's old house on the edge of the cliff. It was so bad that I hid my head under the pillow to stop the sound of its shrieking. But I was still scared. I could feel the floor trembling. And the water in the glass next to my bed slopped around as if shaken by an invisible hand.

Outside, the sea boiled. Huge waves threw themselves at the cliffs in fury. Salt spray whipped against the windows. Fierce gusts flattened the grass in the paddocks.

'Are you scared, Keith?' said a friendly voice. It was Grandad. He sat down on the bed and took my hand. 'It's only a storm,' he said. 'It will be over soon. Try to go to sleep.'

I felt safe while he was there. But I knew that he would soon go away and then I would be on my own again. So I tried to keep him talking. I pointed to his watch. The one they gave him when he retired from the railways. It was a great watch. I loved it. Made out of solid gold. Dependable. Like Grandad.

'What makes it go?' I asked him. 'Does it have a battery?'

'No,' said Grandad. 'No battery.'

'Do you wind it up?'

'Nope.'

That had me puzzled. If you didn't wind it up and it didn't have batteries, how could it go?

'What then?' I asked.

He waved his arm around. 'When you move it the watch winds itself. The movement of your hand keeps it going.'

'What about when you take it off?' I asked.

'It can go for twelve hours. Then it stops. But you only need eight hours sleep. So you can take it off at night.' He gave my head a bit of a rub. 'And sleep is just what you need,' he said. He stood up, smiled and left me alone.

Well, not alone. Grandad's dog, Sandy, was hiding under my bed. Whimpering. Scared of the storm. Sandy wasn't supposed to come inside but we always let her when the thunder started. It's funny how dogs that are really brave turn to shaking jelly when it thunders.

A huge gust of wind buffeted the window. For a moment I thought that the glass was going to break and send sharp spears flying into my room. The rain sounded like a million bullets spitting against the pane.

'Shoot,' I said to myself. 'I'm getting out of here.'

I jumped out of bed and ran down to the lounge. Grandad and Grandma were holding hands in the dark. Watching the lightning tear at the sky. They didn't know that I was there. They didn't know that someone was listening.

'Keith was asking about my watch,' said Grandad.

'You should leave it to him,' said Grandma. 'To remember you by.'

Grandad shook his head. 'I want you to have it, Elsie,' he said. 'And I want you to promise me something.'

Grandma turned her wrinkled face towards him. 'Anything,' she said. 'Anything.'

He waved his arm around. 'Look,' he said. 'I want you to keep it going. Keep it ticking. Don't let it stop. When I die I want you to put this watch on. Its tick will remind you that for all those years my heart was beating close to yours. Promise?'

'Promise,' said Grandma. 'I'll wear it always. I won't let it stop. Not until we meet again.'

I just stood there. Frozen. My heart seemed to miss a beat. Tears started to squeeze out of my eyes. I didn't want Grandad to die. Grandad's aren't supposed to die. Especially when you don't have a mum or dad.

Grandads are meant to be there forever. Laughing at your jokes. Fixing your bike. Flying kites. Bringing you special presents. Reading you stories in bed. Making you feel better in storms.

Grandma put an arm around Grandad's old, bent shoulders. 'I'll listen to it every day,' she said. 'It's ticking now and I'll keep it going. It will never stop. That's my promise.'

I crept back to my room. Suddenly the storm didn't seem to matter any more. What if the roof tore away? What if the windows blew in? What if the whole house was blasted into the sky? What did that matter?

It didn't matter at all. Not when you knew that one day soon your Grandad might not be there.

I lay there under the covers thinking about it. Not hearing the wind.

When Grandad's heart stopped, Grandma was going to take his watch from his wrist and put it on. She was going to keep it going. It was sort of like keeping him there with her. As if the ticking was his heart still beating.

It was so sad.

2

The next day the wind was still blowing but the storm had gone.

Grandad and I struggled along the edge of the cliff, carrying fishing rods. Gulls flew above, hovering in the uprush of air off the sea. Sandy ran from rabbit hole to rabbit hole, sniffing and snorting. Loving every minute.

'I'm taking you to my special spot,' said Grandad. 'It's a long way and no one knows it except me and Grandma. The best fishing hole on the coast. I want you to keep it a secret. Pass it on in the family after I'm gone.'

'That won't be for a long time, will it?' I said.

Grandad didn't seem to hear. He just smiled and changed the subject. 'Here's Fred's Bridge,' he said.

I gasped at the sight. It was one of those cable bridges that are built on two ropes. It stretched high above a gorge. Way down below, the sea was sucking and swelling over black rocks. Every now and then a tremendous wave would thunder into the gorge and send salt spray shooting up almost to the top.

I didn't like the look of it. Not one bit. If there was one thing worse than the wind it was heights.

I looked at the suspension bridge and my head began to spin. The waves below reached up like grasping fingers waiting to pull us into the wild water.

'It's all right,' said Grandad with a laugh. 'You can't fall off. The net would stop you.'

Fred's Bridge had two string walls made out of fishing net. The thought of stumbling against one of them made me feel sick. All right, you wouldn't fall. But how would you feel at that moment of terror as the net gave way under your weight? Just the idea of it made me feel like heaving up my breakfast.

And what if the ropes broke? Like they do in the movies. If that happened we would both be thrown to our deaths.

Grandad walked on to the swaying bridge. 'Come on,' he said.

I watched him cross. The bridge swayed with every step. I waited until he had crossed right over to the other side. Then I put one foot onto the wooden slats. And then the other.

Oh, I couldn't stand it. I couldn't do it. Not just walking across like that. I dropped down on my hands and knees and started to crawl. I made my way forward like a cowardly dog.

'Come on,' yelled Grandad. 'You can do it.'

Finally I reached the other side. Grandad smiled and rubbed my hair. 'Don't worry about it,' he said. 'We all have our own demons to face.'

'Where's Sandy?' I asked.

We both stared across the bridge. Sandy was whimpering and putting one paw on the slats and then backing away. She was too frightened to cross. She didn't like the look of the bridge.

'Go home girl,' Grandad yelled. Sandy just sat there. She was going to wait.

Grandad looked at his watch. 'We'd better get a move on,' he said. 'It's still a long way.'

3

It was too. We walked along the cliff tops for another hour before we stopped. Grandad was puffing. He sat down and rested against a gnarled tree. All of the leaves had been ripped off by the wind. The branches shook like fingers on a dancing skeleton. Nothing could stand up to that wind. It killed everything except the tough grass, which bent and rippled like the surface of the sea.

Clouds ripped across the sky. 'A storm's coming,' said

Grandad. 'The wind is picking up. I think we'd better go back.'

I was really disappointed. We hadn't even started fishing and now he wanted to go back.

Suddenly Grandad cried out in pain. He clutched at his chest and screwed up his face in agony.

'Grandad,' I yelled. 'What's the matter? What's up?'

'My ticker,' he groaned. 'My ticker's playing up.'

I looked at his wrist. 'Your watch?' I shouted.

'My heart,' he said. His face grew white and he clutched his chest with his right hand.

He slumped against the tree with his eyes closed. 'Grandad,' I shrieked. 'Grandad.'

He didn't move. He didn't answer. He was gasping for air with a terrible rasping sound. I looked around for help. But there was no one there.

There was nothing I could do but leave Grandad lying under the bare tree. I ran and ran and ran. My sides ached. A terrible pain stabbed into the left side of my stomach. I gasped and wheezed and fought for every breath.

And with each step the wind grew stronger. Soon it was ripping and tearing at my clothes. My hair was lashing my face. I felt like I was forcing my way through an invisible wall. The wind was my enemy. Pushing me back. Slowing me down. Trying to topple me off the cliff.

I hated that wind.

But I battled against it. Step after step. Leaping, struggling, pushing myself against the terrible storm.

Until at last I reached Fred's Bridge. It's funny how you can find courage when you need it. I ran straight onto the bridge without even thinking. It swayed and rocked wildly but I hardly noticed. I lurched crazily with every step but in no time I reached the other side where Sandy was still waiting patiently. She whimpered and jumped up at me.

'Come on, girl,' I shouted. 'Grandad's in trouble.'

I ran and ran and ran with Sandy at my heels. Many times I stopped and held my side. The pain was sharp and piercing. The wind grew into a shrieking, howling monster. Trying everything it could to stop me.

But in the end I reached the house. I burst into the kitchen and shouted. The words all came out in a rush.

'Grandma,' I yelled. 'Grandad's ticker is playing up.'

4

The people from the State Emergency Service came quickly. They wouldn't let me go with them. They wouldn't let Grandma go either. We had to wait. For ages and ages. The storm whipped and raged and ranted. Night fell.

I wondered if the people from the SES would be able to get across the bridge to Grandad? What if it had been damaged by the wind?

They did get across the bridge to Grandad. But when they reached him his heart had stopped beating. He was dead. There was nothing they could do for him so they had to wait for the storm to end. They had to stay there on the cliff all night with Grandad. That's what the police told us.

Grandma and Sandy and I sat and waited as the hours ticked by. We hugged each other and let the tears mix on our cheeks. We stared out of the window and watched the storm die in the new days' dawn.

In the morning the SES carried Grandad back to our house on a stretcher covered in a blanket. An ambulance was waiting to take him away.

Grandma made me stay inside but she went out and looked under the blanket. I saw her lift Grandad's cold, stiff arm and peer at his wrist. Then she spoke to one of the men. He sadly shook his head.

When she came back I said, 'Was the watch there?'

She threw a glance at the kitchen clock and said, 'He must have dropped it. It will have stopped ticking by now. I won't be able to keep my promise.'

I gritted my teeth. 'I'll get it for you,' I said in a determined voice. 'I'll find it.'

Grandma shook her head. 'No,' she said. 'It's no use. I was supposed to keep it ticking. To never let it stop. To remind me that for all those years his heart had gone on beating next to mine. But now it's stopped and the promise is already broken.'

I didn't know what to say. I just keep thinking of that watch lying there on the cliff top. Silent. Still. With frozen hands. Not ticking. The cruel wind covering it with dust.

I hated that wind.

5

There was a funeral.

And there was a wake where everyone came and brought cakes and casseroles. Friends called in and left cards and flowers. They told stories about Grandad and the old days. There was laughter and tears. Every day for a month people visited or phoned.

But in the end there was just me and Grandma. She had not smiled. Not once since Grandad had died.

She would slowly go about her daily jobs. And when they were done, she would sit on the porch with the wind gently blowing her hair and watch the sea.

But she never smiled. Not once.

'It's the watch,' I said. 'Isn't it?"

She nodded. 'I didn't keep it ticking. I let it stop. I broke my word.'

'You couldn't help it,' I said. 'They wouldn't let you go.'

I wanted to make her happy. I wanted to cheer her up. I wanted to see her smile again. I made her breakfast in bed. I told her stories and jokes. I brought her ropes and buoys and craypots that washed up on the shore. I gave her hugs and read aloud to her.

But nothing worked. Nothing would take the sadness out of her eyes. Or put the smile back on her lips.

Even Sandy's snuffling wet nose and excited barking couldn't cheer her up.

Then one day a terrible thought hit me. What if

Grandma's ticker stopped? What if *her* heart stopped beating? What if she just gave up?

That's when I decided. That's when I made up my mind to find that watch. Even if it *had* stopped ticking.

6

I packed some water and food and started off along the cliff. I didn't tell Grandma. No one knew where I was going. Except Sandy. She trotted a few steps behind me. She didn't chase rabbits or birds. She stayed right with me. Almost as if she knew what was going on.

The wind grew stronger and stronger. Why did it always try to stop me? I lowered my head and pushed my way against it to the bridge.

Or what was left of it.

The wooden slats were still intact. But the netting sides had been ripped out by the wind. They flew like tattered flags from the ropes above. There was nothing to stop anyone falling straight down into the sea. The waves were moving mountains again today. The bridge shook and buckled like a road rearing in an earthquake.

I hid the sight from my eyes with my hands. I couldn't look. I couldn't cross. I couldn't move.

How long I crouched there is hard to say. But then I started to think of Grandma. How many ticks did her heart have left? Could it stop beating just because it was sad?

I crawled out onto the planks. There were no sides.

There was nothing to stop me hurtling down into the clutches of the angry waves below. I closed my eyes and went forward on my hands and knees. But it was too terrifying. I collapsed onto my stomach and moved forward on my belly like a snake instead. I wriggled along the heaving surface, desperately grabbing one plank after another, and dragging my legs behind me. The bridge swayed and rocked with renewed fury in the howling wind.

Slowly, slowly, I inched forward. For one crazy second I thought about throwing myself down just to end the agony. But in the end I beat it. I made it to the other side with my eyes still closed.

Something wet touched my face. Wet and sloppy. It was Sandy. She had followed me across. How she didn't get blown off the bridge I'll never know.

We struggled on against the wind. Sometimes rain squalls would sweep in from the sea and lash my face. My nose and the tips of my ears were so cold that they hurt. But we kept going. I had to find that watch. Even if it had stopped ticking. I felt that it might somehow help Grandma. And keep her going.

I crossed a huge sand dune. The wind picked up the grains of sand and hurled them into my face, like a volley of tiny arrows.

I hated the wind.

7

At last I reached the place where Grandad had died. The lonely tree still clawed at the sky with its bare limbs.

I began to search among the grass and rocks. Grandad had been wearing the watch when I had left him. And the SES had brought him back on a stretcher. So it must be around somewhere. I began to circle the tree, inspecting every inch of ground. I walked slowly, gradually working my way further and further out.

Nothing. No sign of it.

Sandy was snuffling and sniffing herself. Was she looking for rabbits? Or did she understand? Did she want to find the watch too?

After about an hour I stopped and slumped down against the tree just like Grandad had when he'd died. The watch was nowhere to be seen. It was useless. Grandad had died leaning against the tree. He hadn't moved. But the watch wasn't there.

A terrible feeling of emptiness seemed to drain away my strength. I leaned back and closed my eyes. The cold wind buffeted my face.

'Ruff, ruff, ruff.' Sandy began to bark like crazy.

I jumped up to see what she was barking about. 'Good girl,' I shouted. 'You little beauty.'

8

I don't remember much about the journey back. I was so happy.

Once again I had to face the swaying bridge with its broken net. But I wasn't terrified like the first time. I just wanted to get home. I wanted to give Grandma the news.

In my rush across the bridge I slipped and fell sprawling on my face. For a moment I was nearly sick again. But I jumped up and almost ran to the other side. We pelted back along the cliffs to the house.

I burst into the kitchen. 'Grandma,' I shouted. 'I've found Grandad's watch.'

No smile. She didn't even look at it. 'You shouldn't have gone,' she said. 'It was too dangerous. And anyway, his watch stopped ticking long ago.'

'No,' I yelled. 'It didn't. It's still going.'

'Because you put it on your wrist,' said Grandma. 'That has wound it up. It's not the same. It stopped ticking.'

'It didn't,' I shouted. 'Look, it's showing the right time.'

Grandma took the watch from my outstretched hand. 'You didn't reset it?'

'No.'

'But it's been over a month. How could it have kept ticking all that time?'

She smiled when I told her. The biggest smile ever. And I knew her heart would go on ticking for a long time to come.

'Grandad strapped it onto a branch of the tree,' I said. 'The wind kept it moving.'

Outside the clouds scudded across the sky. A sudden strong gust hit the house and made a terrible tremble.

'I love the wind,' I said.

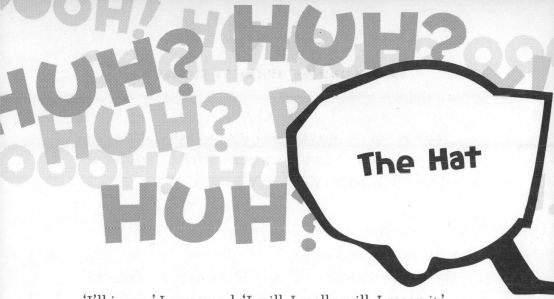

The Hat

'I'll jump,' I screamed. 'I will. I really will. I mean it.'

I stared down at the water churned up by the ferry's huge propeller. Would I fall straight on top of those terrible blades? Would I end up as just a brief red smudge in the ocean? Would I really jump?

Or was I bluffing?

Dad didn't know. 'Don't, Jason. Please don't,' he said.

'Then stop the ferry. Get my hat.'

Most of the passengers were tourists on their way to look at the coral and fish of the Great Barrier Reef. They stared at this real-life drama with wide-open eyes.

'Let him jump,' said a man in a Hawaiian shirt. 'A soaking will do him good.'

'It's only a hat,' said the captain. 'I'm not going back just for that. Time is money. And so is fuel. You should have hung on to it.'

'It's his mother's hat,' said Dad. 'She died three weeks ago. He's not himself.'

I stared at the Akubra hat bobbing way off in the distance. It was upside down, floating like a tiny round boat. Soon it would be out of sight.

'I'm sorry,' said the captain. 'But we're running on tight margins. We can't stop every time a hat blows overboard. It happens all the time.'

I let go of the rails with one of my hands and dangled out over the sea. 'I'm going,' I yelled. 'I'm going to swim back and get it.'

My father slowly took out his wallet. 'How much?' he said to the captain.

2

'One hundred dollars,' said Dad. 'Just for a hat.' He shook his head slowly as the ferry disappeared across the water.

While we walked along the little rickety jetty I hardly noticed the swiftly flowing river. It made its way to the ocean through the mangroves and the wide muddy beach. Even the splashing of rainbow-coloured fish in the swirling water failed to interest me. I hardly saw the crabs as they scurried into their holes at our approach. Normally I would have been racing around checking everything out.

'I'm sorry, dad,' I said. 'I really am. But Mum loved this hat. I feel close to her when I wear it.' I grabbed the wet brim of the wide stockman's hat and pulled it firmly down on to my head.

Dad didn't answer. I guessed that he didn't like the mention of Mum much. He probably didn't like her. She certainly hadn't liked him. I was never allowed to visit him on school holidays. And Mum would always say, 'It's him,' when Dad phoned. She had a special way of saying him which sounded as if she was talking about the most horrible person in the world.

I didn't really know Dad. My own father. And now I was going to live with him. And spend the time in this small camp in the rainforest. Checking on the wildlife and making sure that tourists didn't camp in the National Park or shoot native animals. He was a park ranger. That was his job.

Dad put his arm around my shoulder. 'Come on,' he said. 'I'll show you something special.' We walked past the main building with its wide verandah and across the lawn which swept down to the water.

'Don't swim in the estuary,' said Dad. 'There are crocodiles.'

I gave a shudder. 'I hate crocodiles,' I said.

Dad pointed across the river to a patch of sunlight between some trees.

'Geeze,' I gasped. 'It's huge.'

'Yeah,' said Dad. 'He's big. And he's fast. They can beat a racehorse over a short distance.'

'What do you do if one chases you?' I asked.

'Run like hell. But not in a straight line,' said Dad. 'They are not very good at turning. It slows them down.'

'I wonder if it's seen us,' I said.

As if in answer, the huge beast opened its jaws in a yawn. Then it slid silently into the water and disappeared.

We stopped at a small hutch surrounded by chicken wire. A fine-meshed wire fence surrounded it. It was strong and well made. Not even a mouse could sneak into the enclosure. Dad unlatched the gate and we stepped inside.

The hutch reminded me of Ralph, my pet rabbit back home in Melbourne. I had to give him away when I left.

'Rabbits,' I said excitedly.

'No way,' said Dad. 'We shoot rabbits up here. They're pests. So are the pigs and the feral *rats*.' He said the word rats with a disgusted look on his face. It reminded me of the way that Mum used to pronounce the word, him.

He opened the top of the hutch and carefully took out the most beautiful creature I have ever seen. The hard look fell from Dad's face. He reminded me of a mother staring down at a newborn child.

'This,' said Dad, 'is an Eastern Bilby. A native animal. It's meant to be here. But bilbies are on the edge of extinction. Killed by introduced animals brought in from overseas like pigs and cats and . . . filthy feral rats.'

It was a beautiful animal. About the size of a rabbit with a pointed face and long ears that seemed too big for it. The bilby's nose made it look like a stretched mouse. It waved its furry tail slowly from side to side.

It sniffed Dad's skin. Like a pet.

Dad placed the bilby in my hand and smiled. 'There are only two of this species left alive up here. A male in the zoo in Brisbane. And this one. She's pregnant. Her name is Breeze. I'm trying to introduce them back into this forest. The feral rats and pigs have wiped them out. It's a battle, I can tell you.'

His face looked weary.

'I'll help you,' I said.

Dad grinned at me. His weather-worn brown skin broke into friendly wrinkles. He suddenly pulled the brim of my hat down so that it covered my eyes. 'Come on, Jason. I'll show you around.' From inside the hat I could hear him laughing. I didn't like him touching Mum's hat. But it wasn't the time to say anything.

Nothing would part me from my hat. I would have jumped off the ferry to get it if they hadn't stopped.

Even though I couldn't swim.

3

That night I lay alone in my room on the verandah and listened to the sounds of the forest. The air was warm and only a fly-screen protected me from the dark outside. I left the light on – it made me feel a little safer.

The ceiling had paintings of small green lizards scattered across it. I wondered if Dad had put them there especially for me. It looked like wallpaper.

In the darkness of the rainforest the sounds outside seemed incredibly loud. I was used to trams rumbling down Barkers Road in Melbourne. At night in the city I would never even notice the sounds of squealing brakes and blaring police sirens. But here in this wild and lonely country every rustle seemed to hold a threat.

Suddenly, the wallpaper lizards began to walk. I screamed. They were real and walking upside down on the ceiling, clinging to the paint with little suction cups on the ends of their spidery toes.

Dad raced into the room and then began to laugh. 'You are a city boy for sure,' he said. 'They are geckos. They can't hurt you. They are lovely creatures.'

Dad turned off the light. 'It attracts the mossies,' he told me as he gently closed the door.

Mum's hat dangled from the bedpost. I could see its dark outline in the glow of the huge, soft moon. A tear ran down my cheek and soaked into the pillow. 'Mum,' I moaned to myself. 'Please come back.'

I grabbed her hat and pulled it down over my face to keep out the silent dangers of the night. The hat still smelt of Mum. Even its soaking in the ocean hadn't been able to take that away. No one would ever get that hat away from me. I would go to my grave before I would part with it.

Those and other sad thoughts circled in my head until finally I fell into a deep sleep.

Blam.

I sat upright in terror. What was that noise? Like the slamming of a million doors at the same time. Like the snapping of a giant tree.

I heard the sounds of a struggle and scrabbling feet. Then again.

Blam.

Now I recognised the sound. Even though I had never heard it before. Not in real life anyway. A shot-gun. Someone had fired in the middle of the night. Footsteps approached.

'Sorry, Jason,' said Dad's voice. 'A ruddy feral pig. But it's okay. I got it.'

I shoved on my shoes and staggered outside. Underneath a curtain of hanging vines lay a huge black pig. Its body still steamed with the warmth of its lost life. I gave a shudder.

This place was so brutal. On the one side there was the love of bilbies and crocodiles because they belonged here. And on the other side a scorn for pigs and rats because they didn't.

'I'm feral too,' I said. 'I don't belong here either.'

'No you're not,' said Dad. 'Feral animals are killers. You and me — we are protectors of the weak.'

Dad put his hand on my shoulder and squeezed it. I knew what he was saying. There was nowhere else to go. So I had better get used to it.

4

The next morning Dad raced into my room before I was fully awake. 'Quick, Jason. Get dressed. Something's happened.'

'What is it?'

'Three baby bilbies have been born.'

'Terrific,' I yelled.

'Yes,' said Dad. 'But there's something else.' His face was grave. He was worried. I followed him outside.

We both stared down at the damage to the bilby enclosure. The gate had been flattened and the wire mesh pulled off. The mesh had been twisted into a long rope and dragged off into the forest.

'Who did it?' I exclaimed.

'Not who. What,' said Dad. 'The feral pig that I shot. I thought that it was making a lot of noise. Pigs have enormous strength. Fortunately it didn't get into the hutch. The bilbies are safe.'

'What are you going to do?'

'I have to get some new wire,' said Dad. 'And quick. The pigs won't be back in daylight. But nothing stops feral rats.' He pointed to a patch of tall green grass that stood out against the brown dirt.

'I saw a rat there a couple of days ago,' he said. 'It's the septic tank. I was going to clear it out but I had to . . .' His voice trailed off, 'go to your mother's funeral.'

'What do you want me to do?' I said.

'Stay here while I take the dinghy along the coast to our next ranger's station. There's a roll of new wire there. I'll be back before dark.'

'No worries,' I said. 'Can I see the babies before you go?'

'No. Sorry, Jason,' said Dad, 'but they mustn't be disturbed. The mother has a pouch. They are safe in there. Nice and warm with mother's milk on hand. All you have to do is make sure nothing goes in or out of the entrance to the hutch. Breeze will stay there. There's food and water inside.'

'What about me?' I said. 'How long will you be gone?'

'I'll go and get you something too,' said Dad. 'But you mustn't leave this spot. A rat will be in and out in a flash – they can smell a new birth a mile off. The babies are the first things they eat. A bilby has no defence against rats. I would move Breeze up to the house but I can't risk disturbing her.'

'You can count on me, Dad,' I said. 'Nothing will make me leave here.' I grinned up at him from underneath the brim of my Akubra.

Dad nodded. He came back with a bottle of drink and some sandwiches. And a crowbar.

'What's that for?' I asked.

'If you do see a rat,' said Dad, 'you know what to do.'

I shuddered as he leaned the crowbar against the hutch. 'Okay,' I said hesitantly.

'Good man,' said Dad. 'I should be back in three or four hours.'

He walked down to the jetty and started the outboard on the little dinghy. The putt-putt of the engine drifted across the water as he headed out to sea. He finally vanished around the headland. For a little while I could still hear the sound of the motor. Then it faded and died.

I was alone.

The ground began to return the heat of the rising sun.

The only sound was the occasional buzz of a fly. It's funny how the bush has different sounds at different times. In the morning and evening the birds are noisy and life fills the forest. In the night there are the sounds of secret hunting and feeding. But in the hot hours all is quiet.

I began to grow drowsy. I took a few mouthfuls of water from the bottle and nibbled at a sandwich. I shook my head, trying to keep myself awake. Time passed slowly. I should have asked Dad for a book. For a moment I thought about racing over to the house and getting one. But I had promised not to leave the hutch. Even for a second.

Then the weather began to change. Clouds covered the sun. A tropical breeze sprang up.

Without any warning a fierce gust of wind swept through the clearing. It snatched my hat and sent it bowling towards the river. My blood turned to ice.

In a second it would be gone. Could I follow it?

Could I not follow it? I would only have to leave my post for a few moments. But those words – leave my post – sounded dreadful. Weren't soldiers shot for leaving their post?

But this wasn't war. This was a boy and a hat. Nothing could happen to the bilbies in that short time.

I jumped to my feet and pelted after the hat. It was spinning like a crazy out-of-control wheel on a racing track.

'Oh, no,' I gasped.

A gust carried the hat into the air. In no time it was in the water, floating quickly away from the muddy bank.

I jumped in after it. The mud was soft and I sank up to my knees. In a flash I realised the danger. I tried to lift one leg but straight away the other one sank deeper. The mud was foul and squelchy. It sucked at my legs.

My hat was spinning upside down in the water, just out of reach. The word *crocodile* flashed through my mind.

Panic began to well up in my throat. Then I looked at the hat. My mother's smiling face appeared in my mind. I threw myself into the water and like a dog digging a hole I began to pull myself forward with my hands. I stretched out and reached for the brim of the hat. With two fingers I managed to just nip the edge. I pulled it gently towards me.

Yes. Got it.

With one muddy hand I jammed the hat on to my head and began crawling towards the shore. I reached the bank and ran panting back to the hutch.

Nothing had changed. Or had it? I looked at the small entrance hole. Were the baby bilbies and the mother safe inside? Had something slipped in while I was away? I listened. All was quiet. Too quiet?

Was there a feral creature in there?

There was only one way to find out. Dad had told me not to look at the bilbies. But I had to know. Were they safe?

I lifted the lid and stared inside.

5

Breeze was dead. Her staring eyes did not see. They were dry and milky. I bent down and gently lifted up the still body. Her fur was sticky. Her little legs felt as if they would break if I tried to bend them. One foot had been chewed.

My head seemed as if it had dropped off and was falling down, down, down into a deep well. This was a nightmare. I had deserted my post and the enemy had crept into the camp.

With trembling fingers I began to search for a pouch. Maybe the bilbies were still alive in there. I turned her over and felt in the fur. No pouch. No pouch. Oh, yes, there it was. Facing backwards. It was torn and bleeding where teeth had ripped at it. I felt gently inside with my fingers. There were little teats. But nothing else. My heart seemed to stop beating. The world grew bleak and cold.

The babies were gone. I knew at once that they had been eaten by the rat. Killed before we could even give them names.

The rat was a murderer. It had scurried off to its stinking nest. And I knew where it was.

Red-hot rage flowed through my veins. I had never experienced anything like it before. My whole face was burning. I opened my mouth and screamed in fury at the sky. The sound filled the forest for a few seconds and then died. My skin was cold but inside I was boiling.

Something had taken hold of me. Something inside wanted to explode.

It was hate.

Hate for the filthy skulking piece of vermin that could eat three baby bilbies. The rat's image scurried, red behind my eyeballs. The whole world seemed red. Even the one patch of long green grass that sprouted like an island in the dry house paddock was the colour of the sun.

I grabbed the crowbar that was still leaning where Dad had left it against the hutch and staggered towards the patch of grass.

It's funny how something so healthy and strong can grow out of a foul bog. The grass was lush and moist even though it was the dry season.

I hardly noticed the stench. My boots squelched in the brown soil. Somewhere in there was a hole. A home. A hideout for the rat that had killed Breeze. I parted the grass with furious sweeps of the crowbar. Bubbles plopped and released nauseous gases but I hardly noticed. There. Yes, yes. A wet oozing hole. I shoved the end of the crowbar into it and jabbed in and out with furious shouts.

'Die, die, die,' I shrieked.

The end of the crowbar struck something hard. Maybe a rock. I started to dig but the crowbar wasn't wide enough to lift wet soil. I grabbed a large tuft of grass and began to pull. It was firmly lodged but slowly it began to loosen its grasp.

Splop. It came away with a huge ball of soil dripping from the roots.

There. A concrete pipe. I couldn't see the end but something told me the rat was inside. I struck furiously with the tip of the crowbar. Again and again and again. Small chips and sparks flew into the air. My hands grew red raw and a blister formed on one of my palms.

Chip, chip, chip. I banged and banged and banged. Striking with a fury fuelled by my red-hot hate.

Finally a round crack appeared. Like the lid of a teapot that had been glued in place. I tore at the broken concrete with bleeding fingers.

'Aagh.'

I fell backwards into the bog. My jeans and shirt soaked up the foul water. I floundered helplessly.

A huge rat had jumped out of the pipe. It was black and fat and squeaking. And even worse it was only a metre away from my face.

It suddenly began to jump straight up and down as if cornered. I was suddenly grabbed by a wave of fear and revulsion. I wanted the rat to run away. But it was protecting something. Its lair meant more to it than its life.

Life is nothing to a rat.

It had eaten Breeze's babies as if they were no more than scraps of garbage.

The world once again turned red. I sprang to my feet and began striking crazily at the leaping rodent.

It jumped up and sideways. And then forward, baring its teeth like a dog.

Suddenly it grabbed the end of the bar and began to crawl along it. The thought of its claws and teeth and scabby skin made me feel faint. I dropped to a crouching position and holding the bar parallel to the ground thumped it down. There was a small, sickening crack. The rat twitched and lay still.

I stood up and leaned on the bar. I gasped. The breath was raw in my lungs.

I stared down at the dead rat. Its life had gone in a fraction of a second. And in the same moment hate drained from my frenzied head.

I had never killed anything before. Well, maybe a fly and a few spiders. But not a warm-blooded animal. A mammal – even a rat – is more like a person. It has eyes and ears and skin. It holds food in its paws and chews like a human. It has blood inside. And it gives birth and suckles its young.

Suddenly I felt weak all over. I had killed the rat but it didn't make me feel better. Its dead body reminded me of Breeze, lying stiff and still in the box not far away. Now I was a killer too. I had my revenge. But revenge is not sweet. Revenge is sour.

Inside the pipe I could see grass and straw and bits of chewed-up paper.

The rat had been protecting its nest. My heart slowed. The blood seemed to run backwards in my veins.

I carefully moved the top layer of grass with my crowbar.

'Please,' I prayed. 'Please don't let there be . . .'

It's funny that moment when you realise you have just done something terrible. Something you cannot take back. A deed that you can't undo. You remember. It burns into your brains. And stays there for ever. Somehow I just knew that the rat was a mother. I had just lost my own. I knew what it felt like to be motherless.

I pulled apart the straw. There in the nest, was a helpless, hairless piece of living flesh. The eyelids were still unopened. Thin, veined membranes stretched across its tiny eyes. It moved one leg feebly. It reminded me of a tiny wind-up toy that can only make the same squirming movement over and over again.

What do you call a baby rat? A rattling? I didn't know.

'Ratty,' I said in a whispered voice.

6

I felt ashamed for killing Ratty's mother.

How could I make it up to this helpless creature? I knew what Dad would do. The tiny rat would not last more than a few seconds once he returned. Especially when he found out that the bilbies were dead.

I cradled Ratty in the palm of my hand to keep her warm. I stumbled across the clearing to the house and rushed into my bedroom. I found a small cardboard box and filled it with fluffed-up tissues. Then I put Ratty inside.

What do baby rats need? Milk. Mother's milk. And I didn't have a drop of it.

I yanked open the fridge and grabbed some cow's milk. It was cold. Too cold. I poured some into a cup and warmed it in the microwave for a few seconds. I searched in the medicine cabinet and found a small eyedropper. Just the thing. I hoped.

I drew a few drops of milk into the eye dropper and placed the end in Ratty's mouth. The tiny creature sucked. I couldn't believe it. Even though she was blind and helpless, she could still suck.

But how much should I give it? And how often? After a few drops Ratty seemed to tire of the effort. Milk ran down her hairless little chin. Goosebumps were standing out on her skin.

I quickly covered her up with some tissues – to keep her warm.

A friendly sound drifted across the clearing. Before I even realised what it was a feeling of dread ran down my spine. It was the putt, putt putting of Dad's dinghy.

I watched him tie up to the jetty and begin to drag a roll of wire towards the bungalow. Then he glanced towards the bilby hutch. He dropped the wire and started running.

He burst through the door.

'What are you doing?' he yelled. 'I thought I told you not to leave the hutch. What happened?'

'A rat killed Breeze,' I said with a shaking voice. 'And ate the babies.'

'Why did you leave her unprotected?' said Dad. I could tell he was trying to control his temper.

'My hat blew into the river,' I said softly. 'I had to go and get it.'

There was a long, silent pause. Then he exploded. 'Do you know what you've done? We have one bilby left on the mainland. One. This is the end of the line. There are not going to be any more Eastern Bilbies. All because of you.'

'I'm sorry,' I said. 'I'm really sorry. But Mum's hat . . .'

At that moment Dad lost it. He just freaked out. 'Your hat. Your stupid hat. I'm sick of it. What about all the things I've given you over the years? Can't you think about anything else? Breeze is dead.'

His eyes fell on the cardboard box in my hand.

'What's that?'

'A baby rat,' I said. 'I killed the mother and then I found her in the nest.'

'Hand it over,' said Dad. 'Now. You know what has to happen, Jason.'

'Her name is Ratty,' I said. 'And you're not getting her.'

I turned and ran. Straight down the beach to the water's edge. Dad was right behind me. He had me trapped. I turned to face him.

7

Behind me was the sea, grey and threatening. The choppy surface gave no hint of the terrors beneath. Or the beauty. Butterfly fish and rainbow eels. And sharks. And crocodiles.

In front of me was my furious father.

The wind tugged at my hat. I made a quick grab at the brim with one hand and pulled it further on to my head. I needed both hands to keep Ratty's box from tipping and sending her into the water.

'Give me that rat,' said Dad. 'This is no joke, Jason. You've seen what a rat can do. You saw Breeze dead and stiff. Her babies eaten.'

'Ratty is a pet,' I said. 'I'll keep her in a cage. I'll never let her out. I promise. Please let me keep her.'

'That is not a pet, Jason. That is vermin. That rat will never be tame. It will grow up to be a killer like its mother.'

I looked down into the frail cardboard box at the helpless creature squirming in the straw. It wasn't a rat to me. It was Ratty. It had a name.

'I love her,' I shrieked. 'You're not getting her.'

'Hand it over, Jason,' said Dad. He took a step forward.

I shook my head and began to walk backwards into the water. Quickly it covered my ankles and then my knees. Dad followed.

This was crazy. The world was mad. Dad would do

anything to save a bilby or a crocodile or even a snake. Because they were natives and they belonged. But he could kill a pig or rabbit or a cane toad because they didn't.

I knew he would kill Ratty. And deep down in my heart I knew he might be right.

But I was only a boy and you can't always do what is right. And maybe sometimes what seems right is really wrong. How can you be sure?

I was trapped. If I fled out to sea Ratty and I would both drown.

I put the small cardboard box on the surface of the water. For a minute it floated safely. But then the water began to soak through and I knew it would sink.

I had to give Ratty a chance. I had a choice. A terrible choice.

What is more important? A thing or a life? It is hard to decide, even when the thing has a million memories.

I put the rat in the hat.

Very gently I lowered Ratty onto the surface of the water. An Akubra hat floats. I already knew that.

The breeze was blowing strongly off-shore. The hat began to move quickly out to sea.

Mum's hat, my beloved mum's hat, began to bob out to sea.

Okay, Ratty didn't have much of a chance. The hat would probably tip over. Or a seagull or bird of prey might swoop down and eat the poor creature. Even if the hat washed up on an island there was no one to feed a blind, baby rat. But a tiny chance was better than no chance. Dad would kill Ratty like any other piece of vermin, that was for sure.

Suddenly I heard a strangled cry. Dad looked as if he was about to choke.

'You care that much,' he whispered. 'You'd give up the hat for the rat.'

I nodded. I knew my eyes were filled with tears. Tears of love and hate and anger.

Without a word Dad bent over and pulled off his shoes. Then he ripped off his shirt and dived into the water. He began swimming furiously out to sea, towards the distant hat. His arms churned like crazy propellers.

'Come back,' I screamed. 'Come back.'

I wanted to go after him.

But I couldn't swim.

Suddenly Ratty didn't seem to matter so much. Neither did the hat. Dad was risking his life in the crocodile-infested waters. Was it to save the hat? Was it to save Ratty? What? What?

Now only one thing seemed to matter. My father. I imagined huge jaws and sharp teeth. Box jellyfish. Nameless horrors.

Dad was a good swimmer. His splashing figure grew smaller and smaller until I could barely see him.

'Come back, come back,' I cried.

I strained my eyes trying to understand the story that was unfolding.

Yes, yes. He was coming back. And what was that? Oh, he was wearing the hat. That's why he had gone. To save my hat. He had tipped Ratty into the water. To drown.

These are some things you have to face up to. A father is more important than a rat. Dad was still in danger. At any moment he might disappear beneath the waves. Pulled into the deep. Would he end up as just a brief red smudge in the ocean?

I bit my fists until they started to bleed.

Finally Dad staggered ashore. Water dripped from his sodden jeans.

We stared at each other for seconds that seemed to go on for ever.

'I saved your hat,' said Dad.

I nodded, sad and grateful. 'It's okay, dad,' I said. 'I understand. About Ratty, I mean.'

Slowly Dad took the hat off his head. There, tangled up in his hair was a tiny, squirming creature.

'Ratty,' I screamed.

Dad straightened up and stepped backwards.

'You know,' said Dad. 'When a rat kills a bilby it is not pleasant. Especially when it steals the babies and eats them.'

'I already know all that,' I shrieked. 'Don't rub it in.'

'But I'm still going to let you keep it.' Dad bent his head down and let me take Ratty from his hair.

For a fraction of a second our eyes met. Using no words. But saying everything.

I held Ratty in my fist, trying to warm her up.

Dad opened my shaking fingers and stared at his enemy for the first time. He seemed to be going through some terrible struggle. His lips moved but no words came out.

'You haven't changed your mind, have you?' I croaked.

'Jason,' he cried. 'This isn't a rat. This is the rat's supper. It's a baby bilby. And if we're quick I think we can save her.'

We both turned and ran back towards the house.

I ran so fast that my hat flew off my head.

I just let it go.

Some things in life are more important than a hat. The hard bit is figuring out what they are.

That's what I reckon anyway.

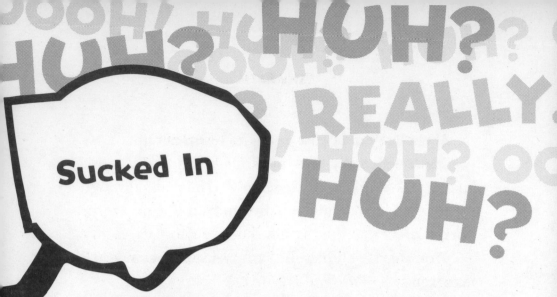

Sucked In

The jar has something floating around inside it. Something awful. Something grey and fleshy. Something foul. Something not alive but not dead either.

A shiver goes down my spine. I wish I could stop peering at the thing in the jar.

But I can't.

The other kids are staring too. Every eye looks at the jar on the desk.

'Okay,' says the new teacher. 'Write a story about this.'

A groan goes up.

The thing in the jar is just another way of getting us to write stories while the teacher cleans out the cupboard.

He probably made it out of a bit of leather or something.

'I can't think of anything,' says Mary Jo.

'Neither can I,' says Helen Chung.

I couldn't think of anything either.

Mr Denton gives a grin. 'Okay,' he says. 'I will make up a story first. That will give you an idea of the sort of thing I want. Then you can have a go.'

This sounds much better.

We all settle down to listen to Mr Denton. But we don't look at him.

We gaze at the thing in the jar. It floats there, silently.

Mr Denton begins his story.

1

Trevor knew that the man in the green coat was going to stick a knife into him. Well, a scalpel anyway. He was going to cut open Trevor's belly and take out his appendix.

'What do you do with them?' asked Trevor as he lay on the operating table.

'With what?' said the doctor.

'Appendixes and tonsils and things. After you cut them out.'

'Burn them,' said the doctor. 'In an incinerator.'

'I want to keep mine,' said Trevor. 'I don't want you to burn it.'

The doctor looked at the nurse from behind his mask. He wasn't too sure what to say. The nurse nodded. 'Okay,' said the doctor. 'I'll put it in a jar for you.'

He pricked Trevor's arm with a needle and the room started to spin.

'Good,' mumbled Trevor, just before everything turned black. 'We must always be together – me and my appendix.'

When Trevor woke up he had stitches across his belly. And a jar next to his bed with something grey and fleshy floating inside it.

Even though his stomach hurt he gave a grin. His

appendix might be out. But it wasn't gone.

He picked up the jar and stared at it. 'You're never leaving me,' he said. 'Never. We must always be together.'

2

When he got home from hospital Trevor put the jar in a safe place and went up to his room.

He took off his dressing-gown and climbed into bed. Then he snuggled down and closed his eyes.

He was just starting to drift off to sleep when a terrible scream came from the kitchen.

Trevor hobbled down the stairs as fast as he could. He found his mother staring into the fridge.

'What's up?' he yelled.

'I'm not having that revolting appendix in there,' said his mother. 'It's disgusting.'

'It's not disgusting. It's part of me. Just like my eyes and brains and that. If you don't like my appendix you don't like me.'

'What have you put it in the fridge for?' she said.

'So it doesn't go bad,' said Trevor.

'It won't go bad, Trevor. It's in formalin. The liquid preserves it.'

Trevor looked at the appendix jar. 'It's best to be on the safe side,' he said. 'It's part of me. I can't let anything happen to it.'

'Well, it's not going in the fridge,' said his mother. 'Someone might think it's a pickle and eat it.'

Trevor nodded. 'You're right,' he said thoughtfully. 'We couldn't have that. Are you sure it won't go bad?'

'I'm sure,' said his mum.

'Good,' said Trevor. 'I'll be able to take it to school with me then. Me and my appendix. We must always be together.'

His mum just sighed and shook her head.

3

So the appendix went to school.

Trevor dumped the jar down on his desk. Everyone stopped talking.

Every eye looked at the jar. Some kids gasped. But most kids just stared. They stared and stared and stared. None of them could stop looking at it.

The jar had something floating around in it. Something awful. Something grey and fleshy. Something foul. Something not alive but not dead either.

A shiver went down every spine. Every spine except Trevor's.

'It's my appendix,' he said. 'Where I go it goes.'

The class was amazed. No one had ever seen an appendix before.

'You'd better leave this on my desk, Trevor,' said his teacher, Mr Birtle. 'No one seems to be able to stop looking at it. We'll never get any work done this way.'

Actually it was Mr Birtle who couldn't stop looking at the jar. He seemed to be mesmerised by it.

'Are you sure this is an appendix, Trevor? I could swear that it was alive. I thought I saw it move.'

Everyone stared at the appendix. It swirled slowly in the yellow liquid.

'Go down to the library, Trevor, and ask for an anatomy book,' said Mr Birtle. 'I want to see just what an appendix looks like.'

Trevor didn't really want to go. He didn't want to leave his appendix behind.

As he walked slowly down the stairs his hands began to feel sweaty. His heart thumped loudly. His head hurt.

He wanted to turn around and run back to the class. He wanted to grab his jar and hold it close to his face. 'We must always be together,' he said to himself. He hurried to the library and started to search for an anatomy book.

Back in the classroom Mr Birtle gasped. The appendix was definitely moving around. Like an angry goldfish, it circled inside the jar.

And in the library Trevor also circled between the shelves like an angry goldfish.

Finally he found what he was looking for. He grabbed the anatomy book and rushed back to the classroom.

Mr Birtle looked up as Trevor entered. 'It's angry,' he said to Trevor. 'It's swimming around and around.'

Trevor rushed over to the jar and peered in. The appendix just floated there. Hardly moving.

A strange look came over Mr Birtle's face. 'It *was*

moving,' he said. 'It stopped when you came back. Go and stand outside the door, Trevor.'

'I don't want to,' said Trevor. 'I don't want to leave it. We must always be together.'

Mr Birtle tightened his lips. 'It doesn't want you to leave either,' he said. 'Go and stand outside the door – it's only for a moment.'

Trevor did as he was told.

He left the room and stood outside. His hands were sweaty. His head hurt. His heart pumped heavily.

He stared in the window and gasped.

The appendix was rushing around inside the jar. It was leaping out of the yellow formalin like a trout on a fisherman's line.

The students all took several steps backwards. They were scared. Something weird was happening.

Trevor rushed back in and grabbed the jar. Straight away the appendix calmed down and simply floated in the formalin.

'We'll give it one more try,' said Mr Birtle. 'Trevor, I want you to go outside, cross the road and go into the milk bar. Count to twenty and then come back.'

Trevor put down the jar and walked slowly out of the door. He trembled as he made his way across the road. The further away he got the worse his head hurt. He wrung his wet hands together. He put his hand on his thumping heart. With shaking legs he walked into the shop and closed the door behind him.

A roar came from the school as thirty people screamed out together.

Trevor didn't even feel his feet touch the ground. He almost flew back to the classroom.

'We must be together,' he screamed.

He fell into the room. Everyone was out of their seat. Backing away from the appendix in horror.

They were all terrified.

Even Mr Birtle.

The appendix was leaping up and down inside the jar, banging against the lid. It sounded like bullets from a crazy machine-gun. The lid trembled under the strain.

Trevor rushed over and grabbed the jar. The appendix fell still. It circled quietly in its fluid. Content.

Trevor smiled at it. Happy. 'You'll never leave me,' he said. 'Never.'

Mr Birtle strode to the front of the class. 'I'll have to take that, Trevor,' he said, snatching the jar. 'Something strange is going on. This could be dangerous.'

'Okay,' said Trevor with a grin. 'If that's what you want.' He turned and walked to the door. The class started to scream in panic as the appendix once again drilled away at the lid.

'Come back,' shouted Mr Birtle. He thrust the jar into Trevor's hands.

'Thanks,' said Trevor. The appendix circled happily. 'We must be together,' said Trevor.

Just then the bell rang and the class headed out for

lunch. 'You wait here, Trevor,' said Mr Birtle. 'I'm going to get the principal.'

4

Trevor looked at his appendix. 'They are going to take you away,' he said. 'They won't let you stay with me, that's for sure.'

The appendix bobbed up and down. It seemed to agree.

'We have to get out of here,' said Trevor. 'We must always be together.' He clasped the jar to his chest and sneaked down the stairs. He crept along the corridor and out of the back door.

Suddenly a hand fell on his shoulder. It was Mr Birtle and the principal.

'I'll have that,' said the principal. He grabbed the jar from Trevor's shaking hands.

Straight away the appendix began to drill up and down at the lid. It hammered so fast that it was just a blur inside the bottle.

'Get it out of the school,' yelled Mr Birtle. 'It could attack the children.'

'No,' screamed Trevor. 'Give it back. Give it back.'

Mr Birtle grabbed Trevor by the arms and held him tight.

'Come back, come back,' screamed Trevor. But it was no use. His appendix had gone.

The principal ran for it, carrying the vibrating jar in

his trembling fingers.

He threw the jar onto the back seat of his car and sped out of the school gate.

The principal's hands shook on the steering wheel. He looked over his shoulder at the appendix which was furiously attacking the lid of the jar.

At any moment the top might burst. What then? The whole thing could explode like a bomb.

He jammed his foot on the brake pedal. Then he grabbed the jar and placed it on the footpath.

Shaking with fear, the principal jumped into his car and hurtled down the street.

He stopped again and looked over his shoulder.

The jar suddenly exploded.

The appendix shot into the air. It turned over and over like a drunken bird.

The appendix was free.

5

Back at the school Trevor struggled to get away from Mr Birtle. But the teacher was too strong. Trevor fought like a wild thing but it was no good. He couldn't slip out of Mr Birtle's iron grip.

Suddenly his body slumped. Lifeless. He drooped like a rag doll in Mr Birtle's arms. Mr Birtle lowered him to the floor. He placed his ear to Trevor's chest. Then he rushed to the cupboard for a rug.

Trevor leapt up and sprinted out of the school. His

trick had worked. He was free.

Free to find his appendix.

And the appendix was free to find him. It slithered along the empty footpath like a wet, foul mouse.

There was not a person to be seen. Only a cat. A large ginger cat. It saw the appendix and it liked what it saw. With one quick spring the cat jumped down from its perch on a fence.

It landed right in front of the appendix.

The appendix stopped.

The cat crouched low.

The appendix quivered. The cat dabbed at the wobbling shape. Its paw seemed to stick to the appendix.

The cat gave three terrified squeals.

'Miaow, miaow, miaow.'

Then it vanished into the appendix.

Sucked up like a rag into a vacuum cleaner. It disappeared as easily and noisily as jelly slurped up a straw. The appendix shivered and continued its journey. It was no bigger. It was no smaller. But it had eaten the cat.

Suddenly the appendix started squealing.

'Miaow, miaow, miaow.'

The appendix copied the cat's last cries. Down the street it went, squealing in a tiny voice.

'Miaow, miaow, miaow,' it squealed.

The appendix rounded a corner and stopped again. An angry dog barred the way. It yapped and flapped and circled the bit of slimy gut that quivered before it.

Suddenly the appendix moved. In a flash it leapt up and fixed itself to the dog's ear. The dog yelped in agony. It tried to shake off the appendix.

'Ruff, ruff, ruff.'

Too late it realised its mistake.

The appendix slurped.

And sucked up the dog without so much as a burp. The dog was gone. Vanished. And the appendix, still small and foul, slithered on its way.

'Ruff, ruff, ruff,' yipped the appendix. It copied its last meal's voice. Over and over.

'Ruff, ruff, ruff.'

It seemed to enjoy the sound of the dog it had eaten for dinner.

Across the road slithered the awful piece of slime. Under a car and down a drain. It seemed to know where it was going.

It did know where it was going.

It was heading for Trevor.

By now, Trevor had run a long way from the school. He panted and looked behind him. There was no one following. He had escaped. But he was out of breath. His head hurt. His hands were damp with sweat.

But he felt a little better.

Somehow he knew that the appendix was on its way. It would never leave him. He sat down in the gutter and waited.

Next to a drain.

'Squeak, squeak, squeak.' A tiny cry. The appendix slithered out of the drain, still imitating its last meal. A meal that it had met in the drain. A rat that had been just a little too curious.

Trevor smiled when he saw the appendix. 'We must always be together,' he said.

The appendix seemed to agree. It slithered up Trevor's leg. Over his jumper. Up his neck. On to his chin.

Trevor opened his mouth very wide.

'We must always be together,' he said.

There was a gulp.

And they were.

'And that,' says the new teacher, 'is the end of my story.'

A shiver goes down my spine. I wish I could stop peering at the thing in the jar.

All the kids in the class sit and stare in silence at the jar on Mr Denton's desk. The horrible grey thing circles silently in the yellow fluid.

'What do you think?' says Mr Denton.

The kids are feeling a bit sick. It's a good story but not one to cheer you up. Everyone claps politely just as the bell rings. The class files out for lunch but no one walks anywhere near the horrible grey thing in the jar.

I hang back until they are all gone. I want to talk to the new teacher about his story.

'There is one thing wrong with that story,' I say.

'Yes?' says Mr Denton.

'If that appendix was swallowed by Trevor,' I say 'how come it is still in the jar on your desk?'

Mr Denton scratches his chin. 'You've got me there,' he says. 'It is a bit of a weakness in the story. But I can't tell you what really happened.'

'Why not?' I say.

'It was too horrible,' he says.

'You can tell me,' I say.

'Sorry,' says Mr Denton. 'But you would never believe me anyway.'

'It's only a story,' I say. 'Isn't it?'

'Is it?' says Mr Denton. He smiles at me and goes off for lunch.

The jar has something floating around inside it. Something awful. Something grey and fleshy. Something foul. Something not alive but not dead either.

A shiver goes down my spine. I wish I could stop peering at the thing in the jar.

But I can't.

I decide to take off the lid and have a good look. The lid is on tight. I can't budge it. I pull open Mr Denton's desk drawer and find a rag.

I twist the top of the jar with the rag and it starts to move. I twist and twist until finally the lid is off.

I look inside the jar. The slimy bit of flesh does not move.

Not at first.

Then, slowly, horribly, it slides out of the jar.

It speaks in the words of its last meal.

'We must always be together,' it says in a tiny voice.

'We must always be together.'

Clear as Mud

I'm undone.

Yes, I know. I'm a fink. A rat. A creep. Nobody likes Eric Mud and it's all my own fault.

But I don't deserve this.

I look in the mirror and see a face that is not a face.

I peel back my gloves and see a hand that is not a hand.

I pull off my socks and see feet that are not feet.

I look down my pants and see . . . No, I'm not going to describe that sight.

Oh, merciful heavens. Please, please. I don't deserve this.

Do I?

1

It all began with Osborn. The nerd.

See, he was a brain box. He always did his homework. He played the piano. He collected insects. The teachers liked him. You know the type.

I spotted him on his first day at school. A new kid. All alone on the end of the bench. Trying not to look worried. Pretending to be interested in what was inside his bright yellow lunch box. Making out that he wasn't worried about sitting by himself.

'Look at it,' I jeered. 'The poor little thing. It's got a lovely lunch box. With a bandaid on it. Has it hurt itself?'

The silly creep looked around the schoolyard. He saw everyone eating out of brown paper bags. No one in this school ever ate out of a lunch box. Especially one with the owner's name written on a bandaid.

Osborn went red. 'G'day,' he said. 'I'm Nigel Osborn. I'm new here.'

He even held out his hand. What a wimp. I just turned around and walked off. I would have given him a few other things to think about but my mate Simmons had seen something else interesting.

'Look,' yelled Simmons. 'A parka. There's a dag down on the oval wearing a parka.'

We hurried off to stir up the wimp in the parka. And after that we had a bit of fun with a kid covered in pimples.

A few days went by and still Osborn had no friends. Simmons and I made sure of that. One day after school we grabbed him and made him miss his bus. Another time we pinched his glasses and flushed them down the loo.

I never missed a chance to make Osborn's life miserable. He wandered around the schoolyard like a bee in a garden of dead flowers. Completely alone.

Until the day he found the beetle.

2

'A credit to the whole school,' said old Kempy, the school Principal. 'Nigel Osborn has brought honour to us, to the town. In fact to the whole nation.'

I couldn't understand what he was raving about. It was only a beetle. And here was the school Principal going on as if Osborn had invented ice cream.

Kempy droned on. 'This is not just a beetle,' he said. 'This is a new beetle. A new species. It has never before been recorded.' He waved the jar at the kids. What a bore.

Everyone except me peered into the jar.

'It is an ant-eating beetle,' said Kempy. 'It eats live ants.' He looked over at me. 'Eric Mud, pay attention,' he said.

I just yawned loudly and picked my teeth.

At that very moment the beetle grabbed one of the ants that was crawling on the inside wall of the jar. The beetle pushed the ant into its small mouth. It disappeared – legs twitching as it went.

Osborn stood there staring at his shoes, pretending to be modest. What a nerve. He needed to be put back in his box.

But that would have to wait. Old Kempy was still droning on. He stopped and took a deep breath. 'This species will probably be named after Nigel Osborn,' he said. 'Necrophorus Osborn.'

'Necrophorus Nerd Head,' I whispered loudly. A few kids laughed.

Kempy when on with his speech. 'This is the only beetle of its type ever seen. An expert from the museum is coming to fetch it tomorrow. Until then it will be locked in the science room. No one is to enter that room without permission. It would be a tragedy if this beetle were to be lost.'

My mind started to tick over.

A tragedy, eh?

Well, well, well.

3

It was midnight. Dark clouds killed the moon. I wrapped my fist in a towel and smashed it through the window. The sound of broken glass tinkled across the science room floor.

Once inside I flashed a beam of light along the shelves. 'Where are you, beetle? Where are you, little Nerd Head?' I whispered. 'Come to Daddy.'

It was harder than I thought. The science room was crammed with animals in bottles. Snakes, lizards, spiders. There were so many dead creatures that it was hard to find the live one I wanted.

But then I saw it. On the top shelf. A large jar containing a beetle and some ants.

I reached up and then froze. Somewhere in the

distance a key turned in a lock. The security guard. Strike. I couldn't get caught. Old Kempy had already warned me. One more bit of trouble and he would kick me out of the school.

I scrambled out of the window. A jagged piece of glass cut my leg. It hurt like crazy but I didn't care. Pain never worries me. I'm not a wimp like Osborn. I ran across the oval and into the dark shadows of the night.

I held the beetle jar above my head. I had done it.

Back home in the safety of my bedroom I examined my prize. The beetle sat still. Watching. Waiting. It was covered in crazy colours – red, green and gold – with black legs. It was about the size of a coat button.

I looked at the ants. They didn't know what was in store for them. Beetle food.

They were queer-looking ants too. I had never seen any like them before. They were sort of clear. You could see right through them. The beetle suddenly grabbed one and ate it. Right in front of my eyes.

It was funny really. This was the only one of these beetles that had ever been found. This could be the last specimen. There might be no more in the world. And in the morning I was going to flush it down the loo. What a joke.

But the next day I changed my mind. There was no hurry. I shoved the jar in the cupboard and went to school.

I played it real cool. I didn't tell anybody what I had

done. You never know who you can trust these days.

Old Kempy was not too pleased. In fact he was as mad as a hornet. He gathered the whole school together in the assembly hall.

'Last night,' he said slowly, 'someone broke into the science room and stole our beetle.' His eyes roved over the heads of all the kids. He stopped when he reached me. He stared into my eyes. But I just stared back. He couldn't prove a thing. He was just an old bore.

But his next words weren't boring. Not at all. 'The School Council,' he said, 'is offering a reward of two hundred dollars for information which leads to the arrest of the thief. Or two hundred dollars for another specimen. Nigel Osborn's beetle was found in the National Park. Any beetle hunters should search there.'

Old Kempy looked at Osborn. 'You needn't worry, Nigel,' he said. 'We have photos. The new species will still be named after you.'

Rats. The little wimp was still going to be famous.

I walked home slowly. An idea started to form in my head. What if I kept the beetle for a few weeks? Then I would pretend I found another one in the National Park. No one would know the difference. And I would be famous. They might even name it after me. Necrophorus Mud.

I raced home and grabbed the jar. The ants were gone. Eaten alive.

I tipped the beetle onto the table and picked it up.

Its little legs waved helplessly at the ceiling. This was the beetle that was making Osborn famous. I didn't like that beetle. I gave it a squeeze.

And it bit me.

4

I yelled and dropped the beetle on the floor. I was mad. 'You rotten little . . .' I said. I lifted up a boot to squash the stupid thing. Then I remembered the two-hundred-dollar reward. I scooped the beetle up and put it back in the jar.

I jumped into bed but couldn't sleep. My finger throbbed where the beetle had bitten me. I had a nightmare. I dreamed that I was the pane of glass in the science room window. And that someone with a towel around their fist punched a hole right through me.

I screamed and sat up in bed. It was morning.

My hand throbbed like crazy. I held it up in front of my face. I couldn't believe what I saw.

A cold wave of fear grabbed my guts. My legs trembled. My heart missed a beat.

I could see right into my finger. From the middle knuckle right down to the tip of my nail was clear. Transparent.

The bones. The tendons. The nerves and blood vessels. I could see them all. It was as if the flesh of my fingertip had changed into clear plastic.

I rubbed my eyes with my other hand. I shook my

head. This was a nightmare. 'Let it be a dream,' I moaned. I rushed to the sink and splashed my face with cold water. Then I looked again.

It was still there.

I was a freak with a see-through finger. I felt faint. The room seemed to wobble around me.

No one in the world had a see-through finger. Kids would laugh. Sneer. Joke about me. People are like that. Pick on anyone who is different.

I couldn't tell a soul. Not my old man. Not my old lady. And especially not Simmons. I couldn't trust him an inch. He would turn on me for sure.

Breakfast was hard to eat with gloves on but I managed it. Then I headed off for school. I stumbled along the road hardly knowing where I was going. I was so upset that I didn't even feel like stirring Jug Ears Jensen. And I hardly noticed the sheila with the pimples. I didn't even have the heart to give a bit of stick to the kid in the parka.

It was just my luck to have Old Kempy for first period.

'I know you're into fashion, Mud,' he said. 'But you might as well face it. You can't use a keyboard with gloves on. Take them off.'

I can tell you my knees started to knock. I couldn't let anyone see my creepy finger. 'Chilblains,' I said. 'I have to wear gloves.'

Old Kempy gave a snort and turned away. I stuck two gloved fingers up behind his back.

5

As soon as the bell rang I bolted into the toilets and shut myself in one of the cubicles. I peeled the glove off my left hand. Perfectly normal. The flesh was pink and firm. Then, with fumbling fingers I ripped off the other glove.

I nearly fainted.

My whole hand was as clear as glass. I could see the tendons pulling. The blood flowing. The bones moving at the joints. Horrible, horrible, horrible. The beetle disease was spreading.

With shaking fingers I ripped at my shirt buttons. I couldn't bear to look. Hideous. Revolting. Disgusting.

I could see my breakfast slowly squirming inside my stomach. My lungs, like two pink bags, filled and emptied as I watched. I stared in horror at my diaphragm pumping up and down. Arteries twisted and coiled. Fluids flowed and sucked. My kidneys slowly swayed like two giant beans.

My guts revealed their terrible secrets. I could see the lot. Bare bones. Flesh. And gushing blood.

I strangled a cry. I felt sick. I rushed to the bowl and heaved. I saw my stomach bloat and shrink. The contents rushed up a transparent tube into my throat and out into the loo.

This was a nightmare.

How much of me was see-through? I inspected every inch of my body. Everything was normal down below. My legs were okay. And my left arm. So far only my stomach, chest and right arm were infected. Blood vessels ran everywhere like fine tree roots.

I wanted to check my back but I couldn't. Simmons and I had smashed the toilet mirrors a couple of weeks ago.

The bell for the next class sounded. I was late but it didn't matter. We had Hancock for English – a new teacher just out of college. He was scared of me. He wouldn't say a thing when I walked in late.

I covered up my lungs, liver, kidneys and bones and headed off for class. So far my secret was safe. Nothing was showing.

All the kids were talking and mucking around. No one was listening to poor old Hancock. He couldn't control the class. One or two kids looked up as I walked in.

Silence spread through the room. Mouths dropped open. Eyeballs bulged. Everyone was staring at me. As if I was a freak.

Jack Mugavin jumped to his feet and let out an enormous scream. Hancock fainted. The class erupted. Running. Rat-scared. Yelling. Scrambling. Scratching. They ripped at the folding doors at the back of the room. Falling over each other. Crushing. Crashing. Anything to get away from me.

What is it? What had they seen? Everything was covered. I checked myself again: hands, feet, ankles, legs, hip, chest, face.

Face?

I rushed to the window and stared at my reflection. A grinning skull stared back. A terrible throbbing spectre. It was tracked with red and purple veins. My jellied nose was lined with wet bristles. A liquid tongue swallowed behind glassy cheeks. My eyeballs glared back at me. They floated inside two black hollows.

That's when I fainted.

6

When I awoke I remembered my dream. Thank goodness it was all over. I grinned with relief and held my hand in front of my face.

I could see straight through it.

I shouted in rage and flopped back on the bed. It wasn't a nightmare. It was real. I ripped away the crisp white sheets. I was dressed in a hospital gown. I pulled it up and examined myself. I was transparent down to the tip of my toes. I was a horrible, see-through, sideshow freak.

I rushed over to the window. A silent crowd had assembled outside. Two police cars were parked by the kerb. Television cameras were pointed my way. The mob stared up at the hospital, trying to catch a glimpse of the unspeakable ghoul inside. Me.

They wanted to dissect me. Discuss me. Display me. I despised them all. Wackers. Wimps. The world was full of them.

The mob would pay hundreds for a photo. Thousands for a story. Maybe millions for an interview. They made me sick.

I knew their type.

I pulled back the curtains and stretched my bare body for all to see. Inside and out. Blood and bone. Gut and gristle. I showed them the lot.

A low moan swept through the crowd. People screamed. Cameras flashed and whirred. Clicking. Clacking. Staring. Shouting.

They leered and laughed. Mocking monsters. Ordinary people.

A doctor hurried into the room carrying a tray. He grabbed me and tried to push me back into bed. But I was too strong for him. I shoved a veined hand into his face and pushed him off. I could feel my fingers inside his mouth. He choked and gurgled as he fell. He scrambled to his feet and fled.

I pulled on my clothes and with shirt flapping swept down the corridor. Nurses, doctors and police grabbed at me weakly. But they had no stomach for it. Like children touching a dead animal they trembled as I passed.

The crowd at the kerb fell back in horror. I raised my arms to the heavens and roared. They turned and ran, dropping cameras and shopping bags. Littering the road with their fear.

I set off down the empty streets. Loping for home. Looking for a lair.

It wasn't far to go. I kicked the front door open and saw my old lady standing there. She tried to scream but nothing came out. She turned and ran for her life. She hadn't even recognised her own son.

I growled to myself. I pushed food into a knapsack. Meat. Bread. Clothes. Boots. A knife.

And the beetle – still in its jar.

I charged out into the backyard and scrambled over the fence.

Then I headed for the mountains.

7

Up I went. Up, up, up into the forest. No one followed. Not at first.

The sun baked the track to powder. The bush waited. Buzzing. Shimmering. Slumbering in the summer heat.

I was heading for the furthest hills. The deepest bush. A place where no one could see my shame. I decided to live in the forest forever.

No one was going to gawk at me. I hated people who were different. And now I was one of a kind.

When my food ran out I would hunt. There was plenty to eat. Wallabies, possums, snakes. Even lyrebirds.

After five or six hours of trudging through the forest I started to get a strange feeling. Almost as if I was being followed.

Every now and then a stick would break. Once I thought I heard a sort of a howl.

I crawled underneath a fern and waited.

Soon the noises grew louder. I *was* being followed.
I grabbed my knife and hunched down ready to spring.

Scatter. Jump. Lollop. Dribble. Would you believe it was
a dog? A rotten half-grown puppy scampered into view.

'Buzz off,' I yelled. 'Scram. Beat it.' The stupid dog
jumped around my feet. I kicked out at it but missed.
It thought I was playing.

The last thing I wanted was a dog. Yapping and giving
me away. I threw a stone at it and missed. The dog yelped
off into the bush.

But it didn't give up. It just followed a long way back.
In the end I gave up. I could teach it to hunt and kill.
It might be useful.

'Come here, Hopeless,' I said.

The stupid thing came and licked my arm. Its tongue
flowed along my clear liquid skin. It didn't seem to mind
that I was transparent. Dogs don't care if their owners are
ugly. Inside or out.

The night fell but I dared not light a fire. I huddled in
a blanket inside a hollow tree. Hopeless tried to get in to
warm himself but I kicked him out. The mutt probably
had fleas.

I found a couple of ants in the wood.

Food.

But not for me. I opened the jar and dropped the ants
inside. Then I watched the beetle stuff its dinner into its
mouth.

I looked at the beetle with hatred. It had caused all this trouble. I was going to make it pay. 'One day,' I said. 'One day, little beetle, I am going to eat you.'

For three weeks I tramped through the forest. Deeper and deeper. There were no tracks. No signs of human life. Just me and Hopeless. We ate possums and rats and berries. At nights we shivered in caves and under logs.

There were leeches, march flies. Cold. Heat. Dust. Mud. On and on I went. The ugly boy and the stupid dog.

Sometimes I would hear a helicopter. Dogs barking. A faint whistle on the air. But in the end we left them far behind. We were safe. Deep in the deepest forest.

I found a cave. Warm, dry and empty. It looked down onto a clear rushing river. There would be fish for sure.

Hopeless liked the cave too. The stupid mutt ran around sniffing and wagging its tail.

It was the first laugh I'd had for ages. Oh, how I laughed. I cackled till the tears ran down my face. To see that dog wag its tail. Its long clear tail. With the bones showing through the skin. And veins weaving their way in and out.

Hopeless had the see-through disease. What a joke. It was catching.

In the morning most of the dog was see-through. The only bit to stay normal was its head. It had a hairy dog's head but the rest of it was bones, and lungs and kidneys and blood vessels. Just like me. I held up a bit of dead possum. 'Beg,' I said. 'Beg.'

It did too. It sat up and begged. But I didn't give it the possum. There wasn't enough to share around.

8

We stayed in that cave for ten years. The three of us. Me, Hopeless and the beetle. I was like Robinson Crusoe. I set up the cave with home-made furniture. In the end it was quite comfortable.

Every day I fed that beetle. Two ants a day. I kept him alive for ten years – can you believe it? And every day I told the beetle the same thing. 'When I am twenty-four,' I told it, 'I am going to eat you. To celebrate ten years in the bush.'

Not once did I think of going back to civilisation. I wasn't going to be a joke. Looked at. Inspected.

And once they found out the disease was catching no one would come near me anyway. They would lock me up. Put me in quarantine. Examine me like a specimen. I could never go back.

I was fourteen when I went into that forest.

And I was twenty-four when I left it.

See, it happened like this. On my twenty-fourth birthday I decided to have a little party. A special meal just for me. Something I had been looking forward to for many years.

I grabbed the beetle jar and made a speech. 'Beetle,' I said. 'I am an outcast. An ugly see-through monster. I have lived here with you and Hopeless for ten years.

In all that time I have not seen a human face. I haven't heard a spoken word. I want to go home but I can't. Now I pass sentence on you. I sentence you to be eaten alive. Come to Daddy, beetle.'

The beetle waved its legs. It almost seemed to know what was going to happen. I tipped it out of the jar and put it inside my mouth. I held up my mirror and watched it roaming about in there. I could see it through my clear, clear cheeks. It sniffed and snuffed. It searched around trying to find a way out. It had a look down the hole at the back but didn't like what it saw. It backed out.

Then it bit me on the tongue.

I screamed and spat the beetle out onto the floor of the cave. I stamped on it with my boot and squashed it into pulp. Then I rinsed my mouth out with water from the creek. I spat and coughed.

The pain was terrible. My tongue started to swell. I held the mirror up to my face. I stuck out my tongue to get a good look because I couldn't see it properly through my cheeks.

I couldn't see it properly through my cheeks?

I couldn't see it at all through my cheeks.

A pinkish blush was spreading over my face. Eyelids. Lips. A nose. My skin was returning to normal. I couldn't see my spine. My skull was covered by normal hair and flesh. My chin sprouted a dark beard.

I just sat there and watched as the normal colour

slowly spread over my body. Skin, lovely skin. It moved down my neck. Over my chest. Down my legs.

By the next day I was a regular human being. Not a kidney or lung to be seen. One bite of the beetle had made me see-through. And another had cured me.

I could go home. I looked like everyone else again.

Hopeless came and licked me on the face. I pushed him away with a scream.

The dog was still clear. I could see a bit of bush rat passing through his stomach.

He was still see-through. What if he reinfected me? Turned me back into a creepy horror? He had just licked my face. I might catch the disease back from Hopeless.

I sat down and thought about it. There was no way I was going to go home unless I was completely cured. I decided to stay for another month. Just to be on the safe side.

Every night I slept with Hopeless. I breathed his breath. I even shared his fleas. But nothing happened. I stayed normal. And Hopeless stayed see-through.

You couldn't get the disease twice. It was like measles or mumps. You couldn't catch it again.

Maybe if the beetle bit you again you would get it. But the beetle was dead. There was no way I would ever be a freak again.

I packed up my things and headed for home.

9

This was going to be great. I would be famous. The return of the see-through man. And his dog.

I would be normal. But not Hopeless. He was still a walking bunch of bones and innards. I could put him on show. Charge hundreds of dollars for a look. People would come from everywhere to see the dog with the see-through stomach. I would be a millionaire in no time. Hopeless was a valuable dog.

It was a tough trip back through the deep undergrowth and rugged mountains.

But finally the day came.

Hopeless and I stood on the edge of a clearing and stared at a building.

It was a little rural school – the type with one teacher and about fifteen kids. It was a perfect place for me to reappear. They would have a phone. They could ring the papers. And the TV.

The man from the mountains could go home in style.

Still, I was worried. I mustn't frighten them. Hopeless was a scary sight. The teacher and kids would never have seen a dog with its guts showing before. I decided to tie Hopeless up. I didn't want anything to happen to him.

But I was too late. Hopeless bounded off across the grass towards the school.

'Come back, you dumb dog,' I yelled. 'Come back or I'll put the boot into you.'

Hopeless didn't take a bit of notice. He charged across the grass and into the school building.

I waited for the screams of horror. Waited for the students to flee out of the building and run down the road. Waited for the yelling and the fainting.

What if the teacher shot Hopeless? I wouldn't have anything to show. A dead dog was no good.

'Don't,' I yelled. 'Don't.' I ran and ran.

Then I stopped outside the window. I heard excited voices.

'Good dog. Good dog,' said a child's voice.

'Here, boy,' said another.

Something was wrong. They weren't scared of him. Surely Hopeless hadn't changed back too. It couldn't happen that quickly.

I charged into the schoolroom.

The teacher and the kids were all patting Hopeless. His guts still swung about in full view. His dinner still swirled in his stomach. The bones in his tail swished for all to see.

But the kids weren't scared.

Not until they saw me.

A little girl pointed at me and tried to say something. Then they began screaming. Shouting. Clawing at the windows. They were filled with horror. They had never seen anything as horrible as me before.

The teacher could see that the kids were terrified.

'Out the back,' he yelled at the children. 'Quickly.'

The kids charged out of the back door and the teacher followed.

I was alone in the schoolroom.

I looked at the pictures of the see-through people on the walls. I looked at the photos of the see-through people in the text books. In India. In China. And England.

I looked at the photo of our see-through Prime Minister. And America's see-through President.

I stared out the window at the see-through children running in fear down the road. Followed by a perfectly normal see-through dog.

And I realised then. As I realise now. That I am the only person in the world who has their innards covered by horrible pink skin.

I am still a freak.

And I don't deserve it.

Do I?

Shake

Is there a heaven?

Some say 'yes' and some say 'no'.

What is it like?

There are hundreds of descriptions. A lot of people believe in Limbo where souls wait until they have earned their place with the angels. Some think we are born again into new bodies.

Many look forward to a life hereafter. Others say it is just a story.

Like this one.

1

'Look at this,' yelled Gavin. He pulled the box gently out of the ground where I had been digging in the vegetable patch.

Even before he wiped away the dirt I could see the colour. Smudged points of ruby red and emerald green hinted at a covering of jewels. A small key was encrusted into the side of the box.

I snatched the whole thing out of Gavin's hand. 'It's mine,' I yelled. 'The carrot patch belongs to me.

The pumpkins are yours. The box was in my patch.'

'Bulldust,' yelled Gavin. 'I saw it first. I found it.' He put his hands around the box and started to pull but I hung on like crazy.

'It's mine.'

'Is not.'

'Is.'

'Boys, boys,' said Dad. 'Stop fighting. This isn't like you.'

It wasn't either. Gavin and I hardly ever fought. We were twins and usually we loved being together. We were so close that we could almost read each other's thoughts. That's how we happened to both discover the box at the same time.

Mum had been planting onions in her row. I was weeding my carrot patch. And Dad was helping Gavin put in some pumpkin seedlings. It was a family ritual. Every Sunday we would work together in the vegetable patch. Mum and Dad had done it for years. And before that Nan and Pop had planted and weeded and watered in the very same garden.

It was a happy place. I don't think there had ever been a fight in the vegetable patch before.

I clung on to the box with both hands and deliberately bumped Gavin with my shoulder. He stumbled backwards and fell to the ground. I landed on top of him. We rolled over and over yelling and struggling. Neither of us would let go of the box.

'Thief,' I yelled.

'Robber,' shouted Gavin.

Suddenly a hand grabbed me by the scruff of the neck. It was Dad. He pulled me to my feet. Mum did the same to Gavin.

'I can't believe this, Byron,' Dad said to me. 'You two are acting like enemies.' He took the box from my hand and gave it a gentle shake. Something rattled around inside.

'Dad's right,' said Mum. 'It doesn't matter what's inside the box. It's not worth fighting over. People are more important than things.'

'It's still mine,' said Gavin.

'You suck,' I yelled at him.

'Both go to your room,' said Dad. 'And don't come down until you're friends again.'

I held my hands out for the box.

'No way,' said Dad. 'Nobody is touching this until you've both calmed down.'

Gavin and I walked back towards the house. Neither of us wanted to leave the box. I was busting to know what was inside. It seemed to be calling me. Gavin felt the same way. I knew he did.

He was probably thinking other things too. About me. We went back to our room and shut the door. Gavin threw himself on to his bed. I did the same on mine.

'It's my box,' we said. We both said exactly the same sentence at the same time. It often happened to us. That's how close we were. Normally. But right at that moment we were not close. It was like we were a million miles away from each other.

It's funny when you are mad with someone that you really care about. Just at that moment you sort of hate them. It's not real. But at the time it seems like it is. That's how I felt about Gavin just then. We were like two horseshoe magnets. Normally the ends stick together so strongly that you can't pull them apart. But if they are turned the wrong way around they push each other off.

He started to speak in an angry voice. 'Why don't you . . .'

'Get lost?' I said, finishing his sentence for him.

Just then the door opened. Dad came in carrying the box. He had rubbed it down and we could see that it was covered in bright jewels.

'They're not real,' said Dad. 'Just cheap glass. The box is made of brass so it's not worth anything. And neither is what's inside.'

'Give it to me, Dad.' I said. 'Please.'

'It's mine,' yelled Gavin.

Dad shook his head. 'Neither of you are getting this box. Not until you make up. Not until you shake hands.'

I looked at Gavin. He was mad at me. I could almost read his mind.

'Shake hands,' ordered Dad.

'No,' we both said at the same time. Gavin shoved his

hands into his pockets and so did I.

'All right,' said Dad. 'If that's the way it's going to be, neither of you can have it.'

He gave a huge sigh and shut the door behind him.

Gavin and I stared at each other without saying a word. Finally, Gavin took one hand out of his pocket and held it out. He wanted to shake.

I shook my head.

'No way,' I said. 'That box is mine.'

Gavin's bottom lip started to tremble.

My stomach churned over. We had never been like this with each other before. We were both upset. I could see he really wanted to make friends. But I wouldn't. I was too stubborn.

Suddenly he rushed out of the room. I heard him stumble down the stairs and out of the front door.

I wanted to yell out for him to come back.

But I didn't.

I never saw Gavin again. Well, not in the flesh anyway.

2

My twin brother Gavin was run over by a car right in front of our house. After I refused to shake hands he rushed out of the front door and straight across the busy road. Maybe he had tears in his eyes from our argument. Maybe he was in so much of a hurry he just didn't look.

Either way it was my fault.

'No it's not, Byron,' said Dad as we drove home from the funeral. 'You can't think like that. If I hadn't sent you to your room it wouldn't have happened. If we hadn't found the box he wouldn't have run on to the road. Life is full of things making other things happen. It wasn't anyone's fault.'

I answered with a trembling voice. 'Gavin held out his hand,' I said. 'And I wouldn't shake.'

Mum put her arm around me and tried to smile. 'Everyone does mean things to the people they love,' she said. 'We all have to get over it.'

That was easy to say. But it didn't happen. Gavin was run over right outside our house. Every time I went in and out of the gate it reminded me of him. All I could think of was shaking his hand and putting things right.

Dad tried to reason with me. 'Byron,' he said. 'When someone you love dies you think you will never be happy again. There is a great big black hole in your life. You cry and ache and hurt inside. But finally a day comes when you can think about them and smile.'

'That day will never come for me,' I said. 'Not until I can shake Gavin's hand.'

A year went by. A whole year. But I couldn't get happy. I just kept thinking about Gavin standing there and offering me his hand. Sometimes I would hold out my arm and move it up and down as if I was shaking with him.

'Sorry,' I would say. 'You can have the box. I don't want it.' I would close my eyes and see us laughing and digging in the garden and having fun like we used to. But when I opened them no one was there.

No one.

Dad was going to throw the box out. He showed me what was in it. A pair of glasses. Just an old pair of granny spectacles. That's what my brother had died over.

'No,' I said. 'I'll keep it.'

The box was a connection to Gavin. For some strange reason I felt as if I could reach him through it. Mum made me put it in the cupboard. She couldn't bear to look at it. In fact Mum didn't even like living in our house anymore. Everything made her sad.

Finally Dad made a decision. 'I think we should move,' he said. 'Buy a new house. Start new memories.'

Mum nodded her head. 'I would like that,' she said. 'I can't bear it here anymore.'

'No,' I yelled. 'No, no, no. I don't want to go.'

I couldn't tell them why. They wouldn't like it. But the truth is I still hoped to see Gavin again. He was connected to the house. I felt as if his spirit was there.

I went to my room and picked up the box. The terrible box. Maybe it would bring me closer to Gavin.

I walked down to the tool shed. I hadn't been inside there for a year. Neither had Mum or Dad. The tools were all covered in cobwebs. Dust lay over everything. Dad's overalls still hung on the peg where he put them on that terrible day. He had never worn them again.

I stared through the open door at the vegetable patch outside. It was overgrown and full of weeds. None of us could bear to dig in it anymore. Dad hadn't even touched his overalls since Gavin died.

I suddenly held out my hand. 'Shake,' I said.

I pretended that Gavin's hand was in mine. But I knew it wasn't.

Finally I decided to have a look inside the box. It couldn't do any harm. I sat on the ground and opened the lid. Then I took out the glasses. I turned them over in my hand. Finally I put them on and stared around.

3

The shed was different. For a second I couldn't quite take it in. Things always look different when you put on someone else's glasses. But this was really strange. The tools were not the same tools. And Dad's overalls weren't the same.

The Victa lawnmower was gone. And in its place was a push mower. An old-fashioned one. There were paint tins I hadn't seen before. There were two metal buckets and the sharpened handle of a spade. Pop had used something like that to plant seeds.

I snatched the glasses from my nose. Everything went back to normal. This was incredible. What was going on?

I was seeing things – that's what.

The glasses had some sort of power. I put them back

on and stared out at the vegetable patch. The weeds had gone. There were neat rows of carrots and beans and tomato plants held up with wooden stakes. Each row had a small seed packet pinned to a peg and placed at the end of the rows to show what was growing there.

Three people were cheerfully working in the vegetable patch. An old man and woman. And a boy. 'Pop,' I gasped. 'And Nan.'

It was my Pop and Nan. But it couldn't be. They were dead.

And so was the boy.

'Gavin,' I whispered.

My head began to spin. I couldn't take this in. What was going on?

Then it hit me. They were ghosts. I was looking at the ghosts of my dead relatives. They were happily working away in the vegetable patch. Just like they had when they were alive. It was a ghost garden, in a ghost world.

I walked over and stood next to Gavin. He was testing tomatoes by squeezing them.

'Don't pick any green ones,' said Nan.

'No worries, Nan,' he said. Gavin laughed in the way that he always did.

This was wonderful. Fantastic. Frightening. The answer to my dreams. This was my chance to make up. To shake his hand. 'Gavin,' I croaked.

He ignored me. He just kept picking tomatoes.

'I'm getting hungry,' said Pop.

'I'll go and put on the soup,' said Nan.

I used to love Nan's soup. Without thinking, I yelled, 'Don't forget me.'

No one heard me. No one answered. They couldn't see me. They couldn't hear me. They didn't even know I was alive.

I went over to Gavin and held out my hand. 'Shake,' I said in a trembling voice. My whole body felt as if it was filled with a zillion volts of electricity. This was my chance to set everything right. I was scared and filled with happiness at the same time.

Gavin lifted his head and looked puzzled. I waved my hand in front of him. It passed right through his head.

'Nan,' said Gavin. 'I thought I saw something.'

'What?' said Pop. 'What did you see?'

'I don't know,' said Gavin slowly. 'I thought I saw something out of the corner of my eye. I thought it was a person.'

Pop and Nan laughed and laughed.

'There's no such thing as a person,' said Nan.

'I don't believe in people,' said Pop.

'Neither do I,' said Nan.

'It's me,' I yelled. 'Byron. Your grandson. I'm real. I am. Gavin, Gavin, it's me.'

They didn't take a bit of notice. Pop started walking towards the shed with his garden fork. Nan followed.

'Stop, stop,' I yelled.

There was no reply.

It was just as if I was a ghost.

They could talk to each other. They could see each other. But I wasn't there. Not to them.

I have often wondered how ghosts felt. Hanging around and not being seen. Watching others do things. Being there at Christmas but not getting presents. Asking questions and receiving no answers. Knowing answers but not being able to tell them.

Now I knew how a ghost felt.

Lonely.

It was the loneliest thing in the world. To be there and not to be included. It was like walking into a new school where no one notices you. Only a million times worse.

I snatched the glasses from my eyes and at once the three ghosts disappeared. Everything went back to normal.

4

What did the ghosts mean when they said that they didn't believe in people? Didn't they know they were dead? Where did they think they came from?

I put the glasses back on my nose. There they were again. A family of ghosts working the vegetable garden. Pop was leaning the wheelbarrow up on its wheel against the shed.

'I believe in people,' said Gavin to Pop. 'We could have lived in another world before this one. Another life.'

Nan shook her head. 'You would remember,' she said. 'You would remember other people who were there. But we don't. No, there's nothing before you are born. How could there be?'

'I feel like I was here once before,' said Gavin.

'That means you would have had to stop living and start again. But we go on for ever,' said Pop, shaking his head. 'You can't stop living.'

I couldn't help yelling out even though I knew they wouldn't respond.

'It's called dying,' I said. 'You get run over. Or sick. Or you just die of old age.' None of them took any notice. They didn't hear a thing.

'I feel like I remember something,' said Gavin. 'But I can't be sure. Maybe I had a sister or something. Before I was born.'

'No,' I screamed. 'Not a sister. You had a brother. A twin. Me. I'm here.'

This was crazy. He couldn't remember being alive.

Gavin stared around, frowning. But he didn't see me.

'That's enough nonsense for one day,' said Pop. 'I'm going inside for a cuppa.'

'Me too,' said Nan.

Just then a face appeared over the back fence. It was another old man. He had a bald head and a big grin on his face. He held up a glass of Champagne.

'Congratulate me,' he said. 'We've had a child. A son, named Ralph.'

'Oh, wow,' said Pop.

'Fantastic,' said Nan. 'Where was he born?'

'Over there behind the apple tree. One minute there was no one. And then there he was. Appeared out of nothing.'

'Isn't nature wonderful,' said Nan. 'I never get used to it. People being born out of thin air.'

Another face appeared. A man of about forty. 'Here he is,' said the neighbour. 'This is my boy.'

'Pleased to meet you,' said Ralph.

'Isn't he polite,' said Pop. 'I like that in a son.'

'He's got your nose,' Nan said to her neighbour. 'You can see he's related.'

Ralph beamed. He was happy with his new family.

This was crazy. The ghosts thought they were alive. They didn't know they were dead. They believed that new-born people just arrived out of the air already grown and talking.

I stared sadly at Gavin. He had a funny look on his face. As if he was sad about something but didn't know what.

Oh, how I wanted to shake his hand, just one last time.

'I'll stay here and plant some more beans,' he said.

'Good boy,' said Pop. He and Nan shuffled inside. The neighbour and his new son, Ralph, dropped back behind the fence. Gavin was alone in the garden. He planted the beans slowly in the soft earth. He could sense something.

I just knew he could. He knew someone was there. Twins are like that. They are closer than other people.

'I'm here, Gavin,' I called.

He looked around, not seeing me.

Without warning another crazy thing happened. A dog appeared. And *appeared* is the right word. An old dog just popped up from nowhere.

Gavin gave a grin. 'Hello, fellah,' he said. 'Welcome to the world.'

The dog gave Gavin a lick and then scampered off. Amazing. A new-born old dog. Somewhere back in my world someone was sad because their pet had died. But the dog couldn't even remember them. It had probably gone off in search of relatives.

I had to jog Gavin's memory. I had to make him see me.

I looked at the row of vegetables. He was kneeling down in a familiar spot. Yes, yes, an idea was coming into my mind. What was it? Of course. I hit my forehead with the palm of my hand. That's where I had dug up the box. In that very spot.

I closed my eyes and sent out a message. A thought message. I put every bit of energy into the one word. Over and over and over I chanted it in my mind. 'Dig, dig, dig.'

After a bit I took a peek. It was working. Gavin wasn't just turning the soil. He was digging a deep hole. Every now and then he would stop and look around as if he thought he was being watched.

He was. By me.

'Aha!' he cried. He had struck something with his spade. It was the box, all covered in dirt with glass jewels peeking through. And a key sticking out of the lock.

He turned the key and opened it. Then he tipped the box upside down. Nothing. Not a thing. He was disappointed. So was I.

Of course. He couldn't find the glasses because I was wearing them. I suddenly whipped them off my face and dropped them into my cleaned-up box. The ghost world vanished. Everything was back to normal. I couldn't see ghosts without the glasses.

I stared into the box. The glasses were shimmering. In a flash they were gone. Vanished. They had gone to another place. And I knew where.

Now, now, this was my chance. I tried to imagine what Gavin would do if the glasses suddenly appeared in his dirt-encrusted box. He would be startled. Scared. But in the end he would put them on. I knew that because that's what I would do. What I had already done. And we were twins. We thought alike.

'Anyway,' I said to myself. 'Things are always appearing out of nowhere in the ghost world. People are even born from nowhere. They are used to things suddenly appearing.'

I waited a bit. Then I stepped into the garden. I hoped that Gavin was standing there wearing the glasses and looking at me. If I could see him with them, maybe he could see me. I held out my hand. 'Gavin, mate,' I said. 'I want to be friends again. Shake.'

There was no reply of course. Or, if there was, I didn't know it. I couldn't see Gavin without the glasses.

I didn't feel a thing. No ghostly hand. No live hand. My plan probably hadn't worked. I had no way of knowing where the glasses were. And even if they had passed into the ghost world they might not work on ghosts. Or Pop might have grabbed them. Or Gavin might be wearing them inside the house while I was out in the garden.

I knew it was hopeless but I put out my hand again and moved it up and down.

'Shake, Gavin. Please shake,' I said.

'Byron, Byron,' said a voice. 'What are you doing?'

I turned around.

Mum was looking at me with tears in her eyes.

5

Mum dragged me inside and made Dad come home from work. She told him what she had seen.

'Byron,' said Dad. 'There are no ghosts. You are not going to see your brother again. You have to live with that. I'd like to shake Pop's hand. Do you think I didn't say mean things to him when I was a boy? Do you think I didn't do horrible things that I wish I could take back? We are all just good people who make mistakes. Hurt others sometimes. We have to live with it.'

'I saw him,' I yelled. 'Through the glasses. And Pop. And Nan. They don't believe in people. They . . .'

'Okay,' said Dad. 'Okay. Give me a look through the glasses. I'd like to see these ghosts.'

I hung my head. 'I can't,' I said. 'I gave them to Gavin. He could be watching us right now.'

Mum put her arm around my shoulder and gave me a soft smile. Neither of them believed me. And I didn't blame them.

'We have to leave here,' said Mum. 'We have to start anew. None of us will get over Gavin's death while we live here.'

'I'm not going,' I shouted. 'I have to shake hands with Gavin.'

Mum and Dad just looked at each other silently. I could tell that they were going to find a new house. Well, I wouldn't be going with them. That was for sure.

I started to walk back to the shed.

'Another thing, mate,' said Dad. 'You'd better stay away from the vegetable patch and the shed. It's just making you upset.'

'No,' I yelled.

'Yes,' said Mum. 'And that's final.'

6

After that Mum and Dad didn't take their eyes off me. When I came home from school they wouldn't let me go outside unless they went with me. I desperately wanted to go down to the shed where the box waited for me. There might be just a chance that Gavin had the glasses and was watching.

I tried to sneak out a couple of times but I always got caught. Mum became more and more desperate to move house. Dad even sold his car to raise some money for a new place.

Sometimes I would stand in my room and talk to Gavin as if he could see me. I would explain who I was and why I wanted to shake his hand. But it was hopeless. I could tell no one was there. I had to get down to the shed.

Then we had the storm. A real ripper. Thunder and lightning. Hail. Water raced down the gutters and poured out of the spouting. Dad rang from the station after work. 'Come and get me,' he said to Mum. 'I'll get soaked walking all that way.'

Mum drove off in her old Ford.

This was it. This was my chance.

I raced down to the shed without even putting on my coat. I was drenched. But I was where I wanted to be.

There was the box. Right where I had left it. I picked it up with shaking hands and opened the lid. Yes, yes. The glasses. They were back. I grabbed them and put them on.

Once again I saw another world. A world where it wasn't raining. There was the shed with the old-fashioned lawnmower. And Gavin. Painting a bike.

It was upside down and he was carefully coating it with red. His favourite colour.

'Gavin,' I yelled. 'It's me.'

He kept painting. He couldn't see me. I had the glasses on. It was a one-way thing. There was no way I could get his attention. I concentrated like crazy. 'Gavin,' I said in my mind. 'Gavin, I am here.'

My ghost brother looked up briefly and then went back to work on the bike.

'Shake,' I yelled. 'Shake.'

He didn't take any notice. I wasn't getting through. My heart was breaking. I couldn't make contact.

I could try putting the glasses back in the box. Then he would have them. But I wouldn't be able to see him. He might not get them. Or Pop might confiscate them.

I could stand there, holding out my hand, shaking nothing for all my life without knowing whether it was being returned. I decided to give it a try anyway. I took the glasses from my face and the ghost world disappeared. I quickly put them in the box. They began to shimmer and then vanished.

'Please pick them up, Gavin,' I whispered. 'Please.' I waited for a bit, giving him the chance to see them. And put them on his nose.

I began to speak into the empty jar. I just hoped he could hear me. 'Gavin,' I said. 'Gavin. Don't be scared. I am not a ghost. No, that's no good. You are a ghost. I am a person. There is such a thing as a person. You were my brother. You died. It was my fault. I want to shake your hand. If you can hear me put the glasses back in the box.

There was a pause. Then a shimmering, like rain running down a window. Suddenly the glasses appeared. I quickly put them on.

Gavin was standing there with his back to me. He didn't know where I was. But he started talking. I walked right through him and turned around so that I could see his ghostly face.

'Person boy, who looks a lot like me,' he said. 'I don't know what died means. I know what born means. But I believe you. I believe I once lived before. Somewhere else. I will send the glasses back. Tell me everything.'

'Yes,' I yelled. 'Yes, I will.'

Once again the glasses vanished and once again I stood alone in the shed. I began to talk. I explained everything. About him dying. About Mum wanting to move. About me wanting to stay. And about the handshake. How I needed to feel his hand in mine. I explained how we were twins.

Then I stretched my hand out and moved it up and down. Somehow I knew that he was doing the same. That he was putting his ghostly hand in mine. But I couldn't see it. I couldn't feel it. It wasn't enough. I wanted to touch him. I had to touch him. I would never be free until I clasped his hand in friendship. Until I was forgiven.

Think. Think. There must be a way around this. Surely

there was some way we could see each other at the same time. I had to find an answer. I was desperate.

Suddenly I had an idea.

'Send the glasses back,' I shouted.

Nothing happened. Not for a bit anyway. Then there was a shimmer and a dull glow from the box. The glasses appeared. I grabbed them and started to push on one of the bits of glass.

Plop. Yes, the lens flipped out. Then the other one. Plop. The wire frame was empty. I had done it. I stared at the two glass lenses. Then I quickly threw one of them into the box. It shimmered and vanished.

I pushed the remaining lens on to one eye and closed the other. It was a lens for one eye. A monocle.

It worked. I could see Gavin through my left eye. He was putting his lens up to his right eye. He could see me.

'G'day,' he said in a cheeky voice.

I choked a reply. 'Hello,' was all I could manage.

This was wonderful. We could see each other. He wasn't ghostly. He was solid like a real person. We grinned in amazement at each other.

Suddenly his face fell. He was staring through the window. Pop was coming and he didn't look pleased. I snatched a glance through my window. Dad and Mum were coming and they didn't look pleased either. They were angry. They were furious.

'Quick,' I yelled. 'Quick. Shake.'

I held out my hand. Gavin took it. It was a firm, warm handshake. Solid. Full of life and love. So good. So good. A wonderful feeling ran from his hand right through my whole body. Everything was okay. I had done it. We had done it. I was happy. Now at last I would be able to remember Gavin and smile.

Dad burst through the door of my world.

Pop burst through the door of Gavin's world.

Pop had his hand out to snatch Gavin's eye-glass. Dad had his outstretched to grab mine.

Gavin had time for one last sentence. 'Goodbye, Byron,' he yelled. 'I . . .'

I heard no more. Dad had grabbed my eye glass. Gavin vanished. Pop vanished.

Dad turned, flung back his hand and threw the glass lens into the air and over the fence. I heard it hit the road. And then a crunch. A car had destroyed the lens.

Dad was angry. 'I'm sorry, Byron,' he said. 'But this has to stop.'

I grinned at him. 'It doesn't matter,' I said. 'It's all over. We shook hands.'

Mum and Dad stared at me, upset.

'We have to leave this house,' said Mum. 'We have to start again.'

In my heart I knew that I would never see Gavin again. Pop would have thrown away Gavin's lens too. Or confiscated it. And mine was destroyed. It was over. I had done everything that had to be done.

Well, nearly everything.

I went over to Mum and Dad and put my arms around them. 'If you want to go to a new house,' I said, 'It's okay with me.

'I'm ready to move on.'

Is that a tape recorder, doctor? Is it switched on? Good. I'll tell you how all this happened. There's nothing you can do to save me. No one can help me now. So I'll tell you how I got into this mess.

I'm not in any pain. I'm just crying because I'll never eat another meal. No more fried kidneys. No more sheeps brains. And no more apple pie.

I didn't look like this before. I was a good looking bloke. A bit plump. A little overweight. Some people even called me fat. Well I couldn't help it. I needed a lot of food. I was born hungry. I had a big appetite.

It was all right for skinny people. They didn't feel hungry. I felt hungry all the time. I needed a lot of food.

When I was fourteen it was especially bad. I was a growing lad and I was always hungry. Everybody tried to stop me eating. My parents tried to put me on a diet. The teachers tried to stop me going to the canteen.

One teacher was really bad. He wrote to my parents telling them not to give me any money. He said that I was spending it all on junk food.

His name was Kerr – Peter Kerr. I hated him. I hated

him because he stopped my canteen money.

I hated another person at that school. A kid called John Mead. Mead called me names. Names like Fatso, Fat Stuff, Large Larry and Skinny. He thought it was funny to call me Skinny.

But I taught Kerr and Mead a lesson. A lesson that they didn't forget in a hurry. It was their own fault. They shouldn't have picked on me for being fat.

The trouble started when we moved to a new house. There was a house in the town that my mother always liked. It was very old. It had history. That's why my mother bought it. She liked old things.

We were told that an old woman lived there long ago. Her name was Mother Scarrow. She was able to cure sick people. This was in the days before there were doctors. Sick people came from everywhere.

Mother Scarrow had all sorts of cures. She had bottles of herbs and potions. She could cure anything. Mumps, chicken pox, pimples, even bad breath – she could cure the lot.

One day the people in the village killed her. They said she was a witch. They broke into her bedroom and killed her with sticks. A week later everyone in the village died. A terrible disease killed them all. Mother Scarrow couldn't help them. She was dead.

I didn't believe that Mother Scarrow was a witch. They probably killed her because she was old and ugly.

My bedroom was the room in which Mother

Scarrow was killed. I wasn't scared about that. I didn't really believe in witches or spells, so there was nothing to be scared of.

But I wasn't happy in this house. Not because of the witch, but because I couldn't get food. That rotten teacher Kerr told my mother not to give me money. He said I needed to lose weight.

I was starving. My mother put me on a diet. I was only allowed to have three eggs for breakfast. No chocolate, no cakes. Three sandwiches for lunch and no milkshakes!

It wasn't fair – I needed food. I thought about food all the time. I couldn't get it out of my mind. I saw food in my dreams. Lovely food, like buns, roast chicken, chocolate cake, spaghetti and apple pie.

I had to do something. I was going crazy! I went to the bank and took out all my spare cash. I went to the shop and bought fifteen bars of chocolate. Then I went to my room and looked for somewhere to hide them and the rest of the money.

The walls of my room were made of large bricks. One of the bricks seemed loose. I took out a knife and started to dig all around it. It soon came out. I looked in the hole. There was something in there.

It was a book, a very old book. On the cover it had a word that I had never seen before. It said 'FPELLF'. Inside were pages and pages of handwriting. It was shaky writing. It looked as if someone old had written it. It was smudged and hard to read.

At first I couldn't understand any of it. The spelling was wrong. Then I realised something. None of the words had the letter 's' in them. Where there should have been an 's', there was an 'f'.

I looked at the cover again. It said 'FPELLF'. It meant 'SPELLS'.

I had found Mother Scarrow's book of spells!

2

I spent a lot of time reading that book. It was slow work, but at last I got the hang of it. Every page had a different spell. There was a cure for every illness you could think of.

Some were spells for things that were not sicknesses at all. There was one for fixing long noses. Another was for ugly faces. One page had a cure for bad dreams.

Then I got a shock. One page was about fat people. I read it carefully. I thought it would be about diets. It wasn't. It was a spell to make you thin. But you could eat as much as you liked!

There was a black feather pressed flat between the pages. It had been there for hundreds of years.

The book explained what to do with the feather. It would help you to lose weight.

The book told you to eat a big meal. Anything you liked. Then you had to pick up the feather and write someone's name. The name of someone you didn't like. This person would get fatter but you would stay thin.

You could write the name in the air, or anywhere else you liked. Your enemy would get the fat from the meal!

I didn't really believe in spells, but I liked the idea of this one. I had lots of enemies. There were plenty of people I would like to make fat. All those people who had called me names. I could pay them back.

I picked up the feather and looked at it. If only the spell was real! I could become thinner and make everyone else fat. I decided to give it a try.

I picked up some more of the money I had taken out of the bank. Then I went down the street to the shops. I went in to Fred's Cafe. I sat down at a table and ordered a meal.

It was a big meal. I started with chicken soup. Then I had a rump steak with eggs, chips, vegetables and onions. I was still hungry so I had more. I ordered a mixed grill – two chops, sausages, eggs, bacon and a salad.

After this I was ready for dessert. I had a piece of apple pie, a plate of ice-cream and some cheesecake.

My money was nearly gone. So I finished up with two cups of coffee, a milkshake and six cream buns.

I felt full. My belt was tight. My stomach was sticking out. I had to undo a button on my jeans. I felt a bit sick. Then I did a loud burp. That made me feel better.

I picked up the feather and wrote a name in the air with the feather. The name was John Mead. He was the kid who had called me Fatso.

Nothing seemed to happen. Then I looked at my

belt. It was loose. I had to do up the button on my jeans. I didn't feel sick now. I felt hungry again!

3

The next day was Monday. It was a school day. For once, I really wanted to go to school. I wanted to see what had happened to John Mead.

Mead was away from school. I was disappointed. Then I found out why he was away. He had a bad stomach ache. He was very sick. The doctor said that he had been greedy. What a laugh!

Now I knew the witch's spell worked.

Every day I ate as much as I could. I ate big meals – *very* big meals. After each meal I used the feather. I wrote Mead's name with the feather. I had some great meals. Trifle, chocolate cake, cream sponge, jelly. I ate everything that is unhealthy.

I started to lose weight. I became thinner and thinner. My parents were very pleased. They thought I was on a diet. They gave me my pocket money back. They were pleased that I had changed my ways.

Mead started to put on weight. He became fatter and fatter. He didn't call me Fatso any more. People started to call him Fatso. He became very large. He had to buy new clothes. His old ones wouldn't fit. Soon he was the fattest boy in the school.

Mead went on a diet. He had to eat healthy, boring food like carrots and apples. I almost felt sorry for him until I remembered what he had called me. I remembered how he used to tease me. I kept eating big meals and writing his name with the feather.

I started to get too thin. I didn't want to fade away altogether. I decided to use the feather less often. I only used it on junk food. Chocolate, chips, those sorts of things.

I didn't use the feather on good food. If I ate an apple I didn't use the feather. If I ate rubbish I did. In this way I developed a healthy body. Mead grew fatter and fatter and got pimples.

Next Mead started playing truant. He would not got to school because the kids all teased him for being so fat.

In the end Mead got into big trouble. His parents said he was sneaking food out of the refrigerator. They had a big row. Mead ran away from home. But the police caught him. They brought him back. That taught him a lesson.

I'd got my revenge on Mead. But there was another person I wanted to punish – Mr Kerr, the Maths teacher.

This teacher had been giving me a lot of trouble. He gave the class a Mathematics test. He only gave me thirty marks out of one hundred. I was bottom of the class. He said I hadn't done my homework.

It wasn't my fault. I had been out to dinner. I went to a Chinese restaurant. I had a big meal. I took three hours to eat it. There was no time for homework.

I decided to use the feather on Mr Kerr. I started at

once. I wrote his name after breakfast, lunch and dinner. I just used snacks to keep my own strength up.

Mr Kerr was not as easy as Mead. He stopped eating when he found he was getting fat. This made it difficult for me. I had to eat more and more.

I ate at every chance I got. I ate in bed, I ate on the way to school, I ate at school and I ate on the way home.

I had huge meals. My parents didn't care any more. I wasn't fat so they let me eat what I liked. My plate was always heaped up. After each meal I wrote Mr Kerr's name with the feather.

At last the spell began to work. Mr Kerr started to get plump. It was getting to him. He was worried. His face became red and he walked around shaking his head. He didn't know why he was getting fat.

Mr Kerr had a little sports car, a red MG. Every day he drove to school in this car. He loved it. He was always looking at it and polishing it.

The girls thought his car was terrific. They thought Mr Kerr was terrific too, just because he was good looking. But I fixed all that. I fixed it for good.

I used the feather all day every day. Mr Kerr became so fat that he couldn't fit into his car. It was too small for such a fat man. He sold the MG and bought a bike. It was funny to see him riding to school on a bicycle. A great fat man on a tiny bicycle. He could hardly stay on it. He thought the exercise would help him to lose weight. Fat chance!

4

A year went by. My body was in good shape. I had a good figure. I had large muscles and a thin waist. I was very healthy, and good looking.

I was fifteen years old. I started to notice girls. One girl in particular. Her name was Sue. She was very pretty.

I decided to ask her out. I asked her to go out to dinner with me. 'No,' she said, 'you are too vain. You're always talking about your body. Looks aren't everything. You should care about whether a person is nice. Not whether they are good looking.'

What a nerve turning me down like that! I went red in the face. It was embarrassing. I decided to teach her a lesson. I decided to use the spell on Sue.

'Looks aren't everything,' she had said. We would see about that.

It was the school holidays. I went home and ate. I ate all day, and most of the night. Then I used the feather. I did this all day for two weeks. I just ate and wrote her name with the feather. I was mad with her, really angry.

When I got back to school I saw that Sue was no different. She still had a good figure. I found out she was doing exercises. She ran to school. She jogged in the mornings. She did push-ups, and sit-ups. She went to classes where they do exercises to music. It's called aerobics. She was fighting the weight, fighting me.

I wasn't going to let her win. I ate more and more. I ate until midnight every night. I used the feather all the time.

In the end Sue started to grow chubby. She couldn't exercise while she was at school. But I kept eating. And writing her name with the feather. She grew as fat as Mr Kerr and Mead. She was my biggest victory.

The funny thing was that everyone still liked her. She was still popular, even though she was fat. I couldn't understand it.

The truth is I still liked Sue myself. She was always smiling. I was crazy, but I decided to give her another chance. I decided that I would tell her how to lose weight. Then she would be grateful. She would want to go out with me.

I went up to her in the school canteen. 'Sue,' I said. 'I can help you to lose weight.'

She looked interested. 'How?' she asked.

Then I made a big mistake. I told her all about the feather. She listened until I had finished. Then she said, 'That's silly. I don't believe it. And even if it were true it would be mean. It would be the meanest thing in the world. And you would be the meanest person in the world.'

'But I can help you', I told her. 'If I stop using the feather you can be thin again.'

'That's not funny,' she said. 'It's a bad joke. Go away and leave me alone.' She turned around and walked off. She had her nose in the air. What a snob!

I decided never to tell anyone else about the feather. No one would like me. I would be unpopular.

Later that day I saw Sue talking to Mr Kerr. I could tell that they were talking about me. She was tapping her head with a finger, like you do when someone is mad, or stupid. She thought I was crazy. I started to feel scared. I didn't want to get caught using the feather. I had made three people fat. They could make a lot of trouble for me.

At lunch time I noticed Mr Kerr watching me. He was watching me eat my lunch. I knew what he was thinking. He was wondering how I could eat eight pies for lunch and still stay thin. I didn't use the feather. I didn't want to get caught.

I was feeling a bit low. Depressed. To cheer myself up I went out for dinner. I went to the Chinese restaurant again. Chinese food was my favourite. I sat down and ordered my meal. This is what I had: Chinese soup, sweet and sour chicken, fried rice, prawns in batter, fish with bamboo shoots, and pork with vegetables. For dessert I had two plates of ice-cream and ten banana fritters.

I looked up and saw Mr Kerr sitting in the corner, watching me.

All he had for dinner was a plate of soup.

I decided that I would have to be careful. I kept the feather hidden. I only wrote with it where no one could see me. In my bedroom with the door closed. Or in the lavatory of a cafe.

For the next three years I kept my secret. I kept Mr Kerr and Sue fat. I wrote Mr Kerr's name on Monday,

Sue's on Tuesday. This left me five more days for other people.

I used the feather every day for three years. I used it on all sorts of people. I even used it on a dog. The old lady over the road had a dog. It was a real pest, always barking and yapping. It was a Corgi, named Charlie.

I used the feather on the Corgi for two weeks. It got so fat that it couldn't walk. It just sat there panting on the door-step. Then it died. The vet said that the Corgi died from a strained heart. He said its heart just couldn't keep such a fat body alive. The old lady bought another dog. It didn't yap so I let it live.

I will only tell you about one or two more of my victims. There were too many for me to remember them all.

One was Mr Peppi. He owned an ice-cream shop. I asked him for a Saturday job. I thought I could get some extra food without paying for it.

'No,' he said. 'You have bad manners. You would scare away the customers. And you eat too much. Everybody knows how much you eat. I would go broke.'

He did go broke. I sent him broke. I made him into the fattest ice-cream man in the country. His wife said he was eating the ice-cream. She thought that was why he was fat. They had a big fight. Then she left him and went to live somewhere else.

Mr Peppi was heartbroken. He didn't open the shop. He just sat there looking out of the window.

The feather was good to me. It was useful. I could punish anyone who was bad to me, any enemy at all.

I even used the feather to help the country. I liked cricket. I often went to watch Test matches. I wanted our country to win the Test series. So I made the opposition's captain fat. It took two months to do it. But at last he was so fat that he couldn't bat or bowl. He was their best player, but was dropped from the team. So we won the series, thanks to me.

5

For four years I ate and then wrote a name with the feather. But yesterday things started to go wrong. It was my eighteenth birthday.

My parents gave me a big party. Lots of food and drink. I ate as much as usual. Then I went upstairs. I wanted to write a name with the feather. I was feeling bloated.

Just for fun I wrote the name of the Prime Minister. Nothing happened. I still felt full. A bit ill actually. I wrote another name – still nothing.

I didn't worry too much. I let out my belt two notches. Then I went back to the party. It was no good, I felt sick. I went back upstairs to my room.

I went over to the mirror and looked at myself. I was getting a pot belly. My stomach was sticking out, hanging over my belt. My legs looked fatter and so did my arms. Even my face looked chubby.

I started to get nervous. Maybe the spell didn't work any more. I would have to go on a diet. A big diet. It would be hard. For four years I had been eating enough to feed an elephant. It would be hard to stop.

I went to the hiding place and took out the Book of Spells. I decided to read it carefully. Maybe I had done something wrong.

There were a lot of spells. Hundreds. I read them all. Some I had not read before. At last I came to the back page. Something was written in small letters. It was difficult to read, but I kept going.

What I read made me frightened. Terrified. The last page told how long each spell lasted. The fat-people spell lasted four years. Then after four years the person who used the feather would get ALL the fat back from ALL the people. Four years of fat. **I was going to get it all back!**

I crawled over to the mat. I started to do push-ups. Then I ran up and down the stairs. *Tried* to run up and down the stairs, that is. I could hardly move. I was in a panic. I didn't want to get fat again. Not after all I had been through.

It was no use. I was getting fatter all the time. I was swelling up like a balloon. My hands looked like rubber gloves that had been blown up. My belt burst. All the buttons popped off my shirt. My jeans split down the seams.

I felt very tired and ill. I lay down on the bed. I was getting bigger by the minute. My legs were expanding.

My skin was tight. I felt as if I was going to burst. I could see myself getting larger as I looked.

My shoes burst open. So did my socks. My toes sprang out like fat bananas. I was twice as big as before. Double the size. I kept growing bigger and bigger. Nothing could stop it.

All my clothes split off. I was like a naked, fat pig. The legs on the bed broke. The bed fell to the floor with a bang. I thought I would stop growing soon but I didn't.

I grew as big as a cow. Then an elephant. I couldn't move. I just lay on my back on the floor. 'Help, help!' I screamed.

My parents ran up the stairs. They couldn't get in the door. I took up the whole room.

My head was like a pea on a pumpkin. It was squashed up against the roof. My left leg crashed out of one of the windows. It filled up the whole window frame. I could see a face in the other window. It was yours, doctor. You can't get in, but at least you have been able to get a tape recorder and record my story.

It is hard to breathe. There isn't much air left. The whole room is taken up by my bloated body.

I am the fattest man in the country. In the world. In the universe!

Well that is my story. That is how I got like this. I can hear men taking the roof off. Other men have gone to get a crane to lift me out.

It's no use, is it doctor?

I know it's no use. I can't last long. My heart won't stand the strain. I'm going to die. Soon.

I hope everything I have said is on the tape recorder. It's important that you get my story. I want the whole world to know what happened. At least I will be famous.

My chest hurts. I have a bad pain. I'm going. I'm dying. These will be my last words:

'BURP – BURRRP!'

'It's just sitting there,' I shout. 'All alone. The only one.'
A little tear rolls down my nose.

Dad and Gramps feel sorry for me. I can tell.

'What did you say it's called?' says Dad.

'An axolotl,' I say. 'It's a fish but it looks like a lizard.
And it's got legs.'

'Just sitting there?' says Gramps.

'Yes. On the bottom of the tank. Not moving. Just
looking. It's got no friends. It's got no family. All alone in
a big tank of water. Just staring.'

'Staring?' says Dad.

'Yes. That's the saddest bit,' I say. 'It's staring at its own
reflection. It thinks there's another one. But there's not.
It's lonely.' Another tear squeezes out of my eye. I feel so
sorry for that axolotl.

Dad stands up without a word and goes out of the
room. He comes back holding an old exercise book. He
puts it in my hand.

'What's this?' I say.

'My diary. From when I was a kid.' He opens it up and
points to some scribbled writing. 'Read this,' he says.

I open the diary and start to read.

1

I couldn't believe what Dad had done. Dead fish in our fish shop are fair enough. But not live ones.

'It's murder,' said my mate Pepper.

'Yeah,' I said. 'Murder.'

We both stared at the poor old crayfish slowly walking on the bottom of the tank.

'The customers will just point at it and say, "I want that one." Then Dad will fish it out and cook it.'

'I read about it in a book,' said Pepper. 'The cook drops them in boiling water. They scream, you know. They scream when the cook drops them in.'

We both stood there staring through the window of Dad's fish and chip shop. The crayfish slowly crawled along the bottom of the fish tank. It didn't know what was going to happen to it.

But we did.

'I can't believe that Dad would do this,' I said. 'I just can't believe it. Not murder.' It was the saddest thing ever.

'What are we going to do?' said Pepper.

I thought for a bit. Then I grinned and stared into the tank. I spoke to the crayfish. Even though it couldn't hear me. 'Crayfish,' I said. 'You are going on a trip. You are going home.'

2

'The sea,' yelled Pepper. 'We can't take it to the sea. That's a hundred kilometres away.'

'So?'

'How are we going to get there?'

'I've got a plan,' I told him. 'The crayfish has to go back to the sea. That's where all the others are. It has to go back to its family and friends.'

Pepper thought for a second or two. Then he whacked me on the back. 'We'll do it,' he shouted. 'Put it there, mate.' We shook hands and laughed like crazy.

That night at two o'clock we crept into the shop with a bucket of water. Everything was quiet. Dad and Mum were upstairs – asleep.

The shop was gloomy in the middle of the night. The dead fish in the window stared at us with unmoving eyes.

I shivered and it wasn't cold. All those dead fish eyes seemed to be staring, staring, staring. What if there were human eyes? Cold, mean, murderous. Waiting to pounce.

'Let's go back,' I said in a trembling voice. 'Let's do it tomorrow.'

Pepper looked at me. 'If we don't do it now,' he whispered, 'we never will.'

'Something's moving,' I said. 'I'm sure something moved.'

'There's only one thing moving around here,' said Pepper. 'And that's it.'

The crayfish slowly crawled around in its tank. Poor old thing.

'Okay Pepper,' I said. 'Grab it.'

'You grab it,' he said. 'It was your idea.'

'What if it bites me?'

'Crayfish don't have claws,' said Pepper. 'So how can they bite?'

In the end I put on some rubber gloves and lifted the crayfish out of the tank. I put it into a bucket of water and stared down.

'It's walking a bit slower,' I said.

'Yeah,' said Pepper. 'We have to hurry.'

I grabbed the bucket and carried it towards the door. Boy was it heavy. Water sure does weigh a lot.

Pepper undid the lock. What a din. It opened with a loud 'clack'.

I looked upstairs to where Dad and Mum were sleeping. Not a sound. We crept out into the dark street.

Boy it's creepy in a country town at night.

Trees rustled in the breeze. Every shadow looked as if it was owned by a murderer waiting to jump out and grab two small boys. I walked in the middle of the street just to make sure that no one could leap out and get me.

'Are you scared?' whispered Pepper.

'Nah,' I said.

'Me neither.'

What a pair of liars. We were terrified.

We walked more and more slowly. The shadows grew

blacker and blacker as we approached Jeremiah's corner. I could see it up ahead. A black alley. The very place where old Jeremiah had died shouting curses at the moon.

He had sworn to come back and haunt the town.

We both stopped and stood still. Silence. Terrible, horrible silence.

'What's up?' said Pepper.

I stared at the alley. So scared I couldn't move my throat.

Pepper started to walk forward. I could tell that he was thinking about the ghost of Old Jeremiah too.

'Arhooo.' A long wail pierced the night.

We ran. Oh, how we ran. Hanging on to that bucket. Fleeing, running for our lives.

And after us came the horrible sound of . . .

'Old Jeremiah's . . . dog,' said Pepper. 'It was only his dog.'

We both laughed. Little nervous laughs.

I looked around. We were out in the dark countryside. 'I'm never going near that alley again,' I said. 'Never'.

With shaking knees we set off on our journey. How I wished I was home in my nice warm bed.

We walked in the middle of the road. Trees hung over us like rows of ghostly giants with outstretched hands.

I put the bucket down. 'Your turn,' I said.

'Already?' said Pepper. 'That wasn't a hundred steps.'

'It was so,' I said.

Pepper sighed and picked up the bucket. 'One,'

I said as he stepped forward with the bucket. We counted every step out as we walked forward. It made us feel a bit braver. Two voices in the night. Counting out our way to the sea.

After eighty-three steps Pepper plonked the bucket down and flopped down onto the road, puffing. 'I can't do any more,' he said. 'My arm's got pins and needles.'

'Okay,' I said. 'Fifty steps each.'

We trudged on. This time I only managed forty-seven steps. I just couldn't go one more. My arm felt like it was falling off.

Pepper looked at this watch. 'Four o'clock,' he said.

'Already?'

'Yep. We're never going to get to the station by six. We're not even half way.'

The moon peeped out for a second and we stared down into the bucket. The crayfish was moving very slowly. Very slowly indeed.

'We've only got two choices,' I said. 'We can cut across country. That will save at least an hour. We can still make the train by six.'

We both looked into the black forest. There were strange noises. And rustling. You couldn't see more than a couple of metres at the most.

'What's the other choice?' said Pepper.

I looked him full in the face. All I could see of his eyes were two small points of light. 'We tip out some of the water to make the bucket lighter.'

3

The bushes were so close together that we had to push through with our legs. Soon we were scratched and bleeding. We were down to ten steps each with the bucket. It seemed to get heavier by the minute. But we couldn't tip any water out. We just couldn't.

'They get oxygen from the water,' said Pepper. 'When it's all used up it will die.'

I couldn't see into the bucket because it was so dark. But I just had a feeling that old crayfish wasn't moving much at all.

On we went. Up and down. Round and round. Sore feet. Aching arms. Stumbling, mumbling and moaning. The sun started to colour the morning sky. I was glad because it meant that we could see where we were going. But I was sad because it meant something else, too.

'We're not going to make it,' I said. 'It's ten to six.'

'Yes we are,' yelled Pepper. There were tears of anger in his eyes. 'I'm not going to let it die. Not after all this.' He grabbed the bucket and started to run.

'Don't,' I yelled.

But it was too late. He stumbled and fell. The bucket lurched and splashed and fell from his hand. Pepper grabbed at it and sat it up straight. But it was too late. Nearly all the water was gone. There was just enough to cover the back of the crayfish. One feeler waved gently. That was the only movement that it made.

We both flopped down onto the dry ground. We

knew it was hopeless. We would never get to the station now. And there was something else, too. Something very bad.

'We're lost,' I said to Pepper. 'Lost in the bush.'

4

The summer sun rose high in the sky. The three of us lay still in the shade of the drooping gum trees. Me, Pepper and the crayfish. We were on the side of a hill. All around was thick bush except for one spot. A rock jutted out like a bald patch on the top of a monk's head.

'There's only one rule to keep when you're lost,' I said.

Pepper nodded. 'Stay put,' he said. 'Wait until they come and find you.'

Blowflies buzzed. Cicadas sang their chirping songs. The minutes and hours crawled by. A thought kept coming into my mind. I pushed it down but it kept coming back. I wondered if Pepper was thinking the same thing.

He was. 'I'm thirsty,' he said.

We both looked at the bucket.

'We can't,' I said. 'We just can't. It would be murder.'

Pepper just nodded his head and flopped back against the tree. He didn't look too good. His eyes were rolling around in his head.

I looked into the bucket. It was hard to tell if the crayfish was alive or dead. Its little beady eyes seemed to stare up at me from the ends of their stalks. One of its legs moved feebly. 'Don't,' it seemed to be saying. 'Please don't.'

Another hour went by. My tongue was like a piece of dry stick in my mouth. My lips were cracked. The day grew hotter and hotter. Flies buzzed around the bucket. Pepper lay stretched out, hardly breathing. I picked up the bucket and took it over to him. 'Drink,' I said.

Every fifteen minutes we scooped out two handfuls each. It was the crayfish or us. We had no choice.

In the end there was no water left. The crayfish lay still in the empty bucket. I picked it up. 'It's warm,' I said. 'Dead as a doornail.'

I pulled a branch from a tree and dropped leaves down over the crayfish so that we couldn't see its lifeless body.

Two hours later a plane circled overhead. We waved and yelled and shouted from the bald rock. Something fell from the plane. A tiny speck that grew larger as it tumbled towards us.

'Run,' I screamed. We bolted for cover under the tree just as the package thumped down onto the rock.

We undid the straps and tore away the plastic cover. There was water, and chocolate and tins of fruit and a huge piece of cake. And a note. 'DON'T MOVE,' it said. 'WE WILL COME AND GET YOU.'

There were five bottles of water all together. After we had drunk as much as we could I went over to the crayfish. I looked up at Pepper and he nodded. I sprinkled a little water onto the crayfish's back. But it was no good. There's no coming back from the dead. Not for a crayfish, anyway.

'I feel guilty,' said Pepper.

I nodded my head. I knew exactly what he meant.

5

Well, the rescue party arrived. Dad was there. So was Pepper's mother. It was a tearful reunion. There was a lot of hugging and kissing and crying. Especially when we told them about how we had been trying to save the crayfish.

Dad just shook his head. He couldn't believe it. 'You donkeys,' he said. 'You soft donkeys.'

It wasn't far back to the road. We had done the right thing by staying put.

Pepper and I jumped into the back of Dad's Land Rover and we headed for town.

We went straight past the fish shop. Straight through town. And out into open country. 'Where are we going?' I said.

'I've talked to Pepper's Mum,' said Dad. 'And we've both agreed. We're taking that crayfish back to the sea.'

'But it's dead,' I said.

Dad smiled. 'We'll take it back anyway,' said Dad. 'It's only right.'

Four hours and three ice-creams later we stood on a lonely beach. The water lapped the golden sand gently.

The sea was blue and welcoming. Dad took the crayfish out of the bucket. He looked at it and pulled up a bit of its shell.

'Don't,' I yelled.

'Trust me,' said Dad. He fiddled around for a bit. Then he put the crayfish down on the sand. Suddenly it started to crawl towards the sea. Its legs went like crazy. It was really going for it. In a second it had reached the shore and vanished into the salty water.

I put down the diary and stare at Dad and Gramps.

It was a good story.

But.

'I don't believe it,' I say.

'Why not?' says Gramps.

'It couldn't be true,' I say. 'There is something that does not make sense.'

They both smile at me.

'What?' says Dad.

'The crayfish went back into the sea. Right?'

'Yeah.'

'So the water in the bucket must have been salt water. Crayfish need salt water. So you and Pepper couldn't have drunk it. And anyway. The crayfish was dead.'

'You're right,' says Gramps. 'I didn't tell your dad the truth for a long time. Not until he grew up. The crayfish was made out of plastic. It was a shop decoration. A toy. I just put a new battery in it.'

I stand up. 'Well,' I say to Dad. 'At least you know how I feel about the axolotl. It doesn't have a battery. And it's all alone in the pet shop. I'm going down to buy it. The poor thing.'

'I thought you might,' says Dad.

'And then I'm taking it back where it came from.'

'I'll help you,' says Dad.

'Promise?' I say.

'Promise,' says Dad with a smile. 'I don't want you running away like I did.'

I head for the door.

'Wait up,' says Dad. 'Where do axolotls come from anyway?'

I give him a big grin.

'Mexico,' I say.

The Spitting Rat

'What's a zuff?' I said to Mum.

'No such thing,' she answered. She took the letter from my hand and read it.

Dear Anthony,

I hope you like the Spitting Rat. Take it to the zough and it will bring you good luck. But whatever you doo, don't tutch it.

Love and Happy Birthday,

Uncle Bill

Mum looked hard at the word *zough* and frowned. 'Bill can't spell for nuts,' she said. 'I think he meant *tough* or maybe *rough*.'

'That doesn't make sense,' I said.

'Bill never makes sense,' said Mum. 'Fancy giving you a dead rat for your birthday.'

The rat stood there stiff and still inside a little glass dome. Its mouth was open in a sort of snarl.

'It's cute,' I said. 'Uncle Bill always gives me great presents.'

Mum gave a sort of snort. 'Bill's up in Darwin getting

into all sorts of foolishness. He knows we're dead broke. And what does he give you? Shoes? Books? A new school uniform? Something useful? Not on your Nelly. He gives you a stuffed rat, for heaven's sake.'

'I like him,' I said.

'I like him too,' said Mum. 'But I'm glad he's in Darwin and we're down here in Melbourne. Fancy giving you a dead rat. He probably got it for nothing.'

I could understand why Mum wanted me to have clothes for my birthday. Life was tough for her. She had been working hard. Too hard. She needed a holiday and I was trying to arrange it.

All I had to do was get three thousand dollars for the two of us to go to Surfers Paradise. I had been saving for two weeks and already had one dollar fifty. Only two thousand, nine hundred and ninety-eight dollars fifty to go.

When Uncle Bill made it big he was going to send us money. But at the moment he was broke too. Sometimes Mum called her brother 'Silly Billy'. But I liked him a lot. He was always having adventures.

I read the letter again. 'The Spitting Rat brings good luck if you take it to a zough,' I said.

'I wouldn't get your hopes up, Anthony,' said Mum.

'I'll test it out,' I said. 'Maybe the luck works without a zough – whatever that is.' I went over to the cupboard and fetched a pair of dice from a game of Ludo. Then I shook them up and threw them on the table.

'Two sixes,' I yelled.

'A fluke,' said Mum with a laugh. She walked out of the kitchen, shaking her head and not even waiting to see what happened.

I threw the dice again and stared. I couldn't believe it. Another two sixes.

The stuffed rat glared out from its glass cage. Was it bringing me luck? I threw the dice once more. They both rolled off the edge of the table and under the sideboard that Uncle Bill gave me last year. I couldn't see if they had thrown up sixes or not. I lay down on my stomach and peered into the dusty space where the dice had stopped. There was something there. A piece of paper sticking out of my cupboard.

I reached under and pulled the dice and the paper out. It wasn't just any old piece of paper. It was a fifty-dollar note.

'Wow,' I screamed. 'Bonus. What luck.'

Just for fun I threw the dice again. Two sixes. Yes, yes, yes. The rat was a lucky rat that was for sure.

I showed Mum the money. 'If the Spitting Rat had not arrived we would never have found this fifty dollars,' I said. 'It brings luck. Now we only have to find another two thousand, nine hundred and forty-eight dollars fifty and we can have that holiday up north in the sun.'

Mum gave me a kindly smile. 'It's a lovely thing you are doing, Anthony,' she said. 'But three thousand dollars is too much for a boy to save all on his own. I'd be just as happy if you did the washing-up now and then.'

Poor Mum. Fancy thinking that me doing the washing-up was going to make her happy. No – I had to get the three thousand dollars. Then she could relax next to a pool in Surfers Paradise. And neither of us would have to do the washing-up.

I sat down and wrote a letter back to Uncle Bill.

Dear Uncle Bill,

Thanks for the Spitting Rat. It is grate. By the way, what's a zough? I am going in a speling compatition today. The prize is a free trip to Surfers Paradice. If I win I am going to take Mum. She needs a rest.

Lots of love,

Anthony

The spelling competition was on that very day. At five o'clock in the Town Hall.

'I'm pretty good at spelling,' I said to Mum. 'I might win the competition.'

Mum read my letter and smiled. 'You're so much like Bill,' she said with a smile.

I could see she didn't think much of my chances. I don't know why. I was a good speller. Still, I had to have a fall-back plan. An idea started to form in my mind. Yes. It was a good idea. I would use the money to make money. Invest it wisely.

I put the fifty dollars and the dice into my pocket and picked up the rat's dome. 'I'm going out for a while,' I told Mum. 'I'll be back soon.'

2

We lived on the top floor of the high rise commission flats. I made my way to the lift and pressed the button for the ground floor. The lift was covered in graffiti and the wall was covered in spit. I hated the look of spit. Yuck.

I stepped out of the lift and made my way to the nearest newsagency. I tucked the rat under my arm and held the glass cage tightly. I wanted to give the rat every chance of passing the good luck on to me.

I put the rat on the counter. 'One five-dollar scratchy please, Mrs Filby,' I said.

Mrs Filby shook her head. 'You have to be over fifteen to buy Lotto tickets, Anthony,' she said.

'It's for Mum,' I said.

It wasn't really a lie. It was for Mum's holiday up north. That's what I told myself anyway.

Mrs Filby wasn't sure but she took the five dollars and gave me the scratch lottery ticket.

I walked over to the playground and sat inside a painted drainpipe with the Spitting Rat and my scratch ticket.

You had to get three numbers the same to win that amount of money. There were four different panels to scratch away and reveal the amounts of money.

I uncovered the first panel. $10,000, $25, $15, $10,000 and . . . wait for it, wait for it, stay calm. Oh, rats. $10. Jeez, that was close. I almost won ten thousand dollars.

I tried the next group. $100,000, $250,000, $250,000, and, and, and . . . $250,000. Yahoo. I had won. Three lots of two hundred and fifty thousand dollars. Awesome. Magic. My heart was pumping like crazy.

Hang on, hang on. Oh no. One of them was twenty five thousand not two hundred and fifty thousand. I felt like someone who was on the end of the queue just as McDonald's closed for the day. No hamburger. Nothing.

I quickly uncovered the third panel. No luck. Rats.

One last window to go. Scratch, scratch, scratch. I did them all quickly without really looking. And then I saw it. Oh yes. Three lots of three thousand dollars. There was no mistake. I blinked and blinked and pinched myself. I had won three thousand dollars.

The Spitting Rat was the lucky rat. That was for sure. I jumped up and banged my head on the top of the concrete pipe.

'Oh, wow, arghoo.' It hurt like crazy. I fell down backwards and smashed into the glass dome of the Spitting Rat. And broke it. It just smashed to pieces leaving the rat standing in the not so fresh air.

What had I done? Would the rat still bring luck? Would it get mad at me?

'Sorry, Ratty,' I said. 'I'm really sorry.'

I patted the still, stuffed rat on its head. As if to make it feel better.

3

That's when it happened. Right when I touched the rat. That's when all my troubles started. I still can't believe that it actually happened, but it did.

The rat took a sharp breath. I heard it quite clearly.

My mouth fell open in surprise.

Yes, the dead rat spat. Right into my mouth.

Oh, yucko. Gross. Foul. Disgusting. I could feel the rat's spit on my tongue. Hot, sizzling, terrible.

I tried to spit it out but I couldn't.

Something took hold of my mouth muscles and I swallowed the rat spit right down into my stomach.

The rat just stood there as if nothing had happened. Silent, stiff and dead as a stone. Its beady eyes stared ahead as if they were made of glass. What am I talking about? They *were* made of glass.

I shook my head in disbelief. Maybe it was a dream. A day-dream. Maybe I had just imagined that the rat spat.

Anyway, it didn't really matter. I still had my Lotto ticket. A three thousand dollar payout was heading my way. And Mum and I were heading for the sunshine. I was stoked. Now it wouldn't matter if I won or lost the spelling competition. I had my three thousand dollars *and* the forty-five dollars change from the fifty.

I picked up the rat and headed back to collect my prize.

As I crossed the street a kid came whizzing past me on a bike. It was Michael Smeds, a boy I knew from school. Suddenly I drew a breath. A sharp little intake of air. My mouth just seemed to have a mind of its own. I didn't want to take that breath. I had no choice.

And I had no choice in what happened next.

I spat.

A little blue bit of spit (yes, blue – and hot) went shooting through the air and hit the front tyre of the bike.

Smeds lost control, started to wobble and crashed into a lamp-post. I went over and helped him. He wasn't hurt but his front wheel was buckled. And it had a flat tyre.

'You spat at me,' he yelled. 'It made me fall. What did you do that for? I'll get you for that. Just you wait.' He started to wheel his bike along the footpath, heading angrily for home.

'I'm sorry,' I called out. 'I didn't mean to slag at you.'

The whole thing was crazy. Hot, blue spit. I must have caught some terrible disease from the rat. I needed help. But not before I collected my three thousand smackeroos.

I walked onto the Yarra River footbridge and looked down into the brown water. It was so peaceful. A bloke and his girlfriend were just passing under me in a small rowing boat.

Suddenly I took a quick breath. I tried to keep my mouth closed. I gritted my teeth. I breathed in through my nose. But it was no good. I lost the struggle.

Phshst . . . A hot, blue gob of spit dropped down towards the boat. Splot. It landed right in the middle near the girl's feet.

4

In a flash a little stream of water began to squirt up inside the boat. It grew stronger and bigger. After a few seconds it was like a broken fire hydrant flooding up into the sky. And then, before I could blink, the boat was gone. Sunk. Sent to the bottom of the Yarra.

The two rowers started to swim for the bank. The man looked up angrily at me and yelled out something. They were good swimmers. They looked fit and strong. They looked as if they could tear a thirteen-year-old kid into pieces without much trouble.

I turned and ran for it. I just belted along without knowing where I was going. Finally I fell panting and exhausted under a bush in the Fitzroy Gardens.

I dumped the Spitting Rat down and tried to gather my thoughts. This was dangerous.

I had spat at a bike and punctured it. I had spat at a boat and sunk it. I never knew when I was going to spit next. It was out of my control.

I had to get away from the rat. Maybe if I put some distance between me and it I would be cured. Maybe its powers wouldn't work at a distance. I shoved the rat under a bush and headed for home.

I was really worried. Even the thought of the winning

lottery ticket didn't make any difference. I had to spit when I didn't want to. It was hot and blue and yucky and burned holes into things.

As I walked I started to imagine things. The spit was powerful. What if a robber or burglar got hold of it? They could escape from jail by blowing a hole. Or put it in a bottle and use it to open a bank safe.

But the spit was powerful stuff. It would probably eat through the bottles. All the crooks in the world would be after me to cough up for them. I would be forced to spit for them day after day. No thanks. No way.

I hurried back to the commission flats and jumped into the lift. I pressed the button for the twentieth floor. The doors banged shut and I started to go up. I was alone in the lift.

The floors whizzed by. Seventeen, then eighteen, then nineteen. Suddenly I took a quick breath. Don't spit. Don't, don't, don't. I put one hand on top of my head and the other under my jaw. I pushed as hard as I could, trying, trying, trying to keep my mouth shut.

My mouth suddenly exploded. I just couldn't stop it. *Kersplot*. A bright-blue bit of spittle sizzled on the floor. Like an egg in a frying-pan it spat and crackled. Suddenly a small hole opened in the lift floor and the spit disappeared.

I could see right down to the bottom of the lift-well. Long cables clanked and clanged. My head started to swim and I felt sick. What if my spit had landed on a cable and eaten through it? I could have fallen to my death.

I was a long way from the Spitting Rat. It didn't seem to make any difference. I was still cursed with its spiteful, spitting spell.

5

I hurried out of the lift and ran to our flat. Mum wasn't home but I wasn't taking any chances. I banged my bedroom door shut and locked it. I needed time to think. A terrible thought was growing somewhere deep inside and I didn't want to let it out.

I tried to figure it out. The blue spit could eat through anything. And I didn't know when it was going to happen. I couldn't stop spitting no matter how hard I tried.

But. And it was a big but. Would the spit have its terrible powers if I tried it on purpose?

I looked around for something I didn't need. A piece of rock that I used to keep the door open. I placed it on the floor. Then I worked up a bit of spit in my mouth and let fly.

Yes. It settled on the rock and began to fizz, bright and blue. In no time at all the rock had gone altogether. There was just a little blue smear left on the floor.

Suddenly I started to suck in, then – *kersploosh*. Another small blue bomb landed on my spelling book. It started to fizz and disappeared.

I was taken with a spitting frenzy. I spat on everything.

My skateboard vanished in a fizzing blue mess. And my photo of Mum. Everything was a target. My bed was riddled with bubbling holes. My desk was drilled right through. The light-shade vanished. My football collapsed with a bang.

Breathe, spit. Breathe, spit. Breathe, spit. I couldn't stop myself. I was out of control.

Finally I fell to the floor exhausted. The spitting spasm had finished.

For now.

6

I heard the front door slam. Mum was home.

Mum.

Now the terrible thought managed to surface. I had to face it. What if I spat at Mum? Oh, horrible thought. No, no, no.

I was dangerous. I was a menace to society. Everything I spat at was destroyed. I could kill people.

There was only one thing to do. I had to go away from human beings. Hide deep in the forest. Or find a deserted island. I would never see a person again. I couldn't even have a dog because I might be seized with a spitting fit and accidentally kill it.

Such was the power of the terrible Spitting Rat. A sad and lonely future stretched before me and I was only a kid.

And what about Mum? What would she do without me? She wouldn't have anyone to cook for. No one's bed to make. No one to eat her cakes.

The door-handle suddenly rattled. 'Are you in there, Anthony?' said Mum's voice. 'What are you doing? Playing with that rat, I suppose.'

'I threw it out,' I yelled through the door.

There was a long silence. 'Sometimes I could murder Bill,' said Mum. 'What was he thinking of? Giving you a dead rat for your birthday.'

Her voice trailed off and I could hear her banging around in the kitchen. She always did the washing-up when she was angry. It made her feel better. She was a good mother. I had to get away before I hurt her.

I took out a pencil and started to write a note. My last message to my mum.

Dear Mum,

I love you very much. For the safety of the world I have to go away and be on my own. Do not try to find me or your life will be in danjer. Here is a winning lotery ticket. I want you to have that hollerday up north in the sun.

Your loving son,
Anthony

I folded up my letter and took out the lottery ticket.

I could feel it coming. Sort of building up inside me. Don't let it. Don't, don't, don't. Too late. I snatched a breath and spat. Right on the Lotto ticket. It fizzled for a second and was gone. Disappeared. Totally destroyed.

I hung my head on the drilled-out desk and let a tear run down my nose.

Now my Mum would never get to Queensland.

Why had Uncle Bill given me that rat? He had let us down. Put my life in danger. Still and all – he did tell me not to touch the rat. It wasn't really his fault.

Anger started to boil inside me. My life was ruined. My money was gone. All because of . . . Not Uncle Bill – no, not him. I wasn't mad at him. It was all the Spitting Rat's fault.

The rage inside me made me think. There was a way I could pay it back. There was a way I could get even. I would get my revenge on the rat.

I ran out of my room and out of the flat before Mum could say a word. Along the corridor to the lift. No way. Down the fire escape – the lift was too risky.

Across the playground. Over the bridge. Up to the bush in the Fitzroy Gardens.

It was time for the rat to get a bit of its own medicine.

7

I found two sticks and lifted the Spitting Rat out of the bushes by holding one on each side of its neck. I was careful not to touch it.

'Now,' I yelled. 'You've ruined my life. But you're not getting off free.'

I snatched a breath. And spat. Straight at the face of

the Spitting Rat. A little blue gob of spit sped at its victim like a bullet.

But the rat was too quick. Without warning it opened its mouth. Fast like a dog snapping at a fly.

Slurp. Swallow. The spit was gone. The rat had taken it back.

Straight away the rat went back to normal. It stood there. Stuffed, still and slightly silly. Just as if nothing had happened.

And I went back to normal too. My mouth felt different. I worked up a bit of moisture and spat on the ground. Normal, clear spit. No spitting and fizzing.

'Okay, Mr Ratty,' I said. 'So I'm cured. But what about my luck? Are you still lucky for me?'

I took out the dice and rolled them. A five and a two.

The luck was gone. No more blue spit and no more money.

I pushed the rat back under the bushes with the sticks and walked sadly home. Now my only hope was to win the spelling competition. Two free tickets to Queensland for the winner. I looked at my watch. I just had time to make it to the Town Hall.

8

There were hundreds of kids in the Town Hall. We were all sitting at desks that had big spaces between them so that no one could cheat.

'Pick up your pens,' said the Spelling Master.

The hall was filled with the sound of two hundred pens being lifted at the same time.

I crossed my fingers and hoped for luck. I hoped the words would not be too hard.

'The gangster fired a bullet. Spell *bullet*,' said the Spelling Master.

'Easy,' I lied to myself. I wrote each letter carefully. B-u-l-l-i-t.

'I went *through* the door. Spell *through*,' said the Spelling Master.

Oh no. This was a tough one. How did you spell through? T-h-r-e-w? Nah. T-h-r-o-o? No way. I couldn't get it. I just couldn't work it out. My head was spinning. Everything was going wrong. I had another try. I slowly wrote down the letters and stared at them. T-h-r-o-u-g-h. That was it. Yes, *ough* says *oo*. Like in zoo. I scratched my head and wondered.

'Aghh,' I suddenly screamed at the top of my voice. I flung my pencil on the floor and ran out of the door. Everyone stared. They thought I was crazy.

9

THREE WEEKS LATER

'Last call for Qantas Flight QF 628 to Brisbane,' said the announcer's voice at the airport. 'This flight closes at 3.50 p.m.'

'Come on,' I said to Mum. 'Let's go.'

We hurried onto the plane. Outside the Melbourne

rain was falling softly on the runway. 'Sunshine, here we come,' I said.

Mum headed down towards the back of the plane.

'Not that way,' I said. 'These are First Class tickets.'

We sat down among the business people wearing suits and balancing computer laptops on their knees. The flight attendant brought us fresh orange juice.

Mum was really curious. 'Come on, Anthony,' she said with a smile. 'I know you couldn't have won the spelling competition. You're no better at spelling than Uncle Bill. So where did you get the money?'

I grinned. 'Spitting Rats are extinct,' I said. 'There are none left alive. A man from the zoo gave me three thousand dollars for it. Just the right amount.'

'The zoo?' said Mum. 'Why the zoo?'

I took out the little note pad that they give you in First Class and wrote a word.

'Zough rhymes with zoo,' I said. 'Like through. Uncle Bill wanted me to take the rat to the zoo. He knew it would bring us luck.'

Mum gave the biggest smile ever. She was so happy to be going on a holiday.

'I like Bill,' she said. 'But he's a bit nutty. I'm glad he lives over two thousand k's away.'

The plane started to speed along the runway.

'Yahoo,' I yelled.

'Where are we going, anyway?' Mum said. 'You can't keep it secret any longer.'

The plane lifted into the air.

'Brisbane first,' I said. 'Then on to Darwin to see Uncle Bill.'

Mum started to laugh like crazy. It was good to see.

Nails

Lehman's father sat still on his cane chair. Too still.

A hot breeze ruffled his hair. He stared out of the window at the island. But he did not see. He did not move. He did not know that Lehman was alone.

But the boy knew. He realised he was trapped. Their boat had sunk in the storm. And their radio had gone with it. There was not another soul for a thousand miles. Lehman was rich. The house was his now. The whole island belonged to him. The golden beach. The high hill. The palms. And the little pier where their boat had once bobbed and rocked.

He had no more tears. He had cried them all. Every one. He wanted to rush over and hug his father back to life. He wanted to see that twisted grin again. 'Dad, Dad,' he called.

But the dead man had no reply for his son.

Lehman knew that he had to do something. He had to close his father's eyes. That was the first thing. But he couldn't bring himself to do it. What if they wouldn't move? What if they were brittle? Or cold? Or soggy?

And then what? He couldn't leave his father there.

Sitting, stiff and silent in the terrible heat. He had to bury him. Where? How? He knew that no one would come. The blue sea was endless. Unbroken. Unfriendly to a boy on his own.

Lehman started to scratch nervously. His nails were growing. More of them all the time.

He decided to do nothing for a bit longer. He sat and sat and sat. And remembered how it was when they had come to the island. Just the two of them.

2

'Is that where we live?' said Lehman.

They both looked at the tumbledown hut on top of the hill. 'We'll fix it up in no time,' said Dad. 'It'll soon be like it was in the old days. When I first came here. As good as new.'

And after a while it was. It was home. Lehman became used to it. Even though he was lonely. Every morning he did his school work. Dad told him which books to read. And how to do his sums. Then he left Lehman alone with his studies. And disappeared along the beach.

Dad searched the shore. But he never let Lehman go with him. He took his camera and knapsack. And his shovel. He peered out into the endless sea. He dug in the golden sand. And every lunch time he returned with rocks and strange objects from the sea.

'One day I'll hit the jackpot,' he said for the thousandth time. 'Maybe tomorrow. Tomorrow I'll find one. Tomorrow will be the day. You'll see.' Then he grew sad. 'There were plenty here once.' He dumped his sack in the corner. It thumped heavily in the floor.

'Let's see what you've got,' said Lehman.

Dad shook his head. 'When I find what I'm looking for, you'll be the first to know.' He picked up the sack and took it into his room. He shut the door with a smile.

Lehman knew what his father was doing. He was putting his finds into the old box. The sea chest with the heavy brass lock. Lehman longed to take a look. He wanted to know what his father was searching for. But it was a secret.

He began to scratch his fingers. Just as Dad came out of his room. 'I've told you not to do that,' said Dad.

'I'm itchy,' said Lehman. 'On the fingers. And the toes.'

'Eczema,' Dad told him. 'I used to get it when I was a boy. It'll go when the wind changes.' But he didn't look too sure. He examined the red lumps growing behind Lehman's fingernails. Then he stamped out of the hut.

3

Lehman stared around the silent bungalow. He was lonely. Dad was good company. But he was a man. Lehman wanted friends. And his mother. He picked up her photograph. A lovely, sad face. Staring at him from the oval frame. 'Where did you go?' whispered Lehman. 'I can't even remember you.'

The face seemed to say that it knew. Understood. But it was only a photo of a woman's head. A woman lost in the past. In her hair she wore a golden clip set with pearls.

During the day, Lehman kept the photo on the kitchen table where he worked. And at night he placed it on his bedside table. It watched over him while he slept.

Lehman sighed and closed his book. He looked up as Dad came back carrying some potatoes from their vegetable patch. 'I'm going early in the morning,' he said. 'Just go on with the work I set you today. I'll be back at lunch time.'

'Let me come with you,' pleaded Lehman.

His father looked at him in silence. Then he said. 'When I find what I'm looking for. Then I'll take you.'

'It's not fair,' shouted Lehman. 'I'm all alone here. Every morning. You owe it to me to tell me what you're looking for. I don't even know what we're doing here.'

'I can't tell you,' said Dad slowly. 'Not yet. Trust me.'

That night, in bed, Lehman's eczema was worse. He scratched his itching fingers and toes until they hurt. He dreamed of dark places. And watery figures. Faces laughing. And calling. Voices seemed to whisper secrets from inside his father's sea chest.

In the morning he stared at his itching fingers. And gasped. At first he couldn't take it in. He had ten fingernails. On each hand. Another row of nails had grown behind the first ones. Clean, pink, little fingernails.

He tore back the sheets and looked at his toes. The same thing had happened. A second row of toenails had burst out of the skin. They pointed forwards. Lapping slightly over the first row.

'Dad,' he screamed. 'Dad, Dad, Dad. Look. Something's wrong with me. My nails. I've got too many nai . . .' His voice trailed off. He remembered. Dad was down at the beach. On another secret search.

4

Lehman had been told never to go down the path to the cove. Dad had told him it was dangerous. And out of bounds.

But this was an emergency. Lehman stared in horror at his hands. He pulled at one of the new nails. It hurt when he tugged. It was real. It was there to stay. He staggered as he ran down the steep track to the beach. Tears of fright and anger streamed down his cheeks. His chest hurt. His breath tore harshly at his throat.

He pounded onto the hot sand and stared along the shore. His father was nowhere to be seen. Lehman took a guess and ran along the beach to his right. He came to a group of large rocks that blocked his way. The only way around was through the water. He waded into the gently lapping waves. The water came up to his armpits. He carefully strode on, feeling gently with his feet for rocky holes.

At the deepest point the water came up to his chin.

But he was nearly round the corner now. Lehman let his feet leave the bottom. He began to swim. He rounded the rocks and splashed into a small cove that he had never seen before.

His father was digging in the pebbles against a rocky wall. At first he didn't see Lehman. Then he looked up. And noticed the dripping figure staggering out of the waves. His face broke into a radiant smile. The look of someone who has found a pot of gold. Then he saw that it was Lehman and his face grew angry.

'I told you never to come here,' he shouted. 'I can't believe that you'd spy on me. You'll ruin everything. Go back. Go back.' He wasn't just cross. He was furious.

Lehman said nothing. He just held out his hands. Turned the backs of his fingers towards his father. There was a long silence. His father's anger melted. He stared at the double row of nails. Silently Lehman pointed to his feet. They both looked down.

'Oh no,' said Dad. 'No. I never expected this. Not really.'

'What is it?' yelled Lehman. 'Am I going to die?'

'No. You're not going to die.'

'I need to see a doctor,' said Lehman.

'No,' said Dad. 'A doctor can't do anything. Not for that.'

'What is it? What's wrong with me? You have to tell me.'

They stared at each other. Both afraid.

Dad sat down on a rock. 'I can't tell you. Not yet. What I'm looking for here. It's got something to do with it. If I find what I'm looking for it will be all right. You won't have to worry. But I can't tell. Not yet.'

'What if you never find it?' said Lehman.

'I will,' said Dad. 'I have to.'

Lehman scratched the back of his hands and up his arms. The itch was growing worse. And spreading.

Dad looked around as if he was frightened of Lehman seeing something. As though he had a guilty secret. 'Go home,' he said. 'I'll pack my things and follow. We'll talk back at the house.'

5

Lehman pushed into the water. His mind swirled. His arms itched. Something was terribly wrong. He turned around and shouted back. 'What's going on? You're not telling. I've got a right to know.'

Tears pricked his eyes. Tears of anger and frustration. Dad hung his head. 'Go back,' he called. 'We'll talk. But not here.'

Lehman swam out into the swell. He passed the furthest rock and headed back to the beach on the other side. Dad was out of sight now. Lehman's feet touched the bottom and he walked through the water past a deep, black cave in the rocks.

Something moved inside.

The world froze. Lehman could hear the blood

pumping in his head. A shiver spread over his skin like a wave. He choked off a cry. Two dark eyes stared out at him. He turned and thrashed through the water. Half swimming. Half running. Falling. Splashing in panic. He fell and sank under the surface. When he came up he snatched a frightened glance back at the black space between the rocks. He caught a glimpse of a man's face. Staring. Watching. Hiding.

Lehman fled along the beach, stumbling in terror, not daring to look behind him. He didn't stop until he reached the bungalow. He rushed inside. The thin walls and open windows offered no protection. But he felt better. His breath slowed. His heart beat less loudly. He looked down the track and wondered if Dad was safe.

He scratched his elbows. And then screamed. More nails had grown. Rows and rows of them. Along his fingers and the backs of his hands. And up over his wrists.

Perfectly formed fingernails lapped over each other. They looked like two gloves of armour.

The world around began to spin. Lehman felt dizzy. His legs wobbled. He looked down. The backs of his toes, feet and ankles were covered too. A gleaming pair of toenail socks grew out of his skin. He opened his mouth to call out. And then fainted onto the floor.

6

When he awoke, the first thing Lehman saw was the

photo of his mother. Her soft smile seemed to have faded. The pearl clip in her hair was dull. Then he realised that his eyes were half closed. He was staring at the world through his eyelashes. He suddenly remembered the nails. Was it a dream? He sat up and found himself on his bed. He stared at his hands. The nails had grown up his arms to his elbows. His legs were covered too. Toenails grew up to his knees.

Dad put out a hand and gently touched his shoulder. 'It's okay,' he said. 'Everything is going to be all right. Don't worry.'

Lehman smiled for a second. Dad was safe. Then he examined the nails. The smile disappeared. He was angry.

'Don't worry,' he yelled. 'Don't worry. Look at my arms. And legs. I'm covered in nails. I'm not normal. What are we doing here? What are you looking for down on the beach?' He stared at the photo next to his bed. 'What happened to my mother? I want to know what's going on.'

The wind rattled the windows and shook the bungalow. A sultry storm was brewing up. Far down below their boat tugged and pulled at the ropes that tied it to the pier.

Dad took a deep breath. 'Okay,' he said. 'It's time I told you everything.' He stood up and shut the shaking window. He raised his voice above the noise of the wind. 'I don't know where to start,' he said.

Lehman held up a nail-covered arm. 'Start here,' he

cried. 'What's happening to me?' As they looked, another row of nails slowly erupted from his left arm, just above the elbow. It was like watching a flower open in fast forward. Lehman felt nothing. It wasn't painful.

Dad stroked the nails gently. As if Lehman was a cat. 'You're not sick,' he said. 'But I think more nails will grow.'

'How many more nails? Will they grow on my face? On my head? On my chest?'

Dad gave a kindly smile. 'Not your face. Maybe the rest of you though. I can't be sure. But I can find out. That's what I'm here for.'

7

There was a long silence. 'Are you looking for that man?' said Lehman.

'What man?' snapped Dad. His eyes were startled.

'I saw a face in the rocks. Down by the point. He was staring at me. Spying.'

'What did he look like?' said Dad. His voice was shrill and urgent.

'I don't know. I was scared. I only saw his eyes. I ran off.'

'This is it,' yelped Dad. 'This is what I've been waiting for. This is the answer to the problem.' He hurried off to the window and looked down at the sea. The waves were crashing now. The wind whipped at them, tearing off their foamy tops and pelting them into the humid skies.

'I'm going,' said Dad. 'Wait here. Everything will be all right.'

'No way,' said Lehman. 'You're not leaving me behind again. I'm coming too.'

Shutters banged and a blast of wind broke into the hut like a violent burglar. Everything shook.

'There's going to be a terrible storm,' yelled Dad. 'You can't come, it's too dangerous.'

'If you go – I go,' said Lehman. He looked his father straight in the eye. They stared at each other.

'This is a once-in-a-lifetime chance,' said Dad. 'He might go. I have to . . .'

'What's it got to do with this?' yelled Lehman. He held up his arms. The nails had crept up to his shoulders. And another row was growing. Budding like an ivory chain around his neck. 'What about me? It's all right for you. Look at your skin. Normal. Look at me. Covered in nails. Don't you care?'

'It's because I care,' said Dad. He had tears in his eyes. He tried to explain. 'When we were here before. When you were young . . .'

'I don't remember,' said Lehman. 'You know I don't.'

'No,' said Dad. 'But you were here. And your mother. And that man. He might. He's our only chance to . . .'

A terrible gust of wind shook the bungalow. Thunder rumbled in the distance. The sky was torn and savage. Dad stared outside. His face as wild as the storm. 'I have to go,' he said. 'Later. I'll explain later.' He ran to the door and vanished into the lashing wind.

8

Lehman followed his father, still dressed in nothing but shorts. He didn't feel the raging wind. Or the stinging rain. He didn't notice the nails still growing and spreading. A worse fear had filled him. He was frightened for his father. Lehman couldn't see him but he knew that he was somewhere ahead. Down the track that led to the beach.

The wind screamed and howled. Tore at his hair. Stung his eyes. He hurried on and finally found his father. He was standing at the end of the track. Staring into the furious waves that dashed up the beach and crashed into the cliff. The rocks in which the stranger had hidden were nearly covered. They were cut off by the surf. There was no safe way to get to them.

Dad peered at the sand that was revealed as the sea sucked back each wave. He measured the distance to the rocks with his eyes. Then he turned and shouted over the noise of the wind. 'Is that where he was? Is that where you saw the man?'

Lehman nodded and then grabbed his father's arm. 'Don't go,' he yelled. 'It's too rough. You won't have a chance.'

Dad snatched away his arm. He waited as a large wave began its sweep back from the beach. He jumped and ran along the sodden sand. His feet made deep, wet footprints which filled with water. The wave raced back into the sea, leaving the beach clear. A new wave ate the old and began its forward rush.

The desperate man was halfway. He sank up to his ankles with each step. The wet sand slowed him to a stumbling crawl. 'Go,' whispered Lehman. 'Go, go, go.' He watched the approaching wave grow. 'Don't,' he said. 'Don't.'

The wave took no notice. It raced hungrily up the beach. It swirled around Dad's ankles. Knocked him from his feet. Buried him in its angry foam.

9

Lehman squinted and peered into the water. His father was gone. The waves were empty. Then he saw a helpless bundle washing out into the deep. Dad raised an arm. And then another. He was swimming far out. His arms flayed. He seemed to be moving into deeper water. He was helpless against the strength of the sea. 'I'm coming,' yelled Lehman. He stepped forward, waiting for the next backwash.

But before he could move, he noticed Dad riding the crest of a wave. Surfing inwards at enormous speed. A tiny, helpless cork rushing forward towards the waiting cliff.

Lehman sighed with relief. And then fright. The wave was too big. It was going to run up to the cliff and kill itself on the rocks. It seemed to gather all its strength. It flung Dad full into the jagged boulders. And then left him, hanging helplessly on a small ledge.

Without another thought, Lehman jumped onto the

sand. He had to get to Dad before the next wave began its run. He made it just in time. He grabbed the stunned man by his shirt and dragged him to his feet. Dad stumbled and leaned on Lehman as the next wave crashed around them.

It sucked and pulled at their legs. Tried to topple them. But Lehman felt a strange strength. It was almost as if the sea had no power over him. He dragged his father back to the steps where they sat sodden and panting. The disappointed waves swirled and smashed below them.

Dad tried to stand. He took a few steps like a drunken man. Lehman noticed a huge swelling on his father's head. A lump as big as a tennis ball. His eyes swivelled and he started to fall.

Lehman grabbed his father by the arm. He managed to drag him, stumbling up to the house. It took all his strength. His sides ached. His chest throbbed with pain. He burst through the door and dumped his father into the chair.

Dad stared out of the window. His eyes were glazed. As the wind dropped and the storm grew still, he held out a shaking arm. He pointed down to the beach. Then he drew a deep breath, shuddered, and was still.

Lehman knew his father was dead. Silent tears trickled down his cheeks and splashed on the nails that covered his chest. He sat there like a sorrowful knight of old. A warrior in a coat of mail. Crying for a friend who had fallen.

10

All night Lehman sat. And all morning. He'd never seen a dead person before. He didn't know what to do. Finally he stood up and walked to the door. He looked out at the sea. He wanted help. But he didn't want anyone to come.

He knew he could never leave the island. Not while he was covered in nails. He couldn't go back to the world. A world that would laugh. Or stare and wonder. He could see himself sitting in a school desk. Raising an encrusted arm.

He walked back into the room and looked at Dad. He had to do it now. Or he never would. He gently closed his father's eyes. They were soft but cold. It was like shutting a book at the end of a story. A book that would never be opened again. But a book that would never be forgotten. Not for as long as the waves beat on the lonely beach below.

Dad would be heavy. Lehman knew that. He had to dig a grave close to the house.

He chose a sandy spot that overlooked the sea. Lehman could just see the rocks jutting out where he had seen the face. He started to talk to his father as if he was still there. Standing by him.

'This is the place,' he said. 'You can see down there. Maybe what you wanted will come. Whatever it was.'

The sand was soft. He dug easily and soon had a shallow trench hollowed in the sand. It came up to his knees. He didn't want to make it too deep. Not because the work was hard. But because he couldn't bear to drop his father into a gaping hole. Something might bump. Or break.

Lehman returned to the silent man. He grabbed his father under the arms and tugged him slowly out of the door. The dead weight was heavy. Dad's feet dragged and bumped down the steps.

Lehman lowered him gently into the grave.

He looked down at the silent figure, stretched out. It was as if he was sleeping peacefully in the sand. Lehman picked up the shovel. But something was wrong. He felt bad. As if he had to do something that would hurt. Then he knew what it was. He couldn't put a shovel of sand on his father's face. Even though he was dead.

He fetched an old newspaper from inside. Then he looked at the gentle face for the last time and covered it with the paper. He filled the hole with sand and smoothed it down. He had no strength left to make a gravestone so he pushed the shovel into the sand. And left it standing as a tall marker.

'Goodbye, Dad,' he said.

Lehmann stood and stared out to sea. The sun glinted on the thousands of nails that covered almost every part of him. He looked like a tall lizard man. Standing. Waiting. Daring an invader to come.

There was no boat on the water. He didn't care. He didn't want anyone to see him as he was, covered in nails.

A great feeling of loneliness filled him. As far as he knew, there was no one else in the world like him.

11

He walked inside and looked in the mirror. His face was clear. But his chest, back, arms and legs were covered in the new nails. He suddenly opened a drawer. And pulled out some nail clippers. He wondered if he would have to spend his life clipping thousands of nails as they grew. He laughed wildly and threw the clippers out of the open window.

It had taken him all afternoon to dig the grave.

The sun was beginning to sink lower in the sky. In an hour or two it would be dark. And he was alone. He wondered if he should lock the windows. And bolt the door. He knew that tonight – when the dark came – he would be frightened.

The face in the cave would come. Creeping. Stealing up the path. Wandering in the shadows. He knew that he would jump at every sound. He would try not to sleep. But in the end sleep would come. And so would the unknown man.

He jumped to his feet. 'You won't get me,' he shouted. 'I'll get you.'

He ran outside and sharpened a long stick with the axe. Now he had a spear. He marched down the path towards the beach. His legs felt weak. His stomach was cold and heavy. He wanted to turn. And run. And hide.

But he forced himself on until he reached the beach. The sea was still and blue. It lapped gently on the sandy beach. The wild waves had gone. Lehman strode along the sand towards the rocks. And the cave.

He shuddered even though the air was warm. He gripped the spear tightly with his nailed fingers. The tide was out and the small cave now opened onto the sand. He reached the entrance and peered into the gloom.

There were soft, dripping noises. And the sound of steady breathing. Someone was in there.

'Come out,' he shrieked. His voice cracked and ended in a squeak. He coughed and tried again. 'Come out, whoever you are.' The words echoed in the cave. Then something moved. He thought he heard a slippery, rustling noise.

His courage fled. He started walking backwards, too frightened to turn around.

12

Three people came out of the cave. If people is the word. Two men. And a smaller one. They wore no clothes. But instead, were covered from neck to toe – in nails.

Lehman felt faint. He couldn't take it in. He wondered if this island gave people the terrible nail disease.

They smiled at him. Warm, friendly smiles. The child giggled nervously. The nail people were wet. They had been in the sea. Water glistened and sparkled from their nails. They shone like neat rows of wet glass.

One of the men pointed into the deep water further out. A swift shadow like a shark circling moved far down. It rushed towards the shore with the speed of a train. Then burst out of the water and back in again.

Lehman caught a glimpse of a sparkling fish tail. And fair hair. It swirled several times. And then climbed onto a rock. A woman with long golden hair. And a fish tail covered in nails.

The men laughed. Their chuckles sounded like bubbles bursting out of the water. Lehman stared at the nails which shivered as they moved. He spoke aloud. Half to himself. Half to them. 'Not nails,' he said, 'but scales.'

He turned back to the mermaid. In her hair, she wore a golden clip, set with pearls. The same pin that he had seen every day in his mother's photograph.

In that moment Lehman knew that while his father had been a man, his mother was a mermaid.

She beckoned to him, calling him out into the water. Then she dived down under the rippling surface. The mermen nodded at him, pointing out to sea. Like Lehman, they had legs rather than a tail.

Lehman walked. And walked. And walked. The waves closed over his head. He opened his mouth and took a deep breath of water. It passed through his new gills with a fizz of bubbles. His head was filled with lightness. And happiness. He began to swim, deep down, following his mother.

Then, for a second, he remembered something.

He burst upwards faster and faster and plunged out of the water like a dolphin. He snatched one last look at the island. And saw, high on a hill, a small mound. A shovel stood pointing to the bright sky above. He knew now why his father had brought him here. A fish-boy could only be happy in one place – the ocean.

Lehman waved goodbye and then plunged down far below the surface. And followed his family out to sea.

Guts

'It likes to eat people,' said Mr Borg. 'It will eat dogs, cats, snakes and even cows. But its favourite food is human beings.'

'It eats people?' I yelped.

'People,' said Mr Borg. 'Loves 'em. It's a real guts.'

My mouth was hanging open. But my sister Danni's teeth were firmly clenched.

'What sort of people?' I asked.

'It's favourite is kids,' said Mr Borg. 'Especially cheeky brats like you two.'

'Get real,' said Danni.

'Oh, yeah,' said Mr Borg in a mean voice. 'Well, go and take a look for yourself. Go and pay a visit to the Lost Mine. In fact do us all a favour and get lost yourselves.'

Mr Borg gave a hearty laugh. He thought this was very funny.

'Ghosts don't eat,' said Danni. 'They can't even pick things up.'

'The Spirit of the Forest is not your normal ghost,' said Mr Borg. 'It doesn't eat with its hands. Or its mouth. But it devours things. Oh, yes. A horrible sound. You should hear it crunch.'

'You're just trying to scare us,' I said. 'So that Dad will leave and sell our land to you. Well, you're not getting it. Ever.'

Mr Borg's dog, Hacker, started to bark and growl and snap at us through the back window of his Jaguar.

Mr Borg scowled. 'We'll see about that,' he said. He flattened the accelerator and drove off in a cloud of dust.

Danni and I walked slowly back to our little farm by the river.

Things were not going too good. Dad made a living by putting up fences for the big land owners. But times were tough in the bush and he wasn't getting much work. We were nearly broke. If things didn't improve the bank was going to sell us up.

'I couldn't stand it if we had to move into a town.' I said to Danni.

She looked around at the little farm that had been our home since the day we were born. 'Mr Borg is not getting this land. This is ours.'

We stared defiantly around our little farm. We had the best spot on the whole river. All around us were the high mountains of the national park. The peaks were covered in tropical rainforest. It was the most beautiful place in the world. I couldn't even bear to think about leaving it.

Mr Borg wanted to build a casino resort. He was a developer of the worst sort.

2

As soon as we stepped into the kitchen I could tell that something was wrong. Dad was walking around the room kicking at things and muttering angrily under his breath.

'What's up?' I said.

He didn't answer for a second or two. He couldn't bring himself to say the words. Finally he spat it out. 'The Land Rover's gone.'

'Where?' shouted Danni.

'Someone nicked it. Last night. I left it down in the bottom paddock. Now all that's left are a few tracks in the mud.'

Danni and I gasped. Without the Land Rover, Dad wouldn't be able to get any work.

'We're finished if we don't get it back,' he said bitterly. 'It wasn't even insured.'

'Who would want the Land Rover?' I said.

'Come on,' said Danni. 'Use your brains.'

'Mr Borg,' I gasped. 'To force us to sell up.'

'Dad,' I yelled. 'Let's go. Let's get him. Let's flatten him. Let's beat the sh-'

Dad shook his head. 'Getting into a fight won't achieve anything. And we don't know that it was Borg who nicked it. And we couldn't prove it anyway. He's not likely to have left it in his backyard.'

'Where then?' said Danni.

'In the river,' said Dad. 'Or at the bottom of a cliff. Maybe down a mine shaft.'

When Dad said that my mind started to tick over.

'I'll have to go to the police,' said Dad. 'Not that it will do any good. We'll never see that car again, that's for sure.'

Dad went off to report the theft to the police. He was going to go to the bank as well. To see if they would extend his loan.

Danni and I walked down to the back paddock and examined the tyre tracks. They didn't tell us much. We followed them along the river and out of the bottom gate. They disappeared down the road.

'If Borg took the car,' said Danni. 'Where would he have dumped it?'

I went over Dad's words in my mind. 'In the river. Or at the bottom of a cliff. Maybe down —'

'A mine shaft,' I shouted.

'The Lost Mine,' said Danni. 'That's why he was telling us all the bulldust about the Spirit of the Forest. A ghost that eats people.'

'That was a story to stop us going there,' I said. 'To scare us off.'

We were so excited. We couldn't wait for Dad to get back so that we could all go up to the Lost Mine and look for the Land Rover.

So we waited. And we waited. And we waited.

Finally, just as the sun was setting, we saw Dad walking home.

Walking.

Of course. He had to walk. Our four-wheel drive was gone. No wonder he was late.

Dad sort of swaggered into the gate, his head held high. But he couldn't fool us. We could tell he was trying to act cheerful so that we wouldn't get upset. He didn't want to talk about it but we finally dragged the truth out of him.

'The bank won't extend our loan,' he said. 'We can't buy a new Land Rover. We can't even hang on to the property. The bank is going to sell us up. But don't worry, kids. Life in the city isn't that bad.'

'Borg will buy our property,' I said.

Dad nodded.

'We know where the Land Rover is,' said Danni.

Dad listened to her story carefully. He let her finish but he kept shaking his head all the way through.

'No,' he said. 'We're not going up to the Lost Mine. It's too dangerous. No one is allowed up there because of the hidden mine shafts. Lots of people have gone there and never been seen again.'

'The Spirit of . . .' said Danni.

'There *is* something odd about that forest,' said Dad. 'But there's no spirit. Borg told you that story so that we *would* go there. If the car is there it means he wants us to find it.'

'Why?' I said.

'So that he can gloat. It will be smashed or down a mine shaft. We will know that he did it but we won't be able to prove a thing.'

'I thought you loved that car,' said Danni.

'Of course I love it,' said Dad. 'That's why I can't bear to find it all smashed and wrecked.' He forced a grin. 'Look, don't be so gloomy, you two. I'll go into town tomorrow. And arrange for the bank to get on with the sale. You never know. We might even get a really good price.'

Danni and I went out onto the porch and sat listening to the crickets chirping in the warm summer air.

'Do you know where I'm going tomorrow?' I said.

Danni gave a grin. 'The same place as me,' she said.

3

Danni and I stared along the narrow track that disappeared into the forest.

'Look,' said Danni. 'Someone's been here. Maybe a fire truck.' She pointed at a set of wheel tracks in the mud.

'Maybe our Land Rover,' I said. I could hardly stop my voice from shaking with excitement.

I hitched up my pack and took the first step into forbidden territory.

'Do you believe that story about the Spirit of the Forest?' I asked Danni.

She shrugged. 'They reckon that this forest is magical. Anyone who hurts the trees or digs holes suffers a terrible fate. All the workers from the Lost Mine just disappeared. Never seen again. No one ever comes up here.'

I didn't say anything. I just hoped the story wasn't true.

We trudged on and on and on. The track wound through deep gullies and over creek beds. Always heading up. Gradually the forest grew denser. The air was hot and clammy.

'We should have left a note,' I said. 'What if we get lost?'

'If we stick to the track we can't get lost,' said Danni.

I gave a shiver. 'We have to turn back by lunch-time,' I said. 'Otherwise we won't get back by dark.' The thought of spending the night on the mountain was making me nervous.

We kept on. With aching legs and blistered feet we forced our way up the mountain. Sometimes we would break out of the forest and find ourselves staring down into the valley. The tiny houses told us quite clearly how far away we were from people. And help.

After another three hours of struggling uphill, the track levelled out and headed into a dark damp gully lined with ferns and moss.

I slumped down onto a log. 'Twelve o'clock,' I said. 'Time to turn back. We need to get home before Dad.'

'Give it one hour,' said Danni. 'One more hour.'

So we did.

And exactly fifty-nine minutes later we saw what we had come for.

'Look,' I screamed.

4

The Land Rover stood in the middle of a quickly flowing stream. The bonnet was up but there was no one around.

On the other side of the water we could see an abandoned mine site. The shaft itself was just a black hole in the side of a cliff. Nearby were a number of sagging sheds with dusty broken windows. The whole area was littered with rusting machinery that had grass and shrubs growing out of it. A huge pile of grey rocks spewed down the cliff face. All sorts of rubbish cluttered the site. Old oil drums, a kettle, a meat safe, a broken oil lamp, several rotting mattresses – the last remaining signs of long-dead miners.

We waded into the stream and I stared at the engine of the Land Rover. 'Water on the distributor,' I said.

'Easily fixed,' said Danni.

We were both so excited. Dad loved this car. We all did. It wouldn't take a second to dry the distributor and start the engine. Danni looked inside.

'Uh-oh,' she said.

'What?' I asked.

'No key. The ignition key is gone.'

Drat. I could dry off the wet ignition leads. And I could drive the Land Rover. No worries. But how to start it up without a key? That was another matter altogether. We had to get going quickly. Before Borg came and found us. Before . . .

'What's that?' said Danni suddenly.

We both stood still with water swirling around our knees and listened.

'A dog,' I said. 'Somewhere far off.'

'Down the mine,' said Danni. 'Let's go.'

'Let's go?' I said. 'Don't be crazy. Anyone could be down there. *Anything* could be down there.'

'That's Hacker,' said Danni. 'Borg's dog. I'd know that growl anywhere. Find the dog and we find Borg. Find Borg and we find the key to the Land Rover.'

My sister had plenty of guts. I was scared but I couldn't let her go alone. We waded across the stream and walked carefully between the tumble-down sheds.

Everything was as silent as a grave. The buildings were overgrown with blackberries and weeds. Totally deserted. A door creaked eerily on its rusty hinges. Almost as if a hidden hand had given it a push.

'Ghosts,' I said.

'Rubbish,' said Danni.

I grabbed her arm. 'I'm not going into the mine until we've thought this through,' I said.

We sat down on a log in silence. After a bit I noticed something moving. A revolting little cane toad. It was creeping through the grass towards a dirty glass jar. Inside the jar was a small piece of steak.

Steak? Where had that come from?

The toad suddenly hopped into the jar. But before it could grab the meat something really weird happened.

The toad gave a terrible shudder and froze. Just stopped dead. Then it began to fade. I could see right through its body. It was only a faint outline, almost as if it was made of mist. Or smoke. Then it vanished.

The jar wobbled and made a noise. It sounded like . . . well, yes, like a tiny burp. Then it vanished too. Into thin air.

'Aaagh,' I screamed.

'What?'

'A toad just vanished. And a jar.'

Danni gave me a little pat on the head. 'If you could make cane toads vanish,' she said. 'You would be the most popular person in Australia. Come on. Let's go.'

5

We shouldered our packs and walked into the mouth of the black mine. A terrible smell filled the air. A foul, retch-making stench.

'Uurgh,' said Danni. 'A dead possum.'

I stared at the rotting corpse and held a tissue over my mouth. The possum's nose had fallen off and its fur was rotting.

Sitting right on top of it was another cane toad. Having a feast. Feeding on the carcass.

'Yuck,' I said with a shudder.

Danni took out her torch and stepped carefully into the darkness of the mine. 'Let's get going,' she said.

The tunnel grew blacker. Water dripped onto the wet

earth beneath our feet. We followed twisted railway tracks deeper and deeper into the mountainside. Suddenly Danni stopped. She was shining her torch on something. A wooden packing case. Inside was a small dead fish.

Danni reached down. 'Well, look at that,' she said.

'Don't touch it,' I yelled.

Something dark flitted past our heads and grabbed the fish. At first I couldn't work out what it was. The fish seemed to be covered by a ball of quivering fur.

'A feral cat,' I gasped.

The cat did not get a chance to eat. There was no mistaking it. Unbelievable as it may seem, in the torchlight we saw what we saw. For a second the feral cat waved its tail. Then it grew still. And pale. Its skin turned clear and for a moment it resembled a small ice sculpture. Then whoosh it vanished into steam. The box trembled and began to fade. It gave a little 'hic' and vanished.

Danni's eyes grew round.

'The fish was bait,' I whispered. 'And the box was a –'

'Ghost box,' said Danni.

'The Spirit of the Forest,' I said. 'It doesn't like mines. Or miners. Or anything that comes here.' We both backed away, pushing ourselves against the wall. It was cold that far underground. But my hands were sweating. I tried to swallow but fear seemed to paralyse my muscles.

I thought about what we had seen. 'The ghost can make itself into any shape,' I said. I reminded Danni about the first cane toad and she shook her head in horror.

'It could turn itself into a jar,' I said in a hoarse voice.

'Or a box,' Danni whispered.

'Any hollow object. It can make itself into that shape,' I said slowly. 'And any living thing that wanders into it is eaten.'

'Turned to vapour,' said Danni.

'No, turned into a spectre,' I said. 'Dead, gone, vanished from this world. Into the next.'

We stared at each other in the light of the torch. Then without a word we both started to run. Scrambling, screaming back towards the entrance. We fled into the blackness, not knowing what cold hand might reach down and grab us. The beam from our torch bounced crazily from the mine's wall.

6

Finally we stopped. Sucking in the cold air with noisy gulps. Trying to see into the gloom.

Danni was peering at something. 'What's that?' she gasped. 'It wasn't there before.'

We stared at a huge steel bank vault. The door hung open. Inside it was empty. Except for something small, made of metal. It glinted in the torchlight.

'A key,' gasped Danni.

'The Land Rover key,' I said. 'Fabulous.' I stumbled forward but this time Danni grabbed me.

'Don't,' she said. 'It's bait. And look. It's not even a real key. You can see through it. It's a ghost key.'

Suddenly a terrible snarling howl filled the air. We turned. And there he was. Not a spectre but our deadly enemy. Borg. And his dog, Hacker. The huge animal bared its long teeth and dripped saliva.

Borg's face was filled with hatred. 'Where's your father?' he shouted angrily.

'Outside,' I lied. 'He'll be here any minute.'

'Good,' said Borg. 'He's the one I want. But you two will do for starters.'

Now I realised what this was all about. Borg knew about the Spirit of the Forest. He wanted Dad to disappear so that he could get our farm. He had lured us up here on purpose.

Borg spoke in a low voice to his dog. 'Back 'em up, boy, back 'em up.'

Hacker lowered his head and growled horribly. Danni and I started to back away towards the vault. The dog was herding us like sheep. Straight into the gaping vault.

'You want the key,' said Borg. 'Go get it.'

Hacker suddenly lunged forward with open jaws. Straight through my legs. Straight into the vault.

Why had he gone past us? Why? Why? Suddenly I realised. The key had been removed because no one took the bait. And in its place was an enormous bone.

The dog grabbed the bone and then gave a terrible howl. His fur stood up on end and began to move like ghostly grass in a breeze. In a flash the dog was nothing but a pale image. Then he vanished.

The vault shimmered for a second. Then it burped loudly and was gone.

Danni and I stood so still that our feet might have been nailed to the ground. The ghost-vault had swallowed the dog. It was a nasty, savage dog. But still and all — it was a dog, a living being. It had perished in front of our eyes.

Borg shook his head. His eyes grew round. Not with sorrow. But with selfish fear.

Without warning he snatched the torch from Danni's hand and ran down the tunnel.

'Come back, come back,' I yelled. 'Give us our torch back.'

The tunnel echoed with his reply. A piercing, hollow laugh. In a flash he rounded a corner and disappeared from sight. We were alone in the pitch dark. Without light.

'I'm scared,' I said.

'So am I,' said Danni. 'But we have to get out of here.'

I silently reached out and felt for her hand. We began to make our way back along the terrible tunnel with our fingers locked together. We bumped into the walls many times. We slipped and slid. But neither of us put into words the fears that gripped our guts. What if somewhere in the darkness lay a ghostly box or cage? Waiting for us to fall inside.

Would we end up disappearing in a burp or a hiccup? Zapped. Vaporised. Swallowed.

7

I don't know how long we stumbled along but finally we came upon a split in the tunnel. We both felt about in the darkness with our hands. There were two passages.

'Which way?' I said. 'Which is the way out? I can't see a thing.'

'I bet these tunnels wander around for miles,' said Danni. 'Some of them might end in the wells and deep holes. If we take the wrong turn we might fall down a shaft and never get out.'

I gave a shiver and gasped at the thought.

'Take a breath,' I said.

'What?'

'Take a deep breath. Through your nose.'

I heard Danni breathe deeply. But I didn't see her smile because it was so dark.

'This way,' she yelled. 'You're a genius, Nelson.'

We hurried on, following the stink of the dead possum.

My mind was filled with crazy thoughts. Was the spirit waiting for us somewhere in the darkness ahead? Had Borg escaped and taken the Land Rover? Was he pushing it into some deep shaft at this very moment? And Dad. Poor Dad. Without his car. Without his children. How would he manage? How would he find the strength to go on?

'Light,' screamed Danni. 'I see light.'

We staggered to the entrance of the tunnel. Or where

the entrance had been. The way was blocked by a door. A door with a brightly lit window. I peered through and saw the most amazing sight.

A small cottage had been built up against the opening of the mine. Inside was an old bush table with rough wooden chairs. A fire burnt in a wood stove. And on the table a roast chicken sat steaming on a plate.

I looked around. Was this a different entrance? No. Because over there against the wall I could see the stinking carcass of the dead possum. Someone had built the cottage right across the way out.

Danni peered in at the roast chicken and licked her lips.

But she wasn't fooled. And neither was I. 'Bait,' was all she said.

We both knew that whoever stepped into that cottage was going to meet a terrible fate. But we had to get out. We had to reach the sunshine. And get to the Land Rover.

I looked around. Then I ran over to the dead possum. I held one hand over my mouth. And with the other I picked up the rubbery nose from where it lay on the ground.

I rushed over to the door, opened it and threw in the nose. 'There,' I yelled. 'You want food. Try that.' I quickly slammed the door shut.

Everything was still. Then the door flew open and the nose shot out and bounced off the mine wall like a bullet. There was a large gurgling noise like someone being sick.

'It only likes live meat,' said Danni.

I scanned the walls of the mine. I needed something alive. But there was nothing. Except Danni. And . . . there, sitting on the ledge. The revolting cane toad. I pulled my hand into my sleeve and grabbed the creepy creature. Then I opened the door of the cottage and threw the toad into the kitchen.

For a second the toad squirmed and then it grew still. And pale. Its skin turned clear and for a moment it was like a sliver of ice. Then *whoosh*, it vanished into steam. The whole cottage trembled and began to fade. It gave an enormous burp of satisfaction. The whole mine shook with the noise. It echoed down the tunnel like a belch in the guts of a giant.

We were safe.

That's what I thought for about two seconds. Until powerful hands grabbed my shoulders and threw me onto the ground. The air was knocked from my lungs and I lay there gasping for breath.

'Thanks,' yelled Borg. 'Good thinking. I couldn't have done it without you.'

He rushed past me out of the tunnel. Danni bent down beside me with a worried look. 'Are you okay, Nelson?' she asked.

I couldn't answer for several minutes. I just couldn't breathe. Finally I managed a couple of words. 'The car,' I gasped.

Danni helped me out into the fresh air and we

made our way towards the river. I had to rest on Danni's shoulder. We moved slowly.

Finally we reached the stream. The Land Rover had gone.

'Borg,' said Danni.

There was nothing more to say. Borg had beaten us to the car. We would never see it again. In my heart I knew that we were only kids and we couldn't defeat a grown man. Not on our own. Borg would destroy the car. And no one would believe us.

We had gone through all this horror for nothing.

We walked sadly back towards the road. Trying to work out why the spirit ate some things and not others.

'The spirit hates anything that harms the forest,' I said. 'Anything foreign. Anything introduced.'

'Cane toads,' panted Danni.

'Dogs,' I said. 'And feral cats.'

'And . . .' said Danni. 'People who want to dig or chop things down.'

We both looked back and then hurried out of the forest as fast as we could go.

8

Dad was waiting for us when we reached home. He was out the front washing the Land Rover in the last light of the day. 'Look,' he yelled. 'It was in Borg's backyard after all. The police found it last night.'

'Last night?' I said.

'Yes,' said Dad. 'Around midnight. I've spent all day cleaning it up.'

'All day,' I said. 'But . . .' I didn't finish the sentence. Danni was shaking her head at me. No one would ever believe our story.

And that is the end of the story. Borg was never seen again.

'What do you think happened to him?' Danni asked me later that night.

I gave a laugh. 'Well,' I said. 'Let's just say that he should have thrown a cane toad into that Land Rover before he climbed into it.'

About the author

The Paul Jennings phenomenon began with the publication of *Unreal!* in 1985. Since then, readers all around the world have devoured his stories. Paul Jennings has been voted 'favourite author' by children in Australia over forty times. He has won every children's choice award in Australia. In 1995 Paul was made a Member of the Order of Australia for services to children's literature, and in 2001 he was awarded the Dromkeen Medal for services to children's literature. In 2007, Paul Jennings' worldwide sales surpassed 8 million copies.

His most recent books include a guide for parents, *The Reading Bug . . . and how to help your child to catch it*, and several *Rascal* story books for early readers. His novel, *How Hedley Hopkins Did a Dare . . .* , was shortlisted for the 2006 Children's Book Council of Australia Book of the Year Award: Younger Readers.

This collection of twenty stories has been hand-picked by Paul from the *UnCollected* series and contains some of his trickiest and most unexpected tales.

This collection of twenty-five hilarious stories has
been hand-picked by Paul from the *UnCollected* series
and is sure to have readers laughing out loud.

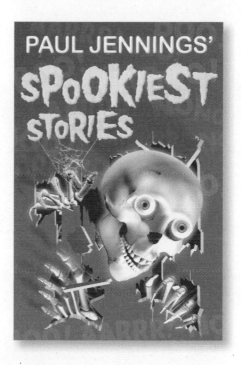